Praise for the Deadly Series

You will be captivated by this beautifully written story and the characters come to life right from the start. *Shelley's Book Case on Deadly Wedding*

I love this series. The attention to detail, the well plotted mystery, and the burgeoning romance in the background provide a captivating look into a fascinating era. *Cozy Up with Kathy on Deadly Wedding*

If you're looking for an all-around good read, this one is for you. *Booklady's Booknotes on Deadly Wedding*

I loved Kate Parker's Victorian Mystery Series. She has a great writing style and her stories feature strong women. I knew I would enjoy this book before I even started reading, but she exceeded all of my expectations. *Escape with Dollycas into a Good Book on Deadly Scandal*

And I'm ever so glad to hear that this is part of a series. It's hard to get enough of our favorite characters, and Olivia definitely ranks on my list. I can't wait to see what she gets up to next! *Back Porchervations on Deadly Scandal*

Kate Parker has hit this one (out) of the park and I am eagerly awaiting the release date of the next. *Kimberlee in Girl Lost in a Book on Deadly Scandal*

Deadly Wedding

Kate Parker

JDP PRESS

Deadly Wedding copyright © 2016 by Kate Parker

ISBN: 978-0-9964831-5-5 [e-book]

ISBN: 978-0-9964831-4-8 [print]

Published by JDP Press

Cover design by Lyndsey Lewellen of
Lewellen Designs

Dedication

To Barbara Connour, Lillian Charves, Sue Schrenk, and all those who have shared their love of a good mystery with others.

CHAPTER ONE

Visiting the ancient Earl of Millhaven was like an audience with the king, except George VI appeared more approachable and less critical. I disliked every visit with the old man, since I knew I'd be found wanting or ignored. I always hoped for ignored.

The old earl sat in his wheelchair, dressed in suit, waistcoat, shirt, tie, and lap rug, and stared at us through faded blue eyes. "Where's Ames and that tea? Ames," he croaked in a sort of bellow.

"He'll be here in a minute, Grandpapa," Celia Eustace, my distant cousin, said in a chipper tone. "Sir Ronald and Olivia have come for the Easter holiday and to help with the preparations for my wedding."

"Who's Olivia?" the old man demanded.

"I'm Olivia Denis. Sir Ronald Harper's daughter," I said, ready to carry out the same conversation we had every time he deigned to notice me.

"Oh."

I thought I'd lucked out and he'd go on to something else.

"Oh, yes. The office worker."

So much for my luck. "Society reporter on a daily London newspaper," I corrected. "*The Daily Premier.*"

"Even worse. A journalist." And then through a wheezy guffaw, "A journalist about ladies' hats."

A dark look from my father warned me not to respond. I waited for the next witticism from the old earl.

"I'd be wearing mourning, too, if I had to prostrate myself for a meager wage."

Age and a title had long ago convinced the old man he could be hopelessly rude. I thought he did it to remind himself he was still alive. I took a calming breath and said, "I suppose you've forgotten I'm wearing mourning because my husband was murdered. It happened last autumn."

I saw the spark of anger flare behind his eyes. "I haven't forgotten, but I thought you had. Glad to see you can follow the dictates of civilized society on occasion."

"More than just occasionally. I did marry him."

My father stirred in his chair. No doubt his fingers itched to put a hand over my mouth. He feared the old earl would throw me out of the house for showing a lack of respect.

I hoped he would. I'd be stuck down here next weekend for Celia's wedding. I didn't want to spend any more time putting up with this fossil and the rest of the inmates in this loony bin.

Ames, the old earl's valet, arrived at that moment with the tea tray, and we all sat in silence while Celia poured. Then my father and Celia started a conversation about the weather while Ames tidied up in the old man's dressing room.

I watched the old earl. I guessed his age at about one hundred. He looked like a frog left out to dry, with wrinkled, papery skin covered with age spots. He didn't appear to pay any attention to any of us. He was probably as bored with conversations about the weather as I was.

Celia set down her delicate china cup and rose to walk over to the old man. Bending over, she straightened his collar.

"That's enough fussing," the old earl said, batting away her hands. "Celia, take your friend and go somewhere else. Sir Ronald and I have business to discuss."

I immediately set down my cup and stood up. "A pleasure as always, Your Lordship."

He didn't look my way or respond. Celia kissed the old man over the sparse, white hair on top of his head and walked away.

At the door, I glanced back to see my father slide his chair closer to the old man's wheelchair. "What did you want to discuss, my lord?"

Celia shut the door, cutting off anything else I might have overheard.

She and I went downstairs while she talked on about flowers and wedding cookies. As soon as we reached the ground floor, I could make out the sounds of an argument. Turning away from Celia, I followed the sounds to the library.

This was Aunt Margaret's favorite room in the Georgian monstrosity. She had added to the collection until the dark- paneled bookshelves were crammed with books, from scholarly hardbound tomes to cheap paperback editions of fiction and poetry with garish covers. The walls were brightened by colorful modernistic paintings done by her brother Walter.

As soon as I opened the door, I knew I wouldn't linger there that day.

Celia's mother, Lady Beatrice, was having a shouting match with Aunt Margaret. Both women were red in the face and glaring at each other through narrowed eyes. They turned toward me as Celia joined me in the doorway.

"Oh, good, Livvy, I'm glad to see you made it," Aunt Margaret said with forced good humor. The light through the big window caught the glistening in her eyes.

"What's wrong?"

"Nothing, dear. Can't sisters disagree?" Aunt Margaret tried to put a light tone in her voice, but I could tell by the way Lady Beatrice walked away, arms folded over her chest, that this was not just some disagreement.

They were both furious.

Celia walked across the room to Lady Beatrice. "Mummy, what's wrong?"

"Nothing, precious. It's only a week until my only child gets married. I'm just having pre-wedding nerves. There's so much to do." Lady Beatrice gave her daughter a hug and then swiped at her eyes.

Aunt Margaret looked relieved at her sister's words. "Come here, Livvy, and let me take a look at you." As I came closer, she looked me up and down. "I still say mourning becomes you. With your auburn hair and creamy skin, you look good in black."

"Thank you, but I really don't like it." It tended to keep men away. One in particular.

"Yes, it does remind everyone around us of the person we lost," Aunt Margaret said, as if she could read my mind. She raised her eyebrows and I gave my head an infinitesimal shake.

Lady Beatrice beamed at me, something she rarely did. "You are going to be able to get off work the day before the wedding? We're going to need your help."

Packing Celia's trunk for her honeymoon. Keeping an eye on the men setting up the tent. All the dogged work Celia didn't want to do, and the servants were already overburdened. "I'll be here, but it may not be until late."

With luck she'd only get married once. Luck I lost at the age of twenty-five when my husband was murdered.

Mother and daughter linked arms. "Celia and I are going into town to pick up some things for her trousseau. Do you want to come along, Olivia?"

They'd probably want me to carry all the packages like some Victorian maid. "I think I'll stay here and help Aunt Margaret with the garden. We want it looking perfect for the wedding next Saturday." I must have caught the fake amiability disease going around because I managed to sound cheerful. "And when you get back, Celia, I want a game of tennis. I brought my racket and your grandfather won't allow us to play on Easter Sunday."

"Golly, no." She laughed. "We'll play right after tea time."

We went through much air-kissing before they left. I noticed a serious look pass between Aunt Margaret and her sister, but they said farewell with great indifference.

After Celia and her mother left, I faced Aunt Margaret. "What is going on?"

"We have a garden that needs tending. You'd better change your clothes." The businesslike Aunt Margaret had returned.

I put on an old day dress, flowered instead of black and likely to scandalize the old earl if he saw me, and found a pair of wellies in the mud room that fit. Then I went out to the garden and found Margaret in the tool shed behind the garage.

I blocked the doorway and asked, "What is going on?"

She handed me a hoe. "There's weeding to be done."

I took the hoe but remained in her path. "Aunt Margaret, I know you're my distant cousin like everyone else here, but you've always treated me like I'm your niece. Or little sister. And you're very dear to me. I know there's something going on. What is it? I only want to help."

"There's nothing you can do. I'm not certain I'd even want you to do anything. But it's certainly not your fight."

She turned me around and gave me a little shove out the door. "However, there are weeds out there by the snapdragons that are calling you. Put on some gloves."

By the time one of the maids brought out a pitcher of lemonade and two glasses to the summerhouse, I'd worked up a good thirst and built quite a pile of weeds. Aunt Margaret stood, hands on her back, and after groaning said, "Come on. We deserve a break. I'm sure the bride is getting one."

"I have no doubt Celia is taking a break right now," I said, following her as I pulled off my gloves.

We sat down in two old chairs in the summerhouse and sighed in unison after we had our first sips of the tart, cold drink. "Is Lady Beatrice the cause of whatever is bothering you?" I asked.

"Livvy, will you leave it alone?" Then she smiled and said, "Where is that young man of yours, Captain Redmond, this weekend?"

"Off doing military things. With Hitler taking over Austria and now threatening the Czechs, he says we're headed for war." The closer I grew to Adam Redmond, the less I liked the word "war."

"Then now is the time for you two to marry. Don't put it off because of the danger." She gave me a wicked smile. "Otherwise, I may just take him for myself. He's a sweetie."

I laughed. Ordinarily, Aunt Margaret was never one to recommend haste in anything. She'd felt I'd married my late husband, Reggie, too soon, and we were engaged for almost a year. "No. I like my job. I'm not ready to go back to being just a housewife again. As long as I'm a widow, I can plead poverty and the need for a job. Married women don't work. Period."

She considered my words. "That changed with the

Great War. If we get into it with Hitler, we will have to go back to letting married women work."

"That's fine for if and when we go to war, but in the meantime, I don't want to sit home all day. I like being busy."

She took a sip of her drink and said, "War will be here soon, whether we like it or not."

It was more than just a fear of boredom. With an honesty I hadn't shared with anyone, I said, "I don't want a war. Adam will be threatened. And after losing Reggie, I don't think I could go through that again."

Her expression changed to worried sympathy. She put a hand over my wrist and said, "Oh, my poor dear. I hadn't thought how insensitive my words could sound. I forgot about Reggie. Of course, you wouldn't forget him or your pain. Please forgive me."

I took a deep breath to stop me from shaking inside at the thought of Adam's death. I had finally accepted Reggie's murder. Adam was alive, gorgeously, invitingly alive. I refused to dwell on what war could do to him. Putting on a smile I didn't feel, I said, "Of course. I can't stay mad at you, Aunt Margaret. You've always been there for me."

"The only cure for this silly talk of mine is more work. Finish your lemonade, and let's go attack more of those weeds. Beatrice will be furious if the garden isn't perfect."

I emptied my glass, put my work gloves back on, and headed back to the flower beds. "You and your sister never seem to agree on anything."

"Let's be generous. Seldom agree. She is rather foolish. That's what finishing school will do for you." Margaret attacked a vigorous weed as if it were a replacement for Lady Beatrice.

I remembered the scene in the library. "But this

morning you were furious with her."

"No. I wasn't furious with her." Then she hacked apart the weed until its roots and stem were in shreds.

I got nothing further out of her, but I felt certain something had made her angry.

The rest of the day was a muted version of every other visit to Millhaven House. Tea, then tennis, then dinner, necessitating three changes of clothes. Only part of the family was in residence, since both of Lady Margaret and Lady Beatrice's brothers were on holiday. I doubted Beatrice's husband, Lord Eustace, had shown his face in his father-in-law's house in a year. And the old earl never left his room.

My father had to be bored, being surrounded by women.

After dinner, we tried talking in the family parlor, a large, high-ceilinged room done in browns and beiges with a cheery fire going in the large fireplace. Celia and Lady Beatrice immediately took over the conversation, going over the same wedding plans we'd heard before.

My father excused himself to spend more time with the earl. Then Margaret said she had a book on Queen Anne she wanted to show me. We escaped to the library where we spent the evening reading and drinking hot cocoa.

It turned out I drank too much hot cocoa, because I woke up in the middle of the night, something I rarely do. Turning on the bedside lamp, I saw it was three in the morning. I pulled on my robe and shoved my feet into my slippers for a dash to the only loo on the huge bedroom floor of the old mansion.

There was a butler's lamp burning near the doorway to the loo that sent up huge shadows at every entrance off the main hallway. The high ceilings swallowed the light, and with every odd turning I made toward the main hall, the light grew brighter. Unfortunately, with a butler's lamp, brighter is relative. I should have packed a torch.

All I needed was a great storm to add to the atmosphere. If anyone had jumped out and said boo, I wouldn't have made it to the facilities in time. As it was, I nearly ran.

I was halfway back to my room when I heard a man's voice. Which was odd, because all the men's bedrooms were on the other side of the house.

I froze, thinking I'd turned the wrong way. But when I looked around, I knew I'd headed in the right direction. I no longer heard the voice. It had to be my imagination.

Then I heard a floorboard squeak.

Terror shot icicles down my body. I dashed back to my room, just off from the hall where Aunt Margaret, Lady Beatrice, and Celia had their rooms. As I shut the door and leaned against it, the squeaks grew closer. Then I thought I heard a heavy footstep.

Or something hit a wall.

I turned out the light in my room and peeked out of my doorway, thinking it could be a burglar. Or Watkins, the butler, responding to a call from one of the residents of the house.

It was dark in the hallway. Too dark to see clearly, but I caught a glimpse of movement. Something, or someone, had passed by. I shivered.

I tried to remember what was further down the hall past my door. Two more guest bedrooms and a servants' staircase going up to the attics and down to the main floor and the basement.

Curious, I stuck my head out further. The air was still and I neither heard anything else nor spied movement.

No one was there.

Then I sniffed. I was reminded of a hospital. Or the morgue.

* * *

After a restless night, I rose and dressed for church early, and then headed downstairs for breakfast. I was the first one down.

Watkins was just seeing to the finishing touches on the serving board. "Tea, Miss Olivia?"

"I'm afraid I'm a coffee drinker in the morning now, Watkins. A consequence of working for a newspaper."

"Fix your plate, and I'll bring a cup over to you."

I took some eggs, toast, tomatoes, and mushrooms, and thought what a treat this was from my usual morning fare. As I sat down and Watkins came over, I said, "Was there a disturbance last night? Was someone ill?"

"Nothing to my knowledge, and the earl is well this morning, according to his valet."

"The house doesn't have ghosts, does it?"

"Ghosts? I don't believe so." If he thought my questions odd, his demeanor didn't show it.

"What's this about ghosts?" Celia asked as she walked in.

"I heard something move down the corridor by my room last night."

She laughed. "Old houses creak. I suppose that's how half of ghost stories begin."

"You didn't have a burglar last night?" I asked Watkins. If one had passed my door last night and I stood by, cowering, I'd feel ashamed.

"There was no sign of someone breaking in and nothing appears to be missing," he assured me as he poured Celia her tea.

"Missing? What's missing?" Lady Beatrice asked as

she walked in.

"Livvy thought she heard a ghost last night," Celia said around a smirk.

"We don't have ghosts." Lady Beatrice's nose went up in the air. "The very idea."

"And Watkins said there weren't any burglars last night, so I don't know what I saw and heard."

"Nothing. You saw nothing. Do you hear me?" Lady Beatrice hadn't spoken to me like that since I was a child.

I wasn't a child any more. There was only one man in the house last night who might have been visiting one of the women.

My father.

I was furious until I thought. His room was on the other side of the house from mine. He wouldn't have left any of the other rooms after a visit and gone down my hallway. It was too far out of his way.

And I'd never noticed my father smelled like a morgue.

But what about Watkins or Ames?

CHAPTER TWO

The following Friday after work, I once again rode out to Millhaven House with my father. I still hadn't asked him if he'd made a midnight visit to any of the ladies of the house the weekend before. I couldn't.

I didn't believe it, for starters. For another, there was that peculiar smell.

We arrived too late for tea and too early to dress for dinner. After I put my things away, I wandered into the back garden, which had been transformed by two huge white tents for the wedding the next morning. The first, butting up to Aunt Margaret's flower borders, held tables covered with cups and plates. The second held a wooden platform floor laid over the tennis court.

As I was standing in the second tent, I heard a man's voice say, "I don't want anything to do with this wedding. I can't stand Grayling. I—"

Another male voice said, "I hope Robert Grayling knows what he's getting into."

I left the tent and covered the short distance to the summerhouse in a few steps. Inside, I found Uncle Humphrey's three sons. Thomas, the oldest and soon to be an Oxford grad, was sprawled in a deck chair looking glum. Charles, the middle son, shorter, stocky, and fair-haired, and also an Oxford student, sat on the table. Edwin, the youngest, still had another year at Harrow before he followed his father and brothers to Oxford.

I greeted them with, "What's wrong with the groom?"

Edwin adjusted his glasses. "Celia's done all right with him."

"Grayling doesn't show proper deference to the future earl," Charlie said at almost the same time.

So that was it. Thom would inherit his grandfather's title someday. But the way the old earl was counting down birthdays, he might outlive Humphrey, his elder son, and Thom, Humphrey's eldest, too.

And the sons of international financiers, like Robert Grayling, tended not to show deference to the aristocracy.

"I think I should warn you. I could hear every word you said from the dance tent."

All three of the boys—though they were hardly boys now—groaned.

"How're the preparations for the big day coming?"

"Oh, lord," the older two grumbled.

"Celia has been pretty dreadful. This morning she ordered Thom to supervise the company putting up the tents, Charlie to supervise the workers putting down the dance floor, and I was to check off the coffee cups and what-have-you that the caterer left here for tomorrow. She said she couldn't do everything at once," Edwin told me. "Then she and Lady Beatrice went to get their hair done."

He paused, glanced at me, and asked in a mystified tone, "How long *does* that take?"

I smiled. Celia had ducked out of any effort for her own wedding. Typical. "Is there a resident ghost in the house?"

I caught a secretive smile cross Charlie's face. He said, "Depends on who you ask," as the other two shook their heads, looking surprised at my question.

"By luncheon yesterday, I ended up being the only one of the family here except for Grandpapa." Edwin glanced at all of us in turn and lowered his voice. "Expect a row tonight."

"Why?" Charlie was immediately interested.

"Mr. Craggett was here."

"So the rumors are true," Thom said.

"What rumors?" My father would have complained about my nosiness, but fortunately, he was inside.

"Grandpapa is changing his will."

"Why? Doesn't your father inherit the lot? He'll be the new earl." That was the way it always worked.

"That's the dirty secret about this title. Very little comes with it. Most of the wealth—land, stocks, investments—is owned privately by Grandpapa. Even Millhaven House isn't entailed. His will determines who gets what when he goes, if he ever does," Charlie said.

"Mother ran into Mr. Craggett when she came home. She went straight up to see Grandpapa and I could hear them shouting from the bottom of the stairs," Edwin said.

"What did they say?" Charlie asked.

"I couldn't hear."

"Drat it, Edwin, you need to pay more attention. This is important," Thom said, springing up to a proper seated position.

"For you," Charlie said.

"For all of us," Thom replied. "This is the money, Grandpapa's private wealth, that will go to different people if the will was changed. Don't you want to know if you benefitted?"

"How was the old will written?" I asked.

"Father gets most of it as the new earl and heir. Aunt Margaret, Uncle Walter, and Lady Beatrice, as Grandpapa's other children, get what's left," Thom said. It sounded like a standard sort of will to me.

"Think the old man disinherited someone?" Charlie asked. He sounded gleeful.

"How do you know the terms of the old will?"

"It's been common knowledge for years now," Edwin said.

"Maybe Mr. Craggett was here about something completely different. Are you sure he was here about a new will?" I asked. I thought the boys were jumping ahead of themselves.

"Watkins took him upstairs and then came back down. About ten minutes later, Ames came down and took one of the maids and the cook up with him. They were upstairs about two minutes. Long enough to witness a signature on a will," Edwin said.

"Oh, my." It did sound like a new will was signed by a very elderly, very rich man. And if someone gained, someone else lost.

"So, who got disinherited?" Charlie said, grinning widely. "And did I get anything?"

We heard her voice before Celia came into the summerhouse, and all three of Humphrey's boys groaned. I wondered how long she'd heard our words.

She walked in, all sunshine and sweetness. "I wondered where you went, Livvy. Come on. You don't have time to talk to the boys. We have a wedding to hold in less than twenty-four hours."

"I thought everything was done or arranged to be delivered tomorrow."

"There's still the packing for the honeymoon. I'll be gone for a month on my travels to South Africa."

"It sounds like a wonderful trip." I admit I was jealous. "So you want my opinion on what you should take?"

"And your help getting it all into the trunks."

That sounded like Celia. I started out of the summerhouse. "I'll see you boys at dinner."

"Have fun, Livvy," Thom said. I could hear the smirk in his tone.

Celia and I went up to her room where every surface was covered with gowns, negligees, shoes, hats, gloves, and dresses for every occasion and in a rainbow of colors. "You're going to get all this into a trunk?"

"Well, two trunks and a suitcase. I think if you start on the gowns, you'll find paper to lay them out on there."

I began on a beaded, light blue number with gauzy short sleeves. "Which shoes and undergarments go with this?"

"Why?"

"To pack them together." I remembered two things at once. Celia hadn't traveled much, and she and her mother had had a ladies' maid until a couple of years before.

"Don't put the shoes on top of the gown. You'll crush it."

I looked at her as if she'd grown a second head. Did she think I was stupid? I grew up with an exacting father and no ladies' maid. I'd packed plenty of trunks in my life.

That problem sorted, I asked, "Does Millhaven House have a resident ghost?"

"No. I thought Mama answered that question last week. Besides, we never found one as children, and I've never heard of one mentioned. Why?"

I again thought of the movement passing my door the preceding weekend. "No reason." As I packed, I tried to recall every detail of the shadowy figure. Whatever it was, it must have been solid. Alive.

Glancing up a while later, I found I had made progress and Celia was sitting and watching me when Lady Beatrice came into the room. "Ah, good. Olivia, Celia, it's time to dress for dinner."

I set down the outfit I was working on. "I'll see you downstairs." I glanced into the other trunk as I passed. Nothing was packed. I escaped, feeling as if I was being used.

I'm sure I was.

There'd been a time, before I'd married Reggie, when I resisted coming out here with my father because of Celia's constant efforts to turn me into her maid. Aunt Margaret had seen what was happening more clearly than my father and put a stop to most of it by the simple expedient of inventing things for me to do with her. The results were pleasant memories of exploring libraries, museums, and ancient sites during my university days and the year afterward until my wedding.

After that, Reggie and I kept busy in London, only visiting Millhaven House for special dinners and taking a taxi back home rather than spending the night in the massive old house.

Over time, I had forgotten about Celia's demanding nature. Until now.

Before dinner, we all collected in the family parlor. I arrived in my slim black beaded gown with slashed sleeves and a keyhole décolletage. Celia's gown was in one of her usual pastel shades, pink this time, that made her look blonder and more delicate.

The men were all in evening jackets and high collars, even Edwin, who looked decidedly uncomfortable.

Aunt Margaret came over to me and whispered, "Father's coming down for dinner."

"Does he do this often these days?"

"No. It's because of Celia's wedding tomorrow."

I wondered if it had anything to do with his rumored changing of his will. "I'm sorry I didn't see you when I arrived."

"I wasn't here. I was at the university library all day, preparing for a lecture in the autumn. Oh, Lord. She's back."

"Who?"

"Amelia. I was hoping she'd stay away at least until the wedding."

Lady Amelia Brooke didn't look like she had a son of twenty-one, but I knew that was Thom's age. She was tall, thin, and wore an envy-inspiring gown of shimmering green. The fabric alone must have cost the earth. Since her husband, Uncle Humphrey, had a high-level position at HM Treasury plus received an allowance as the heir to the old earl, she could afford to be better dressed than the rest of us.

She could also afford to visit every spa known to woman and did so, keeping time's ravages away.

I observed my father and Uncle Humphrey standing by the empty fireplace in close conversation. Neither noticed her walk in.

"Not like that, man," a querulous old voice said, and a moment later, the doors from the front hall swung open and the old earl was wheeled into the room.

We all turned toward him and said a ragged chorus of "Good evening."

"Well? What are you waiting for? Let's go into dinner."

We attempted to form a line according to protocol, but once Lady Amelia walked in next to the wheelchair and Uncle Humphrey escorted in Aunt Margaret, the rest of us followed. There was one more man than woman, and I found myself between Edwin and Thom.

The food was good, but it didn't make up for the lack of conversation. The atmosphere in the dining room was icy, and no one wanted to attempt a word for fear it would be taken wrong. Was it because of the old man's presence, or the possibility of being cut out of the will?

And why was I being quiet? I was a third cousin twice removed, or something. I wouldn't be in the will no matter what. "How are you feeling, Your Lordship?" I asked.

"Who are you?" came out as a scratchy, high-pitched demand.

Here we go again. "Olivia Denis. Sir Ronald Harper's daughter."

"And how do you think I feel?"

"I don't know. That's why I asked." All right. Starting a conversation was a stupid idea.

"Is that your idea of mourning clothes?"

I smiled. There was nothing wrong with his eyesight. "No."

He gave a wheezy laugh. "Well, you're brighter than most of my relatives. Prettier, too." Then he resumed eating, and everyone at the table appeared to give a sigh of relief.

During the next course, I noticed several surreptitious glances shot in my direction. "Doesn't anyone speak during meals if your grandfather is present?" I murmured to Thom.

"Not usually. Afraid to put a foot wrong. Especially after Craggett's arrival today," he said.

"How many people know his solicitor was here today?"

"The three of us," Edwin said, nodding at me and his brother, "plus Charlie, Mother, and maybe Father."

I glanced toward my father, who was sitting across the table. He looked up, but his gaze gave nothing away. The old earl had asked him to stay after Celia and I left last Saturday. Was it to talk about a new will, or whatever reason Craggett was here?

"When will he tell you?"

"Who knows? When he's ready."

We had reached the pudding course when Watkins came in and murmured something to Lady Beatrice. With the lack of conversation at the table, everyone watched her to see what she would do.

She set down her napkin and rose. "If you'll excuse me?"

All the men except the old earl gave a half-hearted rise from their seats. The old earl said, "Why?"

"I need to see to something."

"Does the something have a name?"

I'd have walked out of the room in silence. Lady Beatrice, either because she was trained by her father to obey or because she lived under his roof and ate his food, stood where she was and said, "Lord Eustace."

"Daddy?" Celia said, ready to leap from her seat.

"Sit down, Beatrice," the old man commanded. "He can wait until we finish."

"Oh, good," Thom muttered. "We will now have the longest ending to a dull meal in recorded history."

He might have been right.

The old man toyed with his pudding until I knew there couldn't be anything left in his dish. Then he announced we'd have coffee at the table. I shot my father a look that said I was out of patience. He shook his head and I took a deep breath and prayed for someone to shout "Fire." Or in an old house like this, a rat to run over someone's foot.

At any rate, he only dawdled for another fifteen long, boring minutes before he announced we'd move to the family parlor. "I have an announcement to make. And bring Lord Eustace with you. You are still married to him."

Thom and I looked at each other and we both rolled our eyes.

Celia was the first to bolt from the dining room.

"I didn't know they were speaking to each other," I whispered to Edwin.

"Their only child is getting married tomorrow. I hope they've put up their swords for the occasion," he said, pushing up his glasses and shoving his dark bangs out of his way.

I took my time wandering into the family parlor. The old man's announcement had nothing to do with me. Still, I was nosy enough to want to hear what he had to say.

If he didn't throw my father and me out for not being close-enough relatives.

I sat next to Aunt Margaret and talked to her for a few minutes. On the other sofa, Lady Beatrice and her estranged husband, Lord Eustace, sat with their daughter between them. I noticed Lord Eustace had taken the opportunity to help himself from the whiskey decanter.

Finally, Ames wheeled the old earl into the parlor. The only sounds were the creak of the moving chair and the tick of the large clock against the far wall.

Once he was settled in front of the fireplace with all of us facing him, the Earl of Millhaven said, "As I know some of you discovered already, my solicitor was here this afternoon. I've decided to change my will. And before you all come begging, the new will is already signed and in Mr. Craggett's possession. There's nothing you can do about it."

Around me I heard murmured questions and grumbled worries.

"Are you going to tell us, in broad terms, what it says?" Uncle Humphrey's voice sounded like he was being strangled by his collar.

"You think, because you'll be the next Earl of Millhaven, you have a right to know?" the old man demanded.

"N-no. But it will be up to me to administer this will."

"Oh, you think so, do you?"

What did the old earl have planned? Some final nasty surprise from beyond the grave? That sounded like him.

Aunt Margaret shifted her weight on the sofa next to me before she spoke. "How much of a change is it?"

"A complete rewrite. Totally new terms." The old man gazed at her with an evil grin. "What does that tell you, Maggie? Should you be worried? Should you all be worried?" He wheezed out a cackle.

Then behind me I heard a man's voice say, "How nice. Did you all gather to welcome me home?"

CHAPTER THREE

Uncle Walter. The youngest of the old earl's children.

"Where have you been?" Aunt Margaret said as she walked over to greet him.

"Painting in Deauville and having a lovely time." He kissed her cheek.

"I worry about you." Aunt Margaret had told me she was thirteen when her brother Walter was born. When they lost their mother the following year, she took over the mothering role for the baby.

"Don't. I'm a big boy now."

"Father just told us he's changed his will," she said, stopping his teasing with a single sentence as his eyes widened and his mouth rounded.

"Yes, and it's signed, so don't come crying to me if you don't like it," their father said.

"Wouldn't make much sense. When they read it, you'll be dead." I saw Aunt Margaret wince at her brother's words. "Of course, you'll have to name the next generation because you'll outlive us all."

Then Uncle Walter walked over to pat Celia on the back and wish her well before he picked up his suitcase and walked out of the room.

His father, eyes narrowed, began to roll his chair in the direction his youngest child had gone. Then Ames, standing by, wheeled him out of the room.

Uncle Humphrey said something in his wife's ear. Lady Amelia glared at him and hissed something in return as he walked away.

Aunt Margaret excused herself and left the room right after Humphrey. Lady Beatrice waited a minute before she followed her siblings out.

"They've all gone up to Grandfather's room, the four who were named in the old will. I bet there'll be shouting in a minute," Thom said, dropping onto the sofa where Margaret had sat.

"Going to go up and listen?" I asked.

"Not on your life."

People wandered out of the parlor until it was only Celia and her father and me and my father. "Bridge? We have four," Lord Eustace said, refilling his glass with straight whiskey.

My father shook his head before I could. "I suspect the shouting is finished by now. I think I'll go to bed." He rose.

I did the same. "Good night."

* * *

The house stirred early, and unused to the noises, I rose and dressed to go down to breakfast. I was curious concerning what had been learned about the old earl's will.

I cut across the bedroom level on my way to a side staircase near the breakfast room. My route took me past the old earl's room. Lady Beatrice and the old man's valet stood in the hall outside the door.

"Now Ames, don't be difficult. Surely you don't want to ruin Celia's wedding day, do you? And it won't do any—Olivia! My dear child. Good morning." Lady Beatrice stopped in the middle of berating her father's valet to greet me the moment she spotted me.

Lady Beatrice's hand shook a little as she fussed with her skirt. "I thought that horrid little German was going to put a stop to our festivities when he marched into Austria. Fortunately, Chamberlain had the sense not to go to war with him."

I'd hoped to escape worries about Austria, but even a wedding couldn't stop the incessant talk of war. However, it was odd hearing a political comment come from Lady Beatrice's mouth. She didn't find it a seemly topic for ladies.

"How is the Earl of Millhaven?" I asked, looking from her to the valet. The old man had been expected to die any number of times, but he always confounded medical opinion and recovered.

"You know Father." Lady Beatrice smiled and gave me a pointed look. No lingering allowed.

I decided to take the hint and headed downstairs.

I was halfway down when I heard Lady Beatrice say, "I mean it, Ames. No more of this silliness. We can't let him ruin the wedding."

Celia was in the breakfast room tucking into tea and toast. "Oh, good. As soon as you eat, we can work on packing the trunks."

"At least until I have to dress for the wedding." I helped myself to eggs, toast, tomatoes, mushrooms, and coffee.

"You're going to eat all that?" she asked.

"Yes. Why?" Was food being rationed here? The old earl was supposed to be rich.

"Oh. Nothing." She sighed and went back to her tea.

Edwin came in and piled food up on his plate. "They had quite a row last night in Grandpapa's room."

"Did you hear what they said?" I asked.

"Nothing that tells me anything. Just Father and the aunts saying that he was mad and this wasn't right."

"Lord Millhaven did say this new will is completely different from the old one. What do you think, Celia?" I asked.

"I just want today to go perfectly. There's time to

worry about the will tomorrow."

Edwin continued, "And in the middle of the night, I heard my father, Uncle Walter, and Celia's father arguing."

"Whatever for?" Celia asked.

"I don't know. I heard your mother's name mentioned. My father seemed to be telling your father what to do, or not to do, and Uncle Walter was trying to calm them both down." He shook his head. "Why can't anyone in this family get along?"

"What time was this?"

"Really late. Three or four in the morning." Edwin glanced at the door and fell silent.

Charlie and Thom came in together. Charlie filled up a plate; Thom poured a quick cup of coffee as he was already dressed in his frock coat and carrying his high silk hat. He was gone in five minutes.

Celia watched me eat as she gave another sigh and left the room. I finished my breakfast.

Afterward, I took the side stairs up. When I reached the top, I saw Celia carefully close the door to her grandfather's room and hurry away. I rushed up behind her.

She jumped as she saw me. "Livvy. That's not nice."

"What's not nice? How's your grandfather?"

She trembled. "He's fine. He's not coming to the wedding. Too tiring. Let's get my trunks packed." Pushing away from me, she hurried to her room. I followed.

This time she helped me. The chattering Celia was gone, replaced by a pensive woman.

"What's wrong, Celia?"

"This is our third attempt to reach the altar. The first time, Robert's uncle died. Then we were supposed to get married at Christmas, but last autumn there was that—

that floozy that Robert had a fling with." She finished folding a skirt and laid it in the trunk. "It wasn't until New Year's that he came to his senses."

"Everything's all right now, isn't it?"

"Oh, yes. Everything's fine. I'm just afraid we're jinxed." Her cheerful tone and her smile were forced.

I felt sorry for her.

When it became time to dress, Annabeth Grayling, the groom's sister and maid of honor, arrived to help and I slipped away.

When I returned, in a lavender gown and a wide-brimmed hat, young, serious Annabeth was fussing with the band that would hold Celia's veil on her head. Celia was yelping and telling her to leave it alone. She wasn't going to wear anything so painful.

"May I help?" I asked.

"Oh, Livvy," Celia said, rising from the stool where she'd been sitting. She rushed over to me in her wedding gown, dragging her veil behind her. "What took you so long?"

"I had to dress."

"Please don't report on this disaster in the newspaper," Celia said, holding out her veil as she laughed. She sounded almost hysterical.

Now I knew why I'd been invited for the night before the wedding. Celia and her mother hoped that as a society reporter for a large London daily, I'd get her wedding more column inches in the press.

But what was making Lady Beatrice and Celia so nervous? I'd heard of pre-wedding nerves, but this was a little extreme, even for them.

Annabeth nodded to me as she trailed Celia while gathering up the veil. She was about twenty, with dark brown hair and eyes, and with something solid and unflappable about her.

"It's almost time for the wedding. Now, let's make sure we have a bride." I marched Celia backward and had her sit on the stool in front of her dressing table. Annabeth carried the veil out of the way of our feet.

After I took out all of the hair pins, she relaxed. "That is so much better. I must have welts in my scalp. What is your father doing?"

"I have no idea. I haven't seen him this morning. Should he be doing anything?"

I stopped talking as I set the veil the way I thought it should fit on Celia's head. I put in a few hair pins and then glanced at Annabeth, who came over with more pins.

There was banging on the door. "Celia! We have to leave now. You'll be late for your wedding, my dear."

Celia shrieked and then giggled. "Stay out, Uncle Walter. I'm not dressed."

"Well, you'd better be dressed soon or there won't be a wedding," he shouted back before creaking floorboards said he'd walked away.

I heard a clock downstairs chime the hour as Celia said, "I hope this won't be too much of a strain for you, being a widow and having to watch my wedded joy."

"Oh, good grief," I said around the pins between my lips, thinking of Adam Redmond. I'd rather be courted by him than married to Robert Grayling. To each her own.

Unfortunately, Celia moved, and the fastener I was putting into the veil slipped, hitting her scalp. "Ow. Don't be like that, Livvy."

Annabeth glanced at me in horror, obviously buying Celia's inference that I'd intentionally stuck her. Celia had pulled that trick so many times and in so many ways, I didn't notice it anymore. Well, hardly noticed.

Between Annabeth and me, we made a success of

the veil as the next knock came at the door. "You're officially late for your wedding."

"It's all right, Uncle Humphrey. I'm done. Besides, it's not ten o'clock yet. The clock in the hall is fast."

"By about thirty seconds. And it'll take us five minutes to get to the church. If we run."

"Well, I'm not running. Everyone can wait for me."

That was the Celia I knew.

She rose from the stool and twirled once slowly so we could straighten out her dress and veil. As we did, Lady Beatrice burst in, saying, "Come along, Celia. Who knows how long Robert will wait?"

"He'll wait, Mother," Celia said in a huffy tone.

If the groom knew Celia at all, he expected to wait.

"Here. Your grandfather said you could wear the countess's jewels for the ceremony." She came over and Annabeth and I raised the veil so she could fasten the clasp of the necklace behind Celia's neck. "There. Something old," she said. "And borrowed."

Celia turned around and I heard Annabeth gasp. I'd seen the magnificent necklace before, but I still felt my eyes widen. It was a wide V-shaped bib of diamonds, sapphires, and pearls worth a fortune.

"And something blue," I added, staring at the sapphires. She already wore enough new clothes to cover that category.

"And the silver sixpence is in my shoe. Go on. I'll be down in a minute." Celia made a shooing motion toward her mother.

Lady Beatrice paced the room once, glanced at Annabeth, fluttered her hands, and stomped out, shutting the door firmly behind her.

Celia's blonde hair glittered with the gemstones in the band of her veil. Her dress, a bias-cut satin with lace overlay, must have cost the earth. From habit due to my job on the *Daily Premier*, I was already writing a description in my head.

Annabeth and I squeezed her hands before we all pulled on our white gloves. "Do you have your bouquet?" I asked.

"It's downstairs," Annabeth told me as she hurried from the room. "I'll get it ready."

"And get everyone started toward the church." Celia walked to the door and I straightened her veil as it tried to cling to dressers and discarded clothing. By the time we walked into the hallway, there was no one in sight. Celia put a finger to her lips and went to her grandfather's door.

I followed behind, knowing I was superfluous to the scene that was about to unfold.

Celia hurried over to the bed where her grandfather lay, eyes closed, mouth slack. He looked ill, his coloring gray. Then it hit me. His was the same skin tone I'd seen in the morgue when I'd learned my husband was murdered. "Celia..."

Too late. She shook him and he didn't respond. His mouth hung open but at least his eyes were closed. Her hand hit the covers and she pulled them down. The handle of a knife protruded from the old man's narrow chest. Blood had spilled onto the sheets.

I jerked back and shuddered. She gasped. Then she carefully placed the covers back and turned to me. "Say nothing about this. Come on."

I had to force in a breath to speak. "But we have to call the police." This was murder.

She grabbed my wrist and pulled me along. "After the wedding."

"But..." I stared at the poor wretch in the bed.

"If we tell them now, there will be no wedding. Ever. Now, be quiet. And smile." Ever her mother's daughter, Celia shoved me toward the door.

"This is wrong."

"This is my wedding day. I won't let you or a murder ruin it. And what difference will a few more minutes make?"

Now I knew why she wanted me doing her veil. She wanted me with her as she came downstairs. She wanted a witness for finding the body. And not the groom's sister.

We'd reached the door when I said, "You knew already. You saw he was dead when you came up after breakfast. How long has he been dead?"

Her answer was to shove me out of the room and shut the door behind us, wearing a fierce expression.

"Celia, did you have any hand in this?"

"Of course not. But Robert won't marry me, Livvy, if we postpone the wedding one more time. Don't say a word. And smile." Putting on her best grand dame performance, Celia walked down the stairs. Her family burst into applause as she made the turn in the staircase and came into view.

I had two choices. The legally correct reporting of a suspicious death; or the far more interesting spectacle called *What will the earl's family do?*

I walked down the staircase, knowing I'd decided to keep silent. For the moment.

My brain numb, I helped Annabeth make sure Celia's bouquet was perfect, all my movements automatic. Then Celia took Lord Eustace's arm. "Ready, Daddy?"

"I hope Robert realizes how lucky he is, winning my darling Celie."

Celia nearly dragged her father out the door and down the steps. "We've kept Robert waiting long enough.

One more delay will probably send him packing."

The rest of us had to hurry to keep up. As I took my father's arm and we brought up the end of the procession, he muttered, "Thank the good Lord the church is only at the corner."

Celia was getting married in the village church, once far outside London but now part of the distant suburbs. It was convenient for the guests as well as scenic, with early spring flowers and new greenery all around.

He continued with, "I'm glad you had the decency to at least wear second mourning today. You should still be in black. Reggie hasn't been dead a year yet."

This outfit was far too nice to be considered second mourning by anyone but my father. I would fit in well with the wedding guests.

My sorrow at losing Reggie was none of his business.

It must have been habit that made me defend my actions. "I kept to full mourning for months after we found my husband's killer."

"How many months? Four? Five? And you haven't worn mourning for a single day at that job of yours."

"It's forbidden."

"Balderdash."

At that moment, we walked into the back of the church. We were escorted to the pew behind where Celia's aunts and uncles were seated. Lord Humphrey Brooke and his wife Lady Amelia, the Honorable Walter Brooke, and Lady Margaret Brooke nodded to my father and me.

On this, the happiest day of their niece's life, only Walter appeared unruffled. Humphrey and his wife looked annoyed, and Margaret looked like she suspected Beatrice was up to something that would be to Margaret's loss.

Today's behavior was normal for the Brooke family. But it could also mean they'd already learned the contents of their father's will. And that their father had been murdered.

CHAPTER FOUR

When the groom's parents came down the aisle, they looked like very ordinary, very happy people. Mrs. Grayling's hat was a horrid homage to Edwardian fashions, dwarfing her head.

Then Lady Beatrice was walked down the aisle by Thomas, her oldest nephew. She appeared as relaxed as anyone could be who was hosting an extravaganza.

The organ began to play Mendelssohn and we all rose. Celia looked radiant. I glanced once at Robert, standing by the reverend, and was shocked to see him glare. I swung around and realized Lord Eustace was glowering back at the groom.

Celia, without seeming to look toward her father, jerked on his arm and he changed his expression to a forced smile.

From then on, the wedding went smoothly. Lord and Lady Eustace sat next to each other for ten minutes without open warfare breaking out.

I spent the time wondering how many people besides Celia and me knew the old earl had been murdered.

The weather, so risky in April, shone on the happy couple. After the ceremony, the families lined up in front of the church for photographs, all of the women holding on to their hats in the strong breeze. The first shots were of the bride and groom, who looked relaxed and happy. Everyone applauded as the flash went off.

I was talking to some old school chums when I noticed two men who shouldn't have been there. One was a uniformed constable. The other, who was speaking to

Lord Humphrey, was a man in a brown suit who wore an expression that mixed resignation and determination.

He had to be a police detective inspector.

I excused myself and walked in their direction. After last autumn's experience with Reggie's murder, I wondered how wrong they were going to get everything.

The man I suspected was a police detective was speaking as I stepped close enough to hear his lowered voice. "...No reason to interfere with the wedding feast, which I understand will be held in the garden under a tent."

"Now see here." Uncle Humphrey had always been long on bluster and short on logic.

"We'll use the side entrance. I doubt anyone will notice us."

"I say, man. Can't it wait?"

"I'm afraid it can't."

"Are you certain it's murder?" Uncle Humphrey didn't lower his voice. I clearly heard his words and the shock in his voice.

I felt sure Uncle Humphrey didn't know he'd arrived at the church as the new Earl of Millhaven.

"Olivia, are you eavesdropping?" my father said, walking up behind me.

"Yes. There's been a murder. I just heard Uncle Humphrey say so." I had no qualms about not telling my father I'd already found the murder victim. He hadn't believed anything I'd said when my husband was murdered.

"Some ruffian must have thought the house would be empty during the wedding ceremony and sneaked in, only to meet with a servant to someone's misfortune."

"You think so?" I knew better. The memory of the knife hilt protruding from the bloody pajama top made me shudder.

My father glanced around. "The family's all here."

"Not Millhaven. Not the earl."

"If he'd died, it would have been heart failure or another stroke. No need to call the police." My father gave the officers a glance as they walked away from the churchyard. "You are not to get involved, Livvy."

He'd said the same thing when Reggie was murdered. That time, I had a reason to investigate. "Don't worry. I have no intention of doing so."

Someone had taken care of notifying the police. With luck, any duty I had as an upstanding citizen was already fulfilled.

Too bad I didn't have any luck.

By now, Lady Beatrice and Lord Humphrey were off to one side of the church in a heated pantomime. Celia glanced over at them and looked annoyed just as a camera flash went off.

She was posing for a photograph surrounded by her new husband's family. She turned to face her mother long enough for the photographer to stand up and say something. Robert's expression told me he had snapped at Celia. She glared at him and walked away toward her mother. The photographer shouted, "I'm not finished." I could hear Robert yell, "Celie." His mother looked ready to cry.

Uncle Walter and Aunt Margaret reached their fighting siblings at the same time as Celia. After a few words, they all went in different directions. Aunt Margaret headed toward our group.

"I think we should head back to the house and see how the tent looks for the reception. It's rather chilly out in this wind. Would you like a cup of tea?" she asked, taking the arms of two elderly ladies and marching them along with some care. That was a signal of sorts for the rest of us to fall in behind her.

I saw my father's other arm taken by the widow of an old friend of his, and we made polite conversation as we walked down the street. As we reached the house, I disengaged my arm. "I forgot something from inside. I won't be a minute."

"Livvy," I heard my father say as I ran up the front steps. Before I had a chance to ring the bell, a man with photographic equipment came out the door.

"Oh, are you with the wedding?" I asked, hoping to get an unguarded response.

The young man weighted down with equipment said, "No. I'm with the police. You're having a jollier day than that bloke."

I walked inside to discover Watkins wasn't in view. I could hear voices upstairs, so I went up, telling myself I was headed toward my room if anyone asked. If I were lucky, I'd find a chatty maid.

As I neared the old earl's door, the man who appeared to be a detective inspector came out with Ames, the earl's valet. Surprised, and feeling more than a little guilty, I jumped. They both stared at me as if I'd committed some terrible social faux pas.

"What are you doing here, miss?" the policeman asked.

"I'm staying here. I forgot something in my room." I spoke quickly and pointed. Then I turned to Ames. "What's happened? You're as white as a sheet."

"It's the earl, miss." He looked close to tears.

"Don't tell me he's been murdered."

"How do you know anyone's been murdered?" the detective asked, moving toward me a half step. He was tall and broad shouldered and rather ordinary looking.

"I heard you talking to Lord Humphrey."

"May I trust you not to say anything to anyone, miss? Don't want to ruin the bride's happiest day. What's your name?"

"Olivia Denis. And yours?"

"Detective Inspector Guess."

We nodded and then I turned to the valet. "Now, Ames, you must sit down. This has been a shock. Did his attacker strike you, too?"

"No." He shook his head. "It happened while I was getting my breakfast."

That would have been a couple of hours before the wedding. Ames would have started his day with breakfast before waking the earl with a cup of tea. He'd probably found the old earl stabbed when I saw him with Lady Beatrice. Celia had been in the room after that, and my guess was she'd discovered Millhaven dead.

The detective must have realized how long ago Ames's meal was. He turned to the valet. "What time did you have breakfast? And I want an honest answer this time."

Ames's shoulders slumped and all the air seemed to leave his body. "Her ladyship is not going to be happy."

All the while I wondered why one of Celia's family would kill a sick old man. He surely couldn't have lived much longer. It had to be one of the Brookes. No one else would be sneaking around Millhaven House early on a Saturday morning.

As to who benefitted from the will signed the day before, we'd soon learn when the will was read.

I retreated downstairs to the wedding reception before I was questioned further by the police.

One of Robert's classmates at Oxford who'd been invited to the wedding was a reporter on the national news desk of the *Daily Premier*. We knew each other slightly from work. Somehow, I couldn't force myself to slip him the exclusive on the murder of the earl. At least not before Celia left on her honeymoon.

So instead, we talked about rumors of war and office gossip.

Fortunately, my father was busy with the widow he had escorted back to the house and his cronies, so there was no need for me to have to hide my knowledge about the murder from him.

First came the toasts. Uncle Humphrey, standing in for his father, said the earl was sorry he couldn't attend and was very pleased for his granddaughter and her new husband and wished them well. He gave the loyal toast first, and then said, "To the bride and groom."

I knew the police had told him about the murder. I was impressed he handled his duties so gracefully.

Then Celia's father, Lord Eustace, gave a long-winded, sentimental toast, which gave me time to wonder how he'd come by the bruises on the left side of his face. Despite it still being before noon, the champagne was obviously not his first drink of the day. I was also certain no one had told him about the earl's death.

Mr. Grayling, Robert's father, gave the next toast, welcoming Celia into the family. He seemed relaxed, intelligent, and normal. I wondered how Celia would fit in with a family that was sane.

The best man, a university friend of Robert's, gave the final toast, and then it was announced the food was put out in the other tent. The band had set up during the toasts and began to play the first waltz for the bride and groom. Then the newlyweds danced with the parents, and then the parents danced together. Judging by his reddened coloring and her expression, Lady Beatrice obviously upbraided Lord Eustace as they marched around the floor.

The band must have been warned as the leader quickly called everyone onto the dance floor. Fortunately for all of us wearing high heels, the floor built to cover the tennis court was smooth. No expense had been spared on this wedding. I wondered who had paid for it.

I managed a sedate waltz with the man from the *Daily Premier* while being crushed by the crowd. The dance floor should have been twice its size, but that would have meant building over Aunt Margaret's prized flower garden, and no one was brave enough to do that. As it was, she patrolled the perimeter of the party, ordering people to stop stepping on her Latin-named blooms.

I was twenty-six and realistic enough to know most of the men I'd dance with today might soon be facing German cannons. The thought drained all happiness out of me.

I was by the refreshments table, having a cup of watered-down sherry punch, when Aunt Margaret came up to me. She wore the long string of pearls given to her on her debut into society nearly forty years before, now looped into a knot to make it shorter and fashionable. It went well with her white and green outfit, but not the low-heeled black pumps with the huge bows. Aunt Margaret was willing to follow fashion until it hurt her feet and not an inch further.

My shoes were starting to pinch. I'd have gladly traded with her.

"What do you think of the wedding? Celia certainly looks happy," I said.

"Triumphant is more like it. I didn't think they'd ever marry," Aunt Margaret said, taking a cup of punch. "Ooh, this is dreadful. Must be Bea's doing. Now, is that nice young man of yours here?"

"Adam? No. He's off with the army somewhere."

"A piece of advice, Livvy. You're my favorite niece. Don't let this threatened war rule your life."

"A war wouldn't dare. My father has first call on that."

"Your father loves you nearly as much as I do. Now, go have fun. This dancing is for you young people." She smiled at me as she took my cup and gave me a playful shove toward the dance floor.

I was dancing with Celia's youngest cousin, Edwin, and trying to encourage him despite his stepping on my toes for the fifth time when I heard a cheer go up. We both tried to turn to see what was happening, tangling our feet and bumping heads.

"Annabeth! Olivia! Come up and help me get ready," Celia called out.

"You've been saved," Edwin said, adjusting his glasses.

I shook my head at him and headed into the house. Was I expected to keep the newlyweds out of the earl's room or hand out hankies when the hysteria began?

Celia gave Robert a warm kiss and sent him off to the earl's study on the ground floor to change for their departure. Then she led the way as Annabeth and I followed her up the stairs. "I have to change and finish packing, so I really need your help."

There were still mountains of clothes scattered around the room destined for her trunks and her suitcase. Annabeth shook her head and began to pack a trunk.

I unpinned Celia's veil, undid the tiny row of buttons down the back of her gown, and walked over to help

Annabeth. "Your brother is fond of order and neatness?" I asked as I folded a blouse.

"Very much so. That's how we were raised," she murmured, making quick work of tidying frocks.

"Celia and her mother had a ladies' maid until a couple of years ago. She hasn't developed the skill yet."

The girl frowned. "But you have, and you're part of the family."

"How's it going over there?" Celia asked.

"Fine," I replied. Then I smiled at Annabeth and whispered, "I'm a distant relation. We grew up together from babies because my father and her Uncle Humphrey are third cousins and fast friends. My mother died when I was five, so ladies' maids have always seemed like exotic creatures to me."

Annabeth and I were still packing, while Celia was dressed and smoking a cigarette, when Lady Beatrice came in. "Sit," she commanded her daughter.

Annabeth watched, a scowl on her brow. I knew what was coming and wondered at the wisdom of discussing this in front of the groom's sister. The groom's sharp, observant sister.

Celia sat on the stool in front of her dressing table. "What is going on?"

"I've come to take possession of the countess's necklace," Lady Beatrice said, wrapping up the jewelry. "And I'm very afraid something has happened to your grandfather."

"Another heart attack? Another stroke? We've been expecting something of the sort for ages. It's just awful to think it would happen today." Her eyes welled up, but she seemed calm.

Too calm. Annabeth's scowl lines deepened. I guessed she suspected Celia was acting.

Just as I had when we found the body.

"No. I'm sorry." Lady Beatrice walked over and patted her shoulder. "Your grandfather was attacked. He died of his wounds."

Her bald statement reduced us all to silence. Then Celia's mouth opened and shut a few times. "His wounds?"

"Yes."

"He was murdered? When?"

Did Celia think we were the first two to find her grandfather murdered? Having heard Lady Beatrice and Ames earlier, I guessed we weren't even second.

CHAPTER FIVE

"This morning." Lady Beatrice used her soothing voice, the one that always warned me I'd be punished shortly.

"Oh, no," Celia wailed. "What do I do about wearing mourning on my honeymoon? All my pretty clothes. I don't have enough mourning outfits. It isn't fair."

I winced and Annabeth's jaw dropped at Celia's selfish statement, but she rallied and said, "Celia, may I make a suggestion?"

"Of course."

"Let me tell my brother what happened. I'll ask if he wants you to wear mourning or not, because believe me, once you start wearing mourning, he's going to expect you to follow through with all the customs."

"He believes that once you set a course, you follow through, no matter what?" I asked.

"Yes."

I wondered if she'd also tell him about his wife's sloppiness and lack of feeling for her grandfather. How much did Robert know about his new bride?

"Yes, please, ask him," Celia said.

Annabeth slipped out of the room.

"Under the circumstances, I hope he says no mourning," Celia said to the closed door. "And how long have you known, Mother?"

"I didn't want to say this in front of Annabeth, but he was killed by about eight this morning."

"And you didn't tell me?" Celia rose and walked away from her mother.

I had seen Lady Beatrice and Ames a little before

eight outside the old earl's bedroom. I'd bet anything he was dead then. Celia was in his bedroom about a quarter after eight. She knew, too.

Lady Beatrice murmured, "We couldn't have another delay in the wedding. You'd have been in mourning for six months, and I'll be in mourning for a year. Did you want to delay your wedding for another year? What if Robert ran out of patience?"

"I suspect he might have with some of us already," Celia said, glaring at her mother.

Lady Beatrice was trying to put reasonableness into her tone, but I heard the underlying tension. "You two are so happy together. Of course he's getting impatient. You didn't want to be here while Robert traveled for the bank. Now, what's done is done, and you and Robert are married. Worse comes to worse, Robert will want to delay the honeymoon until you're out of mourning. But that's all." She started forward, sounding as if this was a minor matter.

Celia's eyes narrowed, her face now inches from her mother's. "I had a right to know he was dead."

What a liar. I felt certain she'd found out shortly after her mother.

Lady Beatrice sounded just a little too happy about the fact the ceremony was complete and there was nothing anyone could do about it. "After another woman looked over the bank's assets and decided to try to marry Robert, it's just as well this ceremony is over."

"You've been pushing me to marry Robert since the first time you met him and found out what he does. And how much he has."

"You love him, and he loves you. If he was distracted by another woman's charms, well, that's all in the past."

Robert's determination that once you set out to do

something, you carry it through the whole way could explain why Celia won out over the other woman and why Lady Beatrice was so nervous about the wedding being called off again. I wondered what Annabeth thought of the girl who'd come between Robert and Celia not so long ago.

There was a knock on the door. Lady Beatrice fell silent as I opened it to find Annabeth. "Robert says if you don't mind, a lack of mourning dress would make attending the events in South Africa much simpler."

"That's what I'll do, then," Celia said. "Thank you, Annabeth. I'll be down in a bit. Mother and I have to make some last-minute plans."

I could read on Annabeth's face that she didn't buy Celia's dismissal, but she nodded and left, shutting the door behind her.

"Olivia, there's something you can do for me."

"You have only to ask." I realized a moment too late how dangerous that polite phrase could be when dealing with Celia and her mother.

There was a slight pause while Celia lit another cigarette, and I saw her hands shake slightly. "I won't be here to make sure the police find the killer. You've had experience with this—"

"Celia, I don't—"

"You found Reggie's killer. You can do it again."

"That was my husband. I had a reason to stick my nose into police business. This is your family. Not mine." Just thinking about investigating another murder started my stomach churning.

"I bet Mother agrees with me, and she'll make everyone, family and servants, talk to you."

I glanced at Lady Beatrice as I said, "That's the job of the police."

"You didn't think so when Reggie was killed." Celia began pacing.

"That was different. No one is saying your grandfather killed himself." I wanted no part of this.

"Mother, I won't be here. I want you to have Olivia investigate Grandfather's murder. Make sure the police get the killer. The right killer." Her tone was the verbal equivalent of stomping her foot.

Lady Beatrice walked toward me, her eyes studying me. "Celia told us how you found Reggie's killer. She's right. I want you to find this killer, too. It's the only way we can be sure the police get it right."

"What if it's one of the family?"

"It isn't."

I crossed my arms. "And if it is? Do you want me to hand him or her over to the police?"

She looked at the carpet while Celia watched her, a concerned expression on her face. When her mother glanced back up, I could see the determination in her expression. "Yes."

With Lady Beatrice, that decision could mean only one thing. "You know who did it."

She walked away then. "No. I wish I did. We'll talk after we see Celia off."

"Refresh my memory. How long will you be gone?" I asked Celia.

"A month. Robert has business for the bank to carry out while we're there." She turned to her mother. "No. We'll talk now. What happened to Grandfather?"

Lady Beatrice strode to the window and looked out. "Ames found him when he brought up his morning tea. I was passing by and heard the crash. I thought Father had fallen. I knocked and went in to find Ames patting his cheek and calling his name. We both thought it was his heart."

Turning to face us, she added, "Ames looked down and gasped. I came over and looked. Blood on the covers. We pulled them back and found a knife in his chest."

"Did you recognize the handle of the knife?"

"Unlikely." Her expression was so dramatic that I had trouble believing her. I wondered if I could get the police to show me the knife.

"Was anyone else around when you passed by the door and heard the crash?" I asked.

"No."

I nodded. "You and Ames saw the knife. Then what?"

"I decided the wedding would go on as planned. Ames could call the police once you'd left on your honeymoon. Unfortunately, he called as soon as we all went to the church." She sounded annoyed.

"Did anyone besides you and Ames know about the earl's death before the police were called?"

"I don't think so. Well, maybe."

"You don't think so? Mother. Either they did or they didn't." Celia sounded like she wanted to get to the bottom of her grandfather's death, even if she had to fight her mother's reluctance.

I noticed she didn't mention she and I knew before the wedding. Typical of Celia not to get herself caught in an uncomfortable position.

"I think someone came by the doorway to the room as Ames and I were discussing our options."

"Options? We're discussing a murder. The police won't think much of your options. You find a victim, you report it." I shook my head.

Lady Beatrice ignored my rebuke as she looked down on the garden below. "I don't know if this person heard us talking."

"Celia took me in to see the old earl before the wedding."

The mother turned on her daughter. "You shouldn't have done that. Now you can't say you had no knowledge of his death. Livvy is a witness."

"Livvy won't tell. I've kept her secrets." Celia gave me a victorious smile, and I nodded my agreement. My cheeks heated at the thought of my girlish past sins, and the foolishness of letting Celia discover what I had done.

"Do I have your permission to speak to the servants?" I asked.

"Of course."

"What about your brothers and sister?" This was a complicated family.

"What about them?" Typical Lady Beatrice. My father said she'd been bullying her siblings since childhood.

"They won't speak to me unless they also agree to allow my investigation." And I saw no reason to waste my time on a farce of an investigation. I wouldn't be paid, for starters.

"Leave them to me. We're going to have a family meeting once Celia and Robert and the guests depart."

"I want to be part of this family gathering as well." Celia was wearing a mulish expression that matched her mother's.

"If you don't leave, no one else will, either, dear."

"Robert and I will leave, but then we'll come back."

"Is that wise? Will Robert accept that?" her mother asked.

"He'll have to. I want to tell my aunts and uncles they'll have to accept Livvy investigating Grandfather's murder."

"In front of Robert?"

"Why not? He'll find out Grandfather was murdered

sooner or later. I expect Annabeth has told him already."

Good grief. Celia was planning a good, old-fashioned family fight and setting me in the center of it. Exactly where I didn't want to be. "I hope you don't want me there."

"I do, Livvy. You and your father."

"My father?" She didn't realize how much he would argue against her plans.

"I want him to help convince Uncle Humphrey."

"He didn't like me investigating Reggie's death. I can't imagine he'll be happy for me to get involved in your grandfather's murder."

She smiled. "Leave him to me. Now, are we ready?" She put on her hat and gloves. "I'll be back in an hour, Mother. Have all the guests out of here by then."

I wondered if Celia realized she and her mother used the same tone to order everyone around.

After the bride and groom departed, I went in search of my father. I found him outside in the company of his friend's widow. With any luck, he'd leave with her and I'd face the Brookes on my own.

"Olivia, I imagine you don't remember me."

I hated it when friends of my father started conversations that way. It guaranteed I wouldn't remember them.

She didn't give me time to give an evasive answer. "I'm Martha Gibbons. Your father and I have been friends forever. You don't mind if I steal him away for dinner, do you?" She wore a big smile, knowing I couldn't refuse.

"Not at all." My smile was just as wide. It would solve a big problem for me.

And then, with an inbred sense that drove Celia crazy when we were younger, Lady Beatrice arrived at my shoulder. "Sir Ronald, I need you and Olivia to stay after the other guests have gone. We want your help with a situation."

I caught my father glance from Lady Beatrice to me, a small frown on his face.

"I'm sure we'll be glad to, won't we, Ronald," the widow said brightly.

"I'm afraid the invitation doesn't include you, Mrs. Gibbons. And this is going to take some time. I'm sure you and Sir Ronald can catch up on old times another day." Lady Beatrice took my father's arm on one side and mine on the other and led us away from Mrs. Gibbons, who stood there, her mouth slightly open in surprise.

We were nearly to the door to the house when my father murmured, "No, Olivia. This is one murder you'll avoid."

I looked at my father in surprise. How did he know that Lady Beatrice wanted to involve us?

Once we were inside, she left us on our own in the worn, informal family parlor. It was bigger than the reception tents, but a great deal cozier. My father spent our time waiting by quizzing me on everything I knew about the earl's murder, and I returned the favor by asking about his relationship with Mrs. Gibbons.

He learned the time the body was discovered and how much later the police were notified. I didn't mention Celia and I had also seen the body. I learned what my father heard about the knifing from Uncle Humphrey and nothing concerning Mrs. Gibbons.

The new earl was the last to arrive, except for Celia. "I didn't think I'd ever get rid of him," he muttered, fixing a large Scotch and sitting next to my father.

"Who?" my father asked.

"Eustace. Had his hand out again and wouldn't take no for an answer, cheeky blighter. I told him no one could do anything for him until after the funeral and to have a little compassion."

Then Humphrey looked around the room, all of us seated with our drinks, and said, "What is going on, Beatrice? Father's been murdered, and you've assembled the family in the parlor like we're in some mystery novel."

"Celia wants us to wait for her."

"Celia's on her honeymoon." His voice boomed out so loudly I was sure the servants were getting an earful.

"She said she'd be back in an hour. We just need to be patient."

"Celia's hour is usually two," Walter observed. I noticed he appeared detached, nursing his drink and studying the far wall as if he were used to waiting.

"And why are Ronald and Livvy here?" Aunt Margaret asked.

"All will become clear when Celia arrives."

"If she doesn't forget all about us and take off for her honeymoon and Cape Town. With the countess's necklace," Lady Amelia, Humphrey's wife, added.

"It's already been put back in the safe. Check if you don't believe me," Lady Beatrice said.

Humphrey rose to his feet. "As the new earl, I have duties to perform. Either begin this—absurdity, or I'm leaving."

"Sit down, Uncle. I'm here now." Celia walked in, pulling off her gloves. Robert Grayling walked over to the decanter and poured himself a drink. If this was the groom's first encounter with the bride's family as they really were, he'd need that drink. "Where's Edwin? And Daddy?"

"I didn't think it was necessary for either of them to be here," Lady Beatrice said.

Celia took that with more grace than I expected. She could do without her youngest cousin, but I thought she'd want her father for moral support. Maybe she didn't want to upset her Uncle Humphrey, who, as the new earl, held the reins now. And the purse strings.

Maybe. Everything depended on the will.

Celia walked into the center of the room and said, "Our ship leaves tonight, so I don't have a lot of time. And since I won't be here, I want Olivia Denis to act in my stead to find out who murdered Grandfather."

"That's the job of the police," Humphrey thundered.

"No one is going to replace the police. I want Olivia to make sure the wrong person isn't arrested. She's had experience with this before."

My father, sitting next to me on a sofa, grumbled. I felt like grumbling myself.

"Would someone tell me what's going on?" Thomas, Humphrey's oldest and now next in line to be Earl of Millhaven, asked.

Celia stared at her cousin, who looked away. "Grandfather was stabbed to death. He was found by Ames and Mother about eight this morning. In consideration of my feelings, Ames didn't notify the police until after the wedding had started."

"That's not how it's supposed to be done, Celie," her cousin Charlie said in an amused tone.

I glanced over to see Robert Grayling's eyes narrow. He was definitely taking the measure of his in-laws.

"I know that," Celia said. "I didn't know anything about this until I went to change for our trip. Mother meant well, but she's probably made things more difficult for the police. That's why Olivia should do her own investigation, to make sure everything's done properly from here on out."

"So you're going to let Olivia sniff out our family secrets," Thomas said, grinning.

"Oh, I think she'll figure you out quickly enough," Celia snapped.

"Don't quarrel, children. This can't be fun for Olivia or Sir Ronald," Lady Beatrice said. "Can we all agree to cooperate with Olivia? I'm sure she can be relied on for complete discretion. Something the police can't."

Oh, joy. They didn't want a murderer. They wanted my silence on their secrets.

CHAPTER SIX

I noticed the family members glancing furtively at each other. How many of them knew about the old earl's murder before the wedding? Robert Grayling was watching them with distaste, and my father was glaring at me.

"Livvy, say something," Celia said. I noticed a begging tone in her words.

"I don't want to do this. The only reason I'd consider doing this is as a favor for the bride and groom. And I won't help if any of you don't agree to answer my questions honestly and fully."

I glared at everyone as I looked around the room. "I'm not required to pass on anything I learn to the police. It would be considered hearsay. I won't share any confidences. All I will do is try to make certain the police don't arrest the wrong person and keep Celia informed if anything extraordinary happens."

"Not to be rude, Mrs. Denis, but how can we trust you?" Lady Amelia asked.

"She didn't tell the police anything in her investigation of her husband's death. Nevertheless, she assured that they learned the identity of his killer," my father said. I was surprised but proud that he thought I'd done a good job.

"How on earth did she do that?"

"By putting herself in danger." His grumble told me he didn't approve of my methods.

That wasn't exactly correct. And I had no intention of putting myself in danger to find the nasty old earl's killer.

"I don't expect Livvy to put herself in danger to find

Father's murderer," Aunt Margaret said. "I trust her. I always have. And if she wants to investigate, I'm willing to agree."

"If it means Livvy will be looking out for the best interests of the family, I'm in favor. You can count on my support," Walter said.

"And mine," Lady Beatrice said.

"Oh, but can we be sure she has the best interests of the family in this?" Thomas walked over to the drinks cabinet and poured himself a brandy.

"You can," my father said. "She does, and so do I."

Oh, goody. Now my father was planning to meddle in an investigation I didn't want to be involved in. The look I gave him should have frozen him to his seat.

Not my father. He turned to the new earl. "Humphrey, we only want to help. And Olivia does have a talent for investigating, whether I like it or not."

I recognized that as high praise.

Humphrey turned to his wife. "What do you think?"

"You're the new earl. Stand on your own two feet for a change, will you?" Amelia turned her face away from him.

His face reddening at his wife's rebuke, Humphrey said, "Yes, Livvy, Ronald. You'll have my help in this investigation."

"Well, you won't have mine," Thomas said.

"Why not? It sounds like a lark," Charlie said. "I'll help, and so will Edwin, when we tell him about it. We don't find it necessary to fight our father every step of the way like some people."

Thom shoved him to go along with the dark look he gave his brother.

Lady Amelia said, "I suppose we'll all help you, Mrs. Denis. It's no one in the family, and the sooner we find out who did this, the easier we'll all sleep at night. Otherwise, who knows who'll get murdered next?"

"What nonsense. No one's going to get murdered next," Aunt Margaret said.

"Really? And how would you know that?" Thom asked.

"It stands to reason. Someone knew where Father was and that he'd be alone. He couldn't have been killed by mistake in place of someone else. Therefore, there shouldn't be a next." Aunt Margaret set her teacup down before folding her arms over her bosom.

"He might or might not be the only target, but it's likely the killer is someone in the family or someone who knows the house well." I could tell by the looks aimed at me that they didn't like my reasoning. That was all right. I didn't like my thoughts either. To suspect people you've known all your life of murder was disgusting. But it seemed too likely.

"Someone like Lord Eustace?" Lady Beatrice Eustace said. "That's unthinkable."

"Mummy. Daddy wasn't here last night." Celia couldn't have been more emphatic if she'd stomped her foot. I wondered if her new husband knew about that habit.

"You can never be sure where that man is." Lady Beatrice twisted her fingers.

Lord Humphrey saw the fight that was brewing and said, "I think we're agreed that you are to make some discreet inquiries for us, Livvy."

Blast. I thought they'd refuse. "I'll do it. Please, don't tell me lies. I'm sure I'll have to learn some things people might not want me to know. Rest assured, I don't want to know your secrets and will forget them as quickly as I can be sure they have nothing to do with the murder."

Most of them nodded. I felt sure they'd all lie to me at every opportunity.

"Celia, I'll need an address to write to you in South Africa," I added.

"Surely Celia will be too busy. She'll be on her honeymoon," Lady Beatrice said. Her gaze was icy.

"Robert will be busy with work part of the trip. She'll have enough time to write a letter or two." I looked from Celia to her mother. My expression spoke volumes. *If you don't agree, I won't bother with any investigation, and you can only hope the police get it right.*

Celia walked over to a side table and wrote something down on a slip of paper. When she handed it to me, I read the name of the leading hotel in Cape Town.

"You can reach me there. Thank you, Livvy, for taking this on. Now, if you promise not to murder each other in my absence, I'm going on my honeymoon. Robert?" She strutted over to her husband, who rose and took her arm. He appeared impressed with her performance.

I was impressed, too, but I recognized it as a performance. Celia, the great lady. I wondered if Robert knew what an actress he had married.

"Wait. Before you go, can anyone think of a strange or upsetting event occurring in the last few days?" I glanced at everyone in the room. "Anything that might have angered the earl? Or someone else? Besides the new will, of course."

They all shook their heads or mumbled "No." No one held my gaze.

They were all lying. Or at least very uncomfortable.

With a wave, Celia led Robert from the room.

Lord Humphrey rose. "We've had a wedding and a death in a single day. Could you wait a day or two before you start interrogating us?"

"I have no problem with that," I told him, also rising, "but the police won't be so understanding."

My father and I didn't split up until after dinner, as he invited me to a hotel restaurant with one of the best chefs in London. As soon as I got home, I called the *Daily Premier* and left a message for Mr. Colinswood, an international editor I'd worked with before, about the murder of the Earl of Millhaven under the noses of his family on the day of his granddaughter's wedding.

* * *

After a command performance to stand at my father's side at Sunday service, I dressed to travel by bus into the suburbs to Millhaven House. Yesterday's good weather didn't look like it would last, so I wore my trench coat, a small-brimmed hat, and carried my umbrella.

Watkins let me in and showed me into the formal drawing room. I waited there for a good ten minutes before Lady Beatrice came into the room. I rose and walked over to her.

"I'm afraid you've come on a fool's errand today. We're all trying to come to terms with Father's death." She spoke with a twisting of hands as she looked over her shoulder. I thought we might be in some dreadful play. Lady Beatrice was certainly overacting.

"I'm very sorry for your loss, but there might have been a motive for someone in your family to murder your father."

My words forced her to look at me. "What? That's absurd."

"When a person signs a new will one day and is murdered the next, it is generally thought to be suspicious."

She looked down her nose at me. "Perhaps we don't need you investigating Father's death. The police have torn the house apart well enough without your help."

"Did anyone tell them about the new will?"

"That is none of your business."

I smiled. "I'll take that as a 'No.'"

She moved close to me and lowered her voice as she put a hand on my arm. "You said you wouldn't say anything to the police. That you'd keep our secrets."

Apparently, she'd decided to try a different approach. That wouldn't work, either. "And you said you wanted to find your father's killer. Even if it was a member of your family. And because of this new will, you're afraid that it is." I studied her face. "You know who killed him."

She swung around and walked away from me.

I'd guessed right. Either she knew, or she thought she knew the identity of the killer.

"No. I have no idea who the killer is. But yes, I am afraid it is a member of the family. No one else, except perhaps Ames, would gain." She strode back to me. "It's monstrous to think of a member of our family doing something so—so—"

"Does Celia think she gains under this new will?" I was sure she did.

Her mother nodded, her head lowered.

"Is that why she wanted me to find her grandfather's killer? Because she's sure it's a member of the family?"

Lady Beatrice raised her face and said with all the force I expected from her, "Go away. We don't need you picking over our bones just yet. The funeral isn't until Tuesday. Leave us in peace until then."

With a tight grip on my wrist, she began to drag me across the room.

Then a door behind me opened with a bang and a woman's voice said, "Was it you or your daughter who stole the countess's necklace? It's mine now. Hand it over."

I turned to find Lady Amelia, the new Countess of Millhaven, staring past me.

Lady Beatrice dropped her grip on my arm as she said, "I told you. I put it back in the safe."

"Well, it's not there now. Is it on the ship bound to South Africa or are you hiding it somewhere in the house? I warn you, the necklace is mine and I will have it back." Amelia walked up to Beatrice and glared at her before storming from the room.

Lady Beatrice stood there, looking stunned. I admit I felt the same way.

I was about to slink off when Walter Brooke came in the room and said, "Well, hello, young Olivia. You certainly brighten up the place."

"Thank you, Uncle Walter."

Lady Beatrice grumbled something and walked away.

I'd always called him Uncle Walter, just as I called their sister Aunt Margaret and I'd always called Lady Beatrice by her title. This was a leftover from my childhood and all the time I spent playing here with Celia and her three cousins. "I've come to see if anyone has anything helpful to tell me about your father's murder."

"Helpful? Oh, I doubt that. I doubt that very much."

"What about the new will? Could that have provoked some sort of row?"

Walter glanced at his sister, raising his eyebrows. "A row of that magnitude would have been heard by someone. Several someones, I'd say."

I tried again. "When did you get back from Deauville?"

"You've been paying attention." He smiled to show

there were no hurt feelings. "I arrived at the station at six on Friday and then the ride was oh, half an hour?"

"And you were home all night?"

"Yes. Feeling rather tired. The scene after dinner just made it worse. I went to my room and was asleep right afterward."

"You must have been awake in the middle of the night if you argued with Philip Eustace."

"What?" Lady Beatrice demanded.

"Oh, Bea. I defended you. Humphrey is the one who thinks you should leave the blighter alone." Walter walked past her and dropped into a chair.

She turned on me. "Don't look at me like that."

I kept staring at her, trying not to let my jaw drop any further than it already had. I was certain Lord and Lady Eustace hadn't exchanged a civil word in years.

"We are still married. There's nothing indecent in what we did." Her chin tilted skyward as she warmed up for a full grand dame performance.

"No one said there is." Her brother lit a cigarette.

"Does Celia know?" I huffed out.

"No, and you won't tell her. And Walter, Olivia seems to think there's something wrong with my marriage, but she couldn't manage to wear mourning for her husband for more than a couple of months. And I don't think she ever observed it."

My sigh oozed boredom, a sound I learned from Celia. "We're discussing your husband being in this house Friday night. What time did he arrive and when did he leave?"

Her arms crossed and her nose in the air, Lady Beatrice said, "He arrived a little after midnight and departed after two."

"How did he get in and out?"

"He has his own latchkey."

I stared at her as I realized that meant Lord Eustace could have been in the house at any time. Even at the right time to kill the earl.

Lady Beatrice must have read my mind. "He was long gone before Father was killed. And he wasn't mentioned in either will, so it wouldn't have made any difference to him."

"Could there have been another quarrel between them? Perhaps your father didn't approve of the way your husband was treating you."

"First Father was killed because of the new will, and then he was not. Make up your mind, Olivia." Lady Beatrice made her words a command.

"I don't need to make up my mind about anything. I just need to make sure the police don't hang the wrong person."

"They won't hang the wrong person, Olivia. I'm sure you'll see to that." Walter gave me a gloomy sort of smile.

"Who benefits?"

"Oh, my." Walter straightened the creases in his trousers. "In the old will, Humphrey inherited most of the loot, with legacies for Maggie, Bea and me. In the new will, Humphrey's sons get the lot, but in a company board sort of way. And Celia gets a nice chunk in her own name."

They'd seen the will now. The question was, had they seen it before the murder? "So no one in your generation was named in the new will?"

"Not a bean. Hard for us artistic types."

"How are your paintings selling?" I hated to ask a rude question. And pride might make him exaggerate.

"Not as well as Margaret's poetry. She's starting to get some renown."

"Good for Aunt Margaret. Now, could you explain this

company board setup?" It sounded like a recipe for disaster. Especially since I'd already seen how badly Humphrey, the new earl, and his oldest son Thomas got along.

"They vote on any expenditures, hiring advisors, and so on. It has to be unanimous. Probably because Charlie and Edwin have brains, even if Charlie doesn't always act like it."

"And if one of them dies?"

Walter gave a quiet snort. "I don't know. Wasn't paying that much attention. Especially as Humphrey and Margaret both sounded as if they'd have apoplexy."

"Nonsense, Walter."

He turned on his sister. "It was shameful the way they were shouting at the poor old man in his bed."

So the children had heard the terms of the new will before the old earl died.

"Well, if he hadn't done anything so—extraordinarily wrong, there wouldn't have been anything to shout about."

"It's his money, Bea, or it was, to do with as he liked."

"He was an earl, with properties and responsibilities to the family. He should have thought of that. Instead, so typically, he didn't give his children a thought." Lady Beatrice picked up a vase in a stranglehold.

I fought the urge to duck.

"Why did he write his will that way? It's certainly not normal," I quickly asked before Lady Beatrice launched the vase.

"Perhaps it was an attempt to make Humphrey and Thomas work together for the good of the family," Lady Beatrice said.

"Or maybe he thought about the way we've sponged off him all these years. Maybe he just got tired of seeing us hold out our begging bowls." I noticed as Walter lit another cigarette that his hands shook. He must have been more affected by this argument than I would have guessed by his calm, quiet voice.

"Maybe you've sponged. My husband has supported my daughter and me as much as he was able, and Humphrey has a position in HM Treasury. It's only you and Margaret with your delusions of artistic talent who have had your begging bowls out." She set the vase down with a thud.

Walter rose from his chair. "I've sold a few paintings. I doubt I've taken Dad for as much over the years as you have, supporting your bankrupt husband."

Glaring at each other, the siblings stormed out of the room in different directions.

I hoped the police wouldn't jump to any conclusions, because I was sure they'd find out about the new will.

CHAPTER SEVEN

As I so often did when I came to this house, I went in search of Aunt Margaret.

She was in her favorite spot in the greenhouse, her glasses off, a stray gray hair loosed from her bun, a streak of dirt on her cheek, surrounded by soil, pots, and a plant she was dividing.

"Are you busy?" I asked.

"Never too busy to talk to you. Come in, Livvy, and sit down. How is the newspaper business? Have they figured out yet that the reading public is not made up of idiots?"

Margaret was my favorite of those I called aunts and uncles at Millhaven House because she cared about me. She went into battle with my father and finally convinced him to send me to university, probably because we ganged up on him. She always told me to do what was right for me, which had made her question my marrying Reggie.

And she always had time for me, telling a little girl tales of feminine derring-do in long-ago times and an older girl stories of historical truth involving women of character and bravery.

She often asked me about my job. Today, I ignored her questions. "Celia wants me to make sure the police don't arrest the wrong person in your father's murder. So far, I'm not getting much cooperation."

She set a section of the plant in a pot and turned to look at me. "Why are you doing it?"

"Celia asked me to. And I don't want to see anyone, you especially, being locked up for a crime they didn't commit."

"That's admirable. But what if the killer is Celia? Do you want to see her punished?"

"On the theoretical level, yes, she'd have to be. On the practical level—Celia? Dirty her hands by killing someone? Besides, I was with her when she found the body just before the wedding. He'd been dead a couple of hours by then."

"Are you sure that was the first time she discovered he was dead? Perhaps she took you along for an alibi." Aunt Margaret turned away to tamp down the soil in the pot.

I didn't want to admit how close Aunt Margaret's comments were to my own thoughts. It was far more likely she'd found him dead when I saw her slipping out of his room after breakfast. "It's a possibility."

"I've never understood why you carry out every whim of Celia's. You're smarter than she is. You're better educated than she is. And she may be my niece, but you're a much better person than she is."

I gave the easy answer. The part I wasn't embarrassed to admit. "She's a blood relation. The earl's granddaughter. She belongs here. I'm here by grace and sufferance."

"Not in my eyes, Livvy. I've always envied your mother for having a wonderful child like you."

Surprised, I locked gazes with her. "That's very kind, Aunt Margaret, but the fact remains, this is her family. I have tenuous ties here through my father, and possibly stronger bonds through you by your kindness and generosity."

She gave a most unladylike snort. "You do realize I staked out bragging rights on you and your future when you were six. You can't have a closer relative than that."

* * *

Monday at work, I turned in an article on Celia and Robert's wedding, complete with a studio photo of the couple. Miss Westcott no longer shuddered when I turned in copy, which told me I had graduated to passable society reporter.

Plenty of engagement and wedding notices had come into the paper over the weekend, so I was assigned to writing announcements. By the time I returned to my flat that night, my fingers hurt from pushing down typewriter keys.

The phone rang as soon as I walked in. I said hello and heard Captain Adam Redmond's voice come through the wire to me, crackly and weak.

"Adam, where are you?" I asked before I thought.

"I just called to hear your voice." There was a pause. "I'm still out of town."

With the army, that could be anywhere. With his assignment, intelligence, that could be anywhere in the world. I knew I shouldn't have asked. I swallowed before I said in a bright voice, "I hope you're having a good time. Everything here is the same."

That wasn't true, but this phone call wasn't about the literal truth. It was about our voices touching even if we couldn't.

"Oh, it's been okay here. I don't know what my schedule will be. I'll try to write."

"I hope you do. I always enjoy reading your letters." He wrote about meals, and birds singing, and things we'd seen and done together in London.

"I will, and I'll send you my address, Livvy."

"Good." It wouldn't be his address, but the letter would probably get to him sooner or later.

"It's good hearing your voice."

"Oh, Adam. I'm so glad you called."

"I miss you, Livvy."

"I miss—" There was a noise and the line went dead.

At least I knew he was safe and probably in Britain since he was able to telephone. Oh, never fall for a soldier, I told myself. I hugged the receiver to my chest.

I knew I'd run home every night to check the mail.

* * *

I received permission from Miss Westcott to leave for the day at lunchtime on Tuesday to attend the old earl's funeral. I went home, changed into a dress suitable for mourning, put on a stylish black hat and black gloves, and caught a cab to the church in record time. I arrived at the door to find I'd have to slide into a back pew as the sparse congregation finished the first hymn.

Glancing over, I discovered I shared a pew with men I assumed were police detectives. We nodded to each other.

I recited the responses to the prayers and the Bible readings before settling back to hear the vicar deliver the eulogy. I hadn't realized the old earl had had a second wife that he'd outlived along with the first, that he was a patron of the arts, and that he held ministerial positions in Victorian and Edwardian cabinets. Victorian! How old had the old buzzard been? I'd have to read his obituary.

That made me glance around, but I didn't recognize anyone at this private funeral from my several months working on Fleet Street.

The more I thought, the more I believed the old earl had been in a Victorian cabinet. He had always appeared to be at least ninety as far back as I remembered.

More prayers, and then we rose and sang the final hymn before the old earl was carried out of the church to his final resting place in the graveyard. My father was a pallbearer and glanced over at me as they walked out with the coffin. His frown spoke volumes.

I followed the small group outside for the burial service behind the church. I managed to slip into a spot near my father. We recited the responses to the vicar's familiar words and afterward stood back as the few mourners gave handshakes, air kisses, and pats on the shoulders to the old earl's children.

I noticed Celia's parents moved aside to carry out a hushed conversation. Then Lord Eustace slipped away.

Lady Beatrice made a beeline for me. "Oh, Olivia, I wasn't certain you'd arrive on time. Please come back to the house with your father." It was clearly a command.

I could only hope she wanted to fire me as an investigator. Suspecting a family I'd known all my life of committing murder was disconcerting.

My father joined me as Lady Beatrice moved out of hearing distance. "Well, you certainly cut that close. Where had you been?"

If I told him work, it would only begin another row. I gave him my arm in silence.

It was a short stroll around the church where Celia had been married and then up the street to the imposing house. The three grandsons, Thomas, Charles, and Edwin, were already there along with their mother, Lady Amelia. We went inside with them to the family parlor and waited for the old earl's children to return.

"Drink, anyone?" Thomas asked.

"That sounds good, dear. Brandy, everyone? Just a splash for you, Edwin," their mother said.

"How soon until I can go back to school?" Edwin said, sounding glum.

"Tomorrow. All three of you. Trinity term has already started," Amelia said around my father lighting her cigarette.

"My final term," Thomas said. "And then freedom."

"What will you do afterward?" I asked.

"I don't know. What does one do in that case?" he said as he handed around snifters.

"Get a job," his mother said.

"Let's not rush it." Thomas sounded horrified.

"You will when you discover you need a source of the ready to keep up with your friends," Charlie said, sounding gleeful.

Those were the first words I saw bring any sort of smile to Edwin's lips. I decided the younger two boys weren't in awe of their older brother. They had the brains; he'd get the title.

"I imagine Papa will need me to help change things over to the new regime now that Grandpapa is gone." Thomas poured himself more brandy.

"I doubt it. He's been helping your grandfather with the inner workings of the earldom while working in London for quite some time. Ever since your grandfather first became seriously ill, what was it, three years ago? He has everything well in hand." His mother studied her nails.

Thomas glared at her, his face turning an unhealthy red.

I leaned over to my father and whispered, "Why are we here?"

"We were invited," he muttered.

After a short while, there were voices at the front door and then the new earl, Humphrey, came in with Aunt Margaret, followed by Lady Beatrice, who said, "Walter is seeing off the last of the mourners. He'll be along in a moment."

She picked up a glass half full of brandy sitting on an end table and took a swig. That the glass was mine didn't seem to matter. I let her take it without comment, thinking this was typical of Lady Beatrice.

"Now, Olivia, what progress have you made?" Lady Beatrice asked as she set down my glass.

The majesty in her tone annoyed me. I looked around a room that appeared as if a flock of crows had landed on the furniture. "None, except to learn that everyone knew about the new will. That means there were four people in the house who benefitted when the old earl died who wouldn't have if he'd died a day before. Something I'm sure the police know by now as well."

I hoped she'd fire me for speaking my mind.

"The police find the timing of Celia's honeymoon to be suspicious. Suspicious! She was married and then she went on her honeymoon." Lady Beatrice strode up to where I sat. "You must help us. I don't want her honeymoon ruined."

"Yes. We don't want Celia inconvenienced," Thomas sneered.

"You are a dreadful child," Beatrice replied.

"How inconvenienced she is will depend on whether she's found to be in possession of the countess's necklace," Amelia said. "You'll recall I am now countess. I've contacted the police to search her luggage when she arrives in Cape Town."

"You've done what?" Lady Beatrice shrieked. "How dare you?"

"You better hope my father isn't the next one to die, because then I can throw you out of here." Thomas's smile was ugly.

"It's my home," Beatrice squawked as a chorus of voices said, "Thomas!"

"Better watch out, old boy. You might be the next one," Charlie said. His expression showed he was thoroughly enjoying the argument.

"She didn't take your precious necklace and neither did I, as you well know. You'll have to look elsewhere for the thief. Someone who'll have finished school and doesn't have an occupation," Beatrice said, her smile equally evil.

"What a family," Margaret grumbled. "At least you all behaved at the funeral."

Walter came in then and went straight to the brandy bottle to pour himself a large one. I noticed his hands jerked as if in pain as he did. "I'm glad that's over with. Ah, well. We laid poor old Papa to rest in a manner that he'd find appropriate."

"You seemed to be in a hurry to send him off," Humphrey said, studying his brandy snifter.

Everyone appeared not to hear his words as they shifted uncomfortably in their seats. One, I was sure, had more reason than the rest to be uneasy.

"Mother, can I change clothes and go out?" Edwin asked.

"We have to wait for the reading of the will. Then you may go out. All of you may," Amelia said, looking at her sons.

"I wish they would," Margaret said into her glass.

Once the family solicitor arrived, everyone assembled around the dining room table. For some reason, my father and I were invited to join them. Only Thomas objected, and he was ignored.

I fantasized this was because I had been selected the new earl by King George VI. The thought nearly made me release an inappropriate giggle.

Once we were all seated, the solicitor, Mr. Craggett, opened his briefcase after his somber words of condolence and pulled out a frighteningly thick stack of paper. All three young men began to fidget.

My father glared at me as if he knew I wanted to fidget right along with them.

It turned out we all had to pay attention because the whereases and heretofores made an already complex plan incomprehensible. Celia was left a thousand pounds in her own name. After a couple of small bequests to servants, he recited long, dry paragraphs that said the three boys would manage everything not entailed— Millhaven House, the portfolio, all of the earl's money, and the family's holdings—as a committee. Humphrey made a few scoffing noises and Margaret grumbled, but they kept their voices lowered.

The three boys would have an advisory committee that would act any time their decision wasn't unanimous. The solicitor went on for a distressingly long time on how he, the old earl, wanted the boys to act in concert.

My mind wandered and I almost missed the solicitor saying the advisory committee would consist of four members: Mr. Craggett, Celia, my father, and me. We would serve without remuneration.

"Worse luck that," Thomas said.

"So any time Thom wants money, he needs to come to Edwin and me rather than Mother and Father," Charlie said, nearly whooping with joy.

"If it's family money, everyone will have to come to the three of you," Mr. Craggett said in a solemn tone.

Charlie and Edwin looked at each other with dawning realization of their power.

Thomas looked as if he were measuring them for coffins.

Mr. Craggett finished up reading the will, told the family to contact him if they had any questions or if the advisory committee needed to meet, shook hands, and left.

"Now may we change and go out?" Edwin asked.

"Yes, but be home by dinnertime. We're—" their mother began, but all three had already quit the room.

"Can't get them to listen to you, can you?" Margaret said.

"That's not your problem, is it?" Amelia said as Walter lit her cigarette.

"It is now that they control the purse strings and get to decide if we still have a roof over our heads." Margaret looked around the room and slowly shook her head. "This is going to end badly. Just you wait and see."

"Dear old Maggie. Always gloom and doom," Walter said.

I glanced at my father, judging if he was ready to leave yet. He wasn't.

"I can't imagine all three of the boys wanting any of you out. You can be sure the advisory committee will stop any talk of that sort," my father told those still sitting around the dining room table.

"Can you speak for Celia? She'll protect her mother, but what about the rest of us?" Margaret asked.

I'd had enough of prophesies of doom in the news with the German invasion of Austria. "No one is throwing anyone out."

Aunt Margaret focused her light brown eyes on me. "How can you be certain? None of us can speak for another person."

CHAPTER EIGHT

"I'm not a poet. I'm not an artist." As much as I dabbled in sketching and wrote newspaper copy, I couldn't claim the talents of Uncle Walter or Aunt Margaret. "I live in plain, ordinary, everyday reality. And in that world, no one is going to do anything so dire as to throw any of you out. Not with all the safeguards your father put in place."

Aunt Margaret reached out and took my hand. "The world I grew up in is gone. First the slaughter of half the men I knew in the war. Then the Russians with their ghastly collectives, and now the Nazis burning books. At least when I was a child in the Victorian age, there were certainties. There are no certainties any more, Livvy. Not even that I'll see my garden bloom once more. And I'm frightened."

"I would think you know your nephews well enough not to be worried about being thrown out of your family home. That should be taken as given." I couldn't understand her concern, but I gave her hand a squeeze.

"In his eulogy, the vicar said Father was a patron of the arts. What a laugh. There was no provision in his will for the arts. Not even for the artists in our family." Her voice was a mixture of sorrow and earnestness.

"Come on, Maggie. He didn't mention me, and I inherited the title." Humphrey rose and stalked to the window.

"I'm the oldest. I didn't get a title, or a home, or a legacy. I wasn't mentioned. I received nothing under this new will!" Margaret released my hand, rose from her chair, and with grace, strode from the room with her head held high.

"It is a mean-spirited document," Beatrice said.

"Oh, shut up," Amelia said, lighting a cigarette. "Your daughter got a nice reward for being kind to the old man, even if she's only a girl."

As Amelia's words sank in, I sucked in an angry breath. Her words were ugly, given that she was the mother of the three young men who would decide everyone's future because of the old earl. I was glad Aunt Margaret, once a suffragist, hadn't heard her.

I wouldn't have to tell Celia. I was sure her mother would.

"I'm surprised you don't agree with Beatrice," my father said. "Your father-in-law cut your husband out of making any decisions. In the normal state of affairs, your husband would be the head of the family, not have it led by a committee of three boys."

"Not that it's any of your business, Ronald. Don't let us keep you. Or your daughter." Amelia punctuated her words with a smoke ring.

My father and I rose, and as he said his good-byes to Humphrey and Walter, I spoke to Lady Beatrice.

"She thinks she'll run everything now through the boys," she murmured, looking past me at her sister-in-law.

"They're growing up faster than she may realize," I replied. Boys that age had been known to have minds of their own. And to be murderers.

Somebody had murdered the old earl. As I looked around the Brookes' dining room, I discovered I was having less trouble imagining any of these people in the role of killer.

Aunt Margaret might have killed out of fear or hurt pride, Amelia out of a desire for power to rule over the rest of the family, Lady Beatrice out of anger. Anger also made a good motive for Humphrey. I couldn't find a motive yet for Walter or the boys, but I was beginning to think that I would.

And Celia? She was now in South Africa, away from prying eyes and the questions of the police, except for the wretched necklace. It didn't mean she was innocent.

While I waited for my father to finish his farewells, I cornered Thomas by the front door. "Fancy having a drink in town tonight before you go back to Oxford?" He seemed to be the one the police would focus on first.

"Since I'm leaving for Oxford tomorrow, tonight I'd hoped to spend time with my friends away from the mausoleum."

I'd always thought Millhaven House was a lively old home. Odd how different our impressions were of the same place. "Will you be coming into the West End?" I made my voice as cheery as possible.

"Yes." He sounded wary.

"Perhaps we can meet before you go on to the night's entertainments."

There was a pause before his voice brightened. "Yes. After dinner?"

We settled on nine-thirty at the Dryesdale hotel bar in Mayfair. As my father and I left, I hoped it hadn't taken Thom that long to remember I was on the advisory committee that would approve his allowance.

Perhaps he was debating whether to tell me something important about the murder. No doubt that was more hope on my part than possibility.

After we left Millhaven House, my father and I both changed into evening attire before we went out to dinner at a nice restaurant. I chose a long, slim dress, multicolored on a black background with puffy sleeves and a diamond cutout. I put on some multicolored sparkly earrings and grabbed my black gloves, bag, and evening cape before going out to join my father in the taxi.

I was glad to get out of my mourning clothes. At least when I wore them before, I was mourning my husband. Now, it was for a crotchety old man I hadn't cared for.

His bizarre will hadn't made him any dearer to me, either.

We were eating our soup when curiosity got the better of me. "When the old earl asked you to talk to him privately over Easter weekend, did he tell you about his plans for the new will?"

"He wanted to know if I'd serve on the advisory committee."

"So you knew what was coming today."

He gave me a level stare. "I suspect most of the people who heard the will read already knew what he'd written."

Did someone kill him because they knew what was in the new will, I wondered, or because they didn't?

"Was there anyone who carried a grudge or wanted to revenge a scandal from years ago?"

My father chuckled. "The Earl of Millhaven was not the type to court scandal, even as a young man. I can't imagine any of the politicians he dealt with wanting him dead. They're all dead themselves."

It wasn't until after our main course arrived that my father said, "What did you think of the will?"

"I'd say Celia was lucky. Her husband has enough money that her thousand isn't a motive, and the police should realize it. With all of Thomas's comments about not wanting a job now that he'll be finished with university, he'll have to go to his brothers for money. I don't think Charlie and Edwin will be as generous with him as his father would be. If Thomas hadn't realized it until today, it gives him a good motive to kill one of his brothers in the near future." I gave my father a grim look.

"Not realizing the consequences of the will? Yes, that fits young Thomas like a glove. Kill his grandfather? Or his brothers? I don't think so." My father dug into his dinner.

I stabbed my chop with my fork. I could see how the police would combine Thomas's laziness and his grandfather's will and decide he was the killer. "I hope he has a good alibi."

I needed to talk to Thomas.

"If he did do it, I'd guess his mother drove him to it."

I set down my fork and looked at my father, who'd spoken of murder in such a matter-of-fact tone. "She does seem very happy about the new will. She strikes me as the type to want it in effect as quickly as possible. And she waited a long time to become a countess."

He set his fork down, too. "It must have seemed even longer to her, as much as she dislikes Humphrey."

"An arranged match?"

"Neither one was forced into it, if that's what you mean." He scowled at me. "It's not like we were young during the feudal era. He wanted a smart wife for his governmental career, and she wanted to be a countess. I doubt she'd thought she'd have to wait this long."

"How old was the old earl?"

"Ninety-four, ninety-five. He lived to a ripe old age."

"And then was murdered. You'd think whoever it was would have just waited. He wasn't in good health."

"He was dying," my father said flatly. "The doctors had given him less than six months. His heart was failing."

"Then why kill him?" My voice must have carried,

because people at nearby tables turned and stared. My father and I both gave vague apologetic smiles and leaned our heads closer together.

"Someone hadn't known what the doctors said."

"Surely they all must have known." I couldn't imagine news like that not spreading through Millhaven House.

"No, the old man kept things quiet. I found out from Walter at the wedding reception. Before I learned he'd been murdered." He gave me a dark look then, obviously having guessed I'd known of the murder before him.

This wasn't a race. At least not one I wanted any part of.

"Do we know who the old earl or the doctors told?" I asked. "Presumably we can eliminate them as suspects."

"Only Humphrey and Walter knew. The old man told them and swore them to secrecy."

"And Walter turned around and told you? Why?"

My father studied his cufflinks. "Walter made the comment that Celia's wedding was the only thing keeping the old man going. I asked, 'How long?' He said, 'Less than six months,' and I told him, 'The end of an era.'"

"In front of Mrs. Gibbons?" By now my dinner must have been cold. It certainly didn't look appetizing.

"Heavens, no. She'd gone off to powder her nose with one or two of the other ladies so we were quite alone." Father gave a dismissive wave with one hand.

"How do you know Lord Humphrey knew?" He'd done more sleuthing than I suspected.

"I asked Walter. He said he and Humphrey were invited to a conference in their father's room with the doctor. No one else in the family was to know. The old man's orders."

That raised the question again of who would kill a dying man? If he was dying. "He'd been declared at death's door before and he'd always pulled through. Why would anyone expect this time to be the end?" I asked.

"His heart was slowing down. The doctors said there was nothing else they could do. And he said he was worn out and wouldn't fight any more."

"The earl said that?" It didn't sound like the crusty old man I'd known all my life. In my memory, he'd done nothing but fight.

"It sounds unbelievable, but it's true." My father shook his head.

I was certain the will played some part in it. "He mustn't have liked the way things were going if he bothered to change his will so dramatically with so little time left. I wonder what disturbed him. And I wonder who Humphrey told about his father's health."

"You suspect Amelia knew?"

"Yes. She seemed eager to have the new earl make decisions at that meeting we attended after the wedding reception. If she'd been after her husband to assert himself before then as the heir, he might have told her to shut her up." I couldn't imagine Amelia didn't learn everything of importance in Millhaven House.

He shook his head slightly. "If that happened, I can't see Amelia telling anyone. That would be knowledge she'd keep to herself. Knowledge is power and all that."

"There are a lot of strong personalities living in that house." A house I wouldn't want to live in now. Odd, compared with how I'd wanted to as a child.

With four children in the nursery, it had been a raucous place. Add Margaret's interest in me, and the treats handed out every time I was there, and I'd thought of Millhaven House as heaven.

"Yes. We have our work cut out for us." Having no idea where my thoughts had gone, my father became all business. "How shall we go about dividing this up so we don't question the same person twice?"

Investigating a murder in tandem with my father would be hellish. At least I doubted we'd ask the same questions. "Aren't you going to be uncomfortable, Father, questioning your old friends?"

"Less than I will be seeing one of them hanged unnecessarily. Really, Olivia, I do have some experience questioning people."

"During the war, and they were enemy soldiers."

His nostrils flared, a sure sign I'd annoyed him again. "The principles are the same. I will be busy the next day or two. Why don't you see what you can discover, and then we'll go from there."

After I left my father, I traveled to the Dryesdale entrance to find Thomas already there in his evening attire, his black tie perfect, his top hat tucked under one arm. "Livvy, there you are."

I gave him a bright smile and held out my arm.

He took it and we went in to commandeer a small table in the hotel's main bar. All of the customers were dressed for the evening, although I expected most were waiting on their table in the restaurant. He signaled and a waiter came to take our orders. White wine for me, a sidecar for Thomas.

"Now," he said after our drinks arrived, "I suppose you want to ask me about Grandpapa's murder."

"Who was the first to tell you that you and your brothers would inherit the family's money and property?"

"Mr. Craggett. You were there."

"You mean to tell me the rest of your family knew, and no one told you?" I used a scoffing tone, hoping to rile him.

He took a gulp of his drink and then said, "So much for family loyalty."

"I would have guessed your mother told you."

"Dear old Mummy. She didn't breathe a word of it to me."

"And your brothers said nothing?"

His face turned red and his jovial demeanor crashed. "You mean they knew and didn't tell me? Why, those—"

I held up a hand. "I don't know that they knew. I'm only guessing."

"And you wanted to see my reaction. Did I pass?"

"With flying colors." I guessed he truly didn't know about the new will. "And you were out of the house by the time your grandfather was killed."

"From what I've heard, yes. I left the house to go down to the church before eight."

"Why?"

"Why not?"

"Why did you go down to the church, only one street away, over two hours before the wedding?"

"To make sure everything was set for the wedding."

"Were you the best man?"

He shook his head. "Head usher."

"Why weren't you best man? Celia had his sister as her maid of honor. Why not you as her cousin and close family member?"

"He wanted a childhood friend who went to university with him and is now a business colleague."

"It's all about business with him, isn't it? The best man. The honeymoon, where he also has to travel for business." I wondered if Celia knew what to expect.

"Yeah. It's all about money. Finance. Cost projections." He drained his glass. "Drink up."

"Can't. I have to go to work in the early morning."

"How do you stand it?" He flagged down a waiter and ordered another sidecar, which appeared almost immediately.

I shrugged. "I enjoy my job." Curiosity made me add, "What do you want to do?"

"Nothing."

I blinked. "There must be something you're interested in."

"Cars. Aeroplanes. Boats. Anything that goes fast. Especially aeroplanes."

"Surely you can find some sort of job with your interests."

"Not through my contacts at Oxford. They're just a bunch of dilettantes. Rich, titled amateurs with no idea how to turn anything into a job." He hung his head. "Like me."

"Are they the friends you're going out with tonight?"

"Yeah. We're going to a club or two."

"That's an expensive lifestyle."

He raised his head, defiance in his smirk. "Well, Grandfather was wealthy, and now I am."

"If your brothers will go along with your expenses."

"They will." He sounded more confident than I thought his chances warranted.

"Are your friends expecting you to pick up the tab?"

He shrugged.

"If they do, maybe you need different friends."

"You're brutal," he said in a tone of amazement and annoyance.

It was my turn to shrug. "Truthful. You can find a job involved with aeroplanes, Thomas. You just have to go out and look for it. And ignore your parents," I added when I remembered the arguments I had with my father when I first went to work for Sir Henry Benton. First?

They still cropped up occasionally.

"That sounded like the voice of experience. Uncle Ronald doesn't like you working for a newspaper?"

"Good grief, no."

"The friend I've been visiting on weekends has an aeroplane. He and I are taking flying lessons while I'm there. They'll need pilots for what's coming." He grabbed my hand. "I don't want to end up on a ship like Uncle Walter or in the trenches like my father or Uncle Philip."

"And pilots are glamorous." I winked at him.

"They are indeed."

"It's dangerous."

"War is dangerous. At least flying is exciting, too."

I studied the eager expression on his face. "I'm not to mention this to anyone, am I?"

"No, please don't. They'd try to talk me out of it, and that's such a bore." He stared into his drink, no doubt thinking about the frightening future.

Into the silence, I said, "Why did you really go down to the church two hours before the wedding?"

"I'd had it. Celie and Aunt Beatrice were constantly going into hysterics over what the other had said or done. My parents hadn't said a civil word to each other from the time I came home for term break until we learned Grandfather was dead. Charlie put on his 'I'm a university man now, so I know all the jokes and in-spots' act. Edwin looked at all of us as if we had landed from another planet. And the way we've been acting, he may be right."

Thomas took a swig of his drink before continuing. "After I hung around the church for a while, I walked up to the new housing estate on the far end of the village. Walked around for ages—it's bigger than I thought—and then went back to the church. By then it was nine-thirty and time for me to become the gracious host."

"Did anyone see you leave the house? Or arrive at the church?" I hoped someone had.

"No. I wasn't sneaking out, exactly. I just wanted some quiet. I didn't feel like being sociable."

"Did you see anyone you knew on the street? Or anywhere?"

"No. I was avoiding people. I was feeling like a failure compared to 'Mr. Perfect, I've got money and contacts' Robert Grayling, and I just wanted to go and hide."

"I didn't realize he was that hard to get along with."

He pressed his hands on the table. "He's not hard to take if you're successful. If you're not, he makes you feel small and unimportant. Almost an unnecessary addition to the gathering. But I don't think he does it consciously."

In that case, the marriage of Robert and Celia could be a great partnership or a disaster.

But analyzing Robert wasn't why I'd wanted to talk to Thomas. "Why do you think someone murdered your grandfather? He was old. He'd been sick. He wouldn't last much longer. Why would anyone risk hanging to strike down a sick old man?" I watched Thomas closely.

He shrugged. "I don't know. My mother was desperate to become a countess. But to kill the old earl? No. However, there is one possibility outside the family."

"Who?" No one had mentioned this outsider to me.

"The caterers came on Friday morning with tables and set up the tent, doing all the heavy work. There was this one bull-necked fellow, about my age, who was caught by old Watkins trying to pinch some candlesticks from inside the house.

"I'd slipped out on my job supervising them. When I returned, the bobby on the beat was taking this fellow in and the caterer was firing him. But he would have known when the wedding was and the layout of the house.

Perhaps he slipped upstairs to see what he could filch and Grandpapa confronted him. That was the sort of thing the old earl would do."

I shook my head. "Your grandfather died by eight in the morning. He wouldn't have proven a problem for a burglar at ten."

Thom's shoulders slumped. "Then I guess we're back to me being the favorite to hang." He gave me a weak smile. "But the night is still young and I have friends to meet at a club. Sure you don't want to come along?"

"Certain. I'm one of the world's wage earners now. But if you think of anything else that might help make things less bleak, let me know."

We parted ways at the front door of the hotel, with relief on my part and probably on his, too.

He'd always seemed like a little boy to me. He still did, but now he was a little boy in a lot of trouble.

CHAPTER NINE

The next morning in the office, I saw the policemen from the funeral the day before talking to Miss Westcott. She glowered in my direction as she sent them over to my desk.

They identified themselves as Detective Inspector Guess, who'd been called in during Celia's wedding, and Detective Sergeant Peterson and asked if they could have a word. I agreed and glanced at my colleagues. They were all studiously ignoring us, their ears aquiver. I suggested we go outside.

Fortunately, it was only cloudy when we reached the pavement. "This must be about the Earl of Millhaven's murder."

"We've been told you're investigating it," Guess said. "Why would you do that?"

"Celia Eustace Grayling is off on her honeymoon, but before she left, she asked me to make sure you don't hang the wrong person. I'm not investigating anything. I'm watching your investigation."

Peterson offered me a cigarette. I shook my head before he lit one for himself. He was about my age, thin, with a new- looking fedora and raincoat.

Inspector Guess said, "Do you think that's wise, getting involved in another murder?"

"You know about my husband's murder?"

"Yes." He watched me out of deep blue eyes that appeared not to miss a detail. He wasn't much older than his sergeant, but I guessed he was much cleverer. And while his clothes appeared rumpled, I thought he was the handsomer of the two.

Intelligence did that for a man.

"That's why Celia thought I was the perfect person to keep an eye on your investigation. And to ask questions of her family."

"Are you asking questions of her?"

"I will when she returns. If you haven't found the guilty party before then."

"Why do you think someone would murder a dying man?" Inspector Guess asked.

"Either they didn't know he was dying, or they didn't care because they were so angry or determined to get what they wanted at that instant." A kinder thought occurred to me. "Or they didn't want to see him suffer."

He nodded to himself. "Which do you think it is in this case?"

"I don't know. And I don't envy you trying to find out."

"When did you discover you were part of the advisory committee for spending Brooke money?"

"When the will was read."

"Were you surprised?"

"Yes, I was." I made the mistake of looking into Inspector Guess's eyes. My fear of one question must have shown.

And he knew immediately what that question was.

"When did you discover the old man was dead?"

I knew I had no choice but to tell him the truth. "Immediately before the wedding. Celia ran into her grandfather's room on her way downstairs to go to the church and I followed, trying to keep her train from catching on things. As soon as I saw his color, I knew he was dead."

"And Mrs. Grayling?"

"She shook him. When he didn't respond, she shifted

the covers and found the knife."

"What time was this?"

"Shortly after ten. Celia was late for her wedding."

"And you immediately called the police."

"You know that didn't happen. She told me not to say a word, that the wedding must go on as planned."

He raised his eyebrows beneath his fedora.

"I learned that the wedding had been postponed twice, the second time because of a woman who had come between them. Celia and her mother were determined to see this wedding go through before there was another delay because of mourning customs."

"They were afraid the groom would escape if given another chance?" Guess asked.

"That's putting it a little crudely, but yes. I believe you received a call within a few minutes of the wedding starting from the earl's valet, Ames."

"Yes. The family told you?"

"I saw you in the church yard after the service talking to Uncle Humphrey. You may know to keep your voice down, but he doesn't." I wondered if Peterson should be taking notes. He wasn't, and he wasn't adding anything to our discussion, either.

"Uncle Humphrey? You're a relative then?"

"Distant cousins. My father and Uncle Humphrey are third cousins who went to school together, served in the trenches together, work for the government together. They've always been close friends. Which is why Celia and I have known each other forever. And why I wouldn't act to destroy her wedding by insisting we call the police."

Guess nodded. "You'd better get back inside before that dragon you work for comes looking for you."

He'd taken Miss Westcott's measure.

In a spurt of disloyalty I'd never have given voice to when we were younger, I added, "She didn't admit it, but I had the feeling Celia already knew her grandfather was dead."

"Why?"

"I saw her come out of her grandfather's room at a quarter past eight. Possibly twenty minutes after her mother and Ames found the old earl dead. And then, despite being late for her wedding, Celia dragged me into the room with her grandfather. She didn't call out from the door. Instead, she walked over to the bed."

"None of that means she knew before you two went in there," Inspector Guess said.

"What better way to get me to investigate the old earl's murder than to involve me before the police are notified? Celia has always been good at obligating people to carry out her wishes." At least obligating me.

"You've known her a long time," the detective said.

"Celia's a year younger than me, but I've known her as long as I can remember. We went to the same girls' school. Saw each other every time my father and I would go to Millhaven House because she lived there."

"You were jealous."

I knew he'd know if I wasn't honest. "Growing up, I suppose I was. She belonged. She had the family connections. The social rank. I was there on sufferance. She made it clear in little ways that I was being accepted by the others on her say-so."

I looked Inspector Guess in the eye. "It wasn't until the wedding that I realized how much I dislike her."

I spent the rest of the day at the typewriter, beating out my anger through my fingers on birth, engagement, and wedding announcements.

* * *

Friday, I was assigned to cover a fashion show with Jane Seville, my favorite photographer on the *Daily Premier* staff. She'd been helpful when I first arrived at the newspaper and we'd been friends ever since. By the time the show finished at three, I had all my notes written up for a story.

"Jane, I have a stop to make before I go back to the paper. I'll see you later?"

"Of course. They have some good shops around here. I think I'll make the best of it."

We waved and went our separate ways. I took the Underground as close as it would take me and then caught a bus to reach Millhaven House in what used to be the village but was now just another high street in the suburbs.

I rang the bell and the door was answered by Watkins. I was surprised by how much he had aged. Perhaps I should pay attention to the staff as well as the family. "Is Lady Amelia or Lady Margaret at home?" I asked, giving him my social card.

"Lady Amelia is in the parlor, if you'll follow me, miss."

I walked down the hall and waited while he announced me. Then I strolled in to find the new countess reading a ladies' magazine. The doors shut behind me.

"Lady Amelia, I'm so glad to find you at home. I'm afraid we need to go through those pesky questions so I can keep the innocent from running into legal trouble." I walked over to her, taking off my gloves.

She gestured to a chair near hers. "I don't think this will do any good. In fact, I don't think it's a good idea."

"I agree. I consider this a waste of my time. What difference does it make to me if one of your sons is hanged for his grandfather's murder? They certainly had the best motive."

I found the shocked look on her face reward enough.

"They didn't know about the new will until after the wedding." She turned her attention back to her magazine.

"That's not entirely true."

"Well, Thomas didn't know. We've had trouble enough getting him to focus on finding a job without him thinking he can live off the estate's proceeds."

I took a guess. "The other two knew."

She took a cigarette out of a gold box on the side table and lit it, inhaling deeply before she said, "So what if they did? They're still children."

"More grown up than you may think."

"I hope you didn't come here to discuss my children."

"No. I hoped to find out what you were doing the morning of Celia's wedding from the time you awoke until the wedding started."

"That is easy. I had breakfast in bed, read my correspondence, and then rose at nine to dress."

"What time did your tray arrive?"

"A quarter past eight. By the time I had my eyes open, he was already dead and I was countess." She looked pleased with her story.

So far as I knew, her story was true. How I wished I could poke a hole in it. "No sounds wakened you in the night?"

"No. I took a pill and slept straight through." Her Cheshire cat grin widened.

"Any thoughts on why anyone would kill your father-in-law?"

"None."

"That's what amazes me. Why anyone would kill a man who'd be dead in six months?"

Her smile turned into a smirk. Her composure was perfect. "It does seem like going overboard, doesn't it?"

She had known. Humphrey had told her. Now to find out who else had known.

"Any luck in finding the necklace?"

Her expression darkened. "No. The police have searched here and in Cape Town. Nothing. And that bloody thing's worth a fortune."

"Is it insured?"

"Of course. That's the only reason I haven't murdered my sister-in-law. Yet."

When I left the parlor, Watkins said, "Lady Margaret would like to speak to you. She's in the library."

"Thank you." Two interviews in one afternoon. I hoped this meant I would be done with investigating soon. Then I realized I wasn't any closer to the answer than I was on the day of the murder.

As long as I had the butler's attention, I asked, "What can you tell me about the burglar who tried to steal the candlesticks on Friday?"

"Oh, I don't think he was a burglar, miss. He was one of the laborers working for the caterer. I think he just saw an opportunity and took it."

"That's a generous interpretation, since you're the one who caught him."

Watkins's attitude would have made aristocrats proud. "If he were a decent burglar, he would never have been caught." Then with more humility, he said, "I'm not as speedy as I once was. No, I think it was his first attempt to do something so stupid. I hope he learned his lesson."

"You saw the caterers on Friday. Do you think any of them could have slipped back in early Saturday morning and killed his lordship?"

"No. You see, miss, the police checked and there was

no sign of anyone breaking in. I don't unlock the doors until after the servants have breakfast. And by then Ames had gone up to find his lordship—" He hung his head.

"How long have you worked for the family?"

"Since the reign of King Edward. Er, the seventh." To cover either his embarrassment over the possible misunderstanding or his thoughts on the short, disastrous reign of Edward VIII, he quickly added, "I was hardly more than a lad then. And of course they took me back after the war."

"Then you know this family well. Does the earl's murder surprise you?"

"Yes. He was very old. Why not wait for nature to take its inevitable course?"

"Can you think of anyone with great need or impatience?"

"Indeed I cannot, miss."

"Did he have any visitors or messages from outside the family recently?"

"Other than Mr. Craggett, there's been no one from outside the family writing or visiting his lordship in a year or two. Possibly longer."

The house had a small staff, and I was certain they'd all keep to the same story. Nevertheless, I said, "I'd like to speak to the maids. The live-in staff."

"Will it be a lengthy interview?"

"Not at all."

"Then perhaps if you come at six, we'll have had our tea, and Patty doesn't start her evening off until seven."

"Six it is. Thank you."

As I entered the library, I remembered again how masculine a space it had been until Aunt Margaret transformed it. She'd hung colorful modern paintings done by her brother, Walter, to lighten the dark paneling.

Delicate, lacy curtains covered the windows in place of heavy, dark draperies. The carpet was a solid, muted pink. The Queen Anne-style furniture had light, graceful curves.

"What do you think?" Aunt Margaret asked, looking up from her desk, her pince-nez perched far down on her nose. Her graying hair was scraped back in a neat bun and she wore a baggy gray sweater over a well-ironed white blouse.

"What a wonderful space," I said, and not for the first time.

She smiled at me. "Yes, it is, but I meant about Father's death."

"Right now, I'm trying to find out where everyone was that morning."

She took off her glasses and gestured for me to sit. Fortunately, she hadn't developed the habit of stacking books on chairs. I took the nearest one, an armchair with a firm back and a seat upholstered in a shade to match the carpet, and carried it over to the desk.

She started speaking immediately and a little too fast. "I rose early that morning. I do every day. I dressed and wrote for a while. The maid brought me breakfast, which I ate while I continued to work. After she took the tray away, I dressed for the wedding and joined the family downstairs."

"What time did these things occur?"

"The same time that morning as every morning."

Good grief. I hated people to play games with me, especially Aunt Margaret. Why would she be cagey about something so simple? "Specifically."

"Then you must ask specific questions. I rose at seven, dressed, and began writing. At eight-thirty, the maid brought the tray. She took it away at nine and I finished dressing for the wedding. At nine-thirty, I joined the family downstairs. I hope that's specific enough for you, because I really wasn't watching the time."

"Yes. Thank you. Did you hear anything unusual? An argument? A voice that was unfamiliar?"

She scowled. "You subscribe to the random maniac wandering in and murdering my father theory? That's an idea worthy of Celia. I've always thought you brighter than that."

I glared back. "I don't subscribe to any theory, as you put it. I'm trying to gather as many facts as possible. Who knows what fact may save a member of the family from being hanged for a murder they didn't commit?" If I had to fight Aunt Margaret for the answers to my questions, I'd leave this place with a tired brain.

"My room faces the back of the house. I wouldn't have heard any sounds from my father's room." She paused and added, "Unless he'd been shot. I believe I would have heard a gunshot."

Aunt Margaret was usually so forthright. What had happened that everyone in this house found it necessary to hide their actions? Were they all in this together?

CHAPTER TEN

I tried to remember the layout of the upper floors. "Your room overlooks the back garden."

"Yes. I had a grand view of the top of the reception tent where ordinarily I would watch you and the other young people play tennis." Aunt Margaret smiled ruefully. "I'm afraid I can't help you."

There was no sense trying to pry information out of her that she didn't want to reveal and decided to change the subject. I glanced at a shelf behind her and saw a familiar volume of poetry, published a few years before. "I loved *Grasses in the Wind.*"

Her smile spread across her face as she reached back, pulled out the volume, and stroked the cover. "I'm afraid you're one of the few who read it."

"Then I'm one of the lucky ones. Your imagery is fascinating. Reggie would quote from it to me." One of the many reasons I married him was because he appreciated my aunt's poetry.

She studied my face for a moment. "I hope that's a comfort to you."

"Yes. The pain is still a little raw, but yes, that memory is a comfort." I wondered if the ache from seeing my husband on a morgue table would ever go away.

"I'm glad my poems have meant something to you."

"When is the next volume coming out?" I was eager to read it, but Aunt Margaret never let me read her work ahead of the publication date.

"In the summer. Or so my publisher tells me."

I tried a quick change of topic. "Is there anything you can think of that was out of the ordinary in the time leading up to your father's death?"

Her face reddened as her expression shaped into a scowl again. "That terrible will. At least with Humphrey, you know where you stand. Now we have to deal with those children of his. My father never mentioned Beatrice, Walter, or me in this new will. Shameful."

I thought the old sinner was a great deal worse than shameful. "I heard at the funeral that your father was politically active during Victoria's reign. I don't think he ever left it in his mind."

"The Victorians have a lot to answer for, not the least of which was their abysmal indifference to the intelligence and capability of women. You're lucky you're young in this modern era, Livvy."

Such a talented, proud woman. I remembered the stories she had told me as a girl about the marches she went on with the suffragists. "Your father must have hated your association with the Pankhursts and their fight for women's rights."

"I was their friend and supporter. That was something my father could never forgive. Not that it would have made any difference in the end." She looked at a point far beyond the library. "I was the eldest, but a girl. Humphrey, timid, foolish Humphrey, was a boy and would get it all."

"At least he doesn't seem to be a halfwit like many of the aristocracy." I wasn't sure how she'd react to my comment.

"No, Olivia, he's not. We're not as inbred as many of the older houses." She looked down at her desk. "Is that all? I'm afraid I'm terribly busy today."

"Yes, unless you can tell me why anyone would murder a dying man."

Her expression could best be described as frozen.

"He was dying? But then—" She pulled her sweater more tightly around her.

"Then what?"

She looked at me and put on a quizzical expression. "Then why would anyone want to murder him? That seems bizarre."

I could feel a frown forming on my face. "Do you know something that might be helpful?"

"Nothing at all. And now if you don't mind—"

"Of course." I stood. "I'll see you later when we can chat some more." She knew something useful concerning who killed her father. I guessed she wouldn't share it since she was in sympathy with whomever she suspected. Someone who was a blood relative, while I was just a distant cousin. Never mind her claims of great affection for me, they were family. "Is Ames still here?"

"No. He left after the funeral and reading of the will. I suppose he realized all he'd get were his quarterly wages and his legacy of fifty pounds."

"Do you have his address?"

"He's staying with his sister. I know his address is here somewhere." She flipped through her diary and then wrote down an address in Salisbury on a slip of paper.

She handed it to me, and I thanked her. If the old earl's valet didn't kill him, he'd be a good source of information on this secretive household. I suspected this was one interview where I should take my father along.

And if I hurried, I'd be able to turn in my story to Miss Westcott before she felt the need to murder me.

* * *

It was six fifteen before I returned to Millhaven House. I spoke to Patty first, who had a date at the pictures with her young man. She was the downstairs maid and had nothing to tell me. She'd been there a year and "keep to myself, thank you very much."

The other maid, Betsy, had been there three years and did the upstairs. Things went along fine until I said, "So you change the linens and towels and send them out to be laundered. Do you do this every day?"

"Yes," barely made it past her lips.

"What is it you don't want to tell me? Is someone ill?"

"That's the family's business. I'll have to ask Mr. Watkins if I should answer any questions like that." She kept stubbornly to that one reply.

Watkins had disappeared. I was left wondering what Betsy knew. I was certain it was something I needed to find out.

* * *

Esther Powell, Sir Henry's only child and my friend since school days, met me that Saturday for a day of shopping. We worked our way through Selfridge's, a milliner, and a shoe shop before Esther declared it was time for tea. Or lunch. Something a little more sedentary.

I was more than willing to agree, since while I was carrying fewer parcels than she was, I could tell Esther had something on her mind. Two motherless girls thrown into the foreign land of a boarding school, we had quickly grown close. After all this time, I could still tell when something bothered her.

We walked down Oxford Street to a restaurant that did a wonderful shoppers' lunch. Unfortunately, half of England was shopping that spring day, which carried hints of summer in the air. The restaurant had a line going out the door and I suspected everywhere in the shopping area would be the same.

"Let's try one of the hotels. They're less likely to draw a crowd of shoppers." As we walked away, I said, "What's wrong?"

"It's my aunt."

"Ruth? The woman I met in Berlin?"

"No. She was the middle daughter. My mother was the oldest. It's the youngest, Judith. She and her family live in Vienna."

I shuddered, never wanting to hear the name of that city again. "Edward Hawthorn used to travel there every few months while he was giving the Germans our secrets. Before he murdered Reggie. I've never been to Vienna, but apparently, now it's more staunchly Nazi than Germany."

I responded before I thought. This was why I'd been hired by Sir Henry for his newspaper. I never would have found Reggie's killer without their support. Lacking a good paying job, I'd have had to move home with my father, and that would have been a disaster. I didn't have a great deal of choice in whether I traveled to Vienna, if Esther and Sir Henry wanted me to.

Esther was kind. "I hope you don't have to visit them. Right now, the city is in confusion. My aunt and her family had to register to get their exit visas, but apparently there wasn't any trouble with that. Then her husband lost his job in a bank.

"Now the government says all Jews will have to register their wealth. There are new regulations every day, and there's a lot of violence against Jews. They're frightened. They're trying to get entry visas into England. Everything depends on what Daddy can work out with the Home Office."

I took a deep breath. "I hope everything goes well for them, Esther. I'm sure your father can get them visas."

I could tell Esther was frightened for them.

Esther gave me a shaky smile in reply. She suggested the Dryesdale hotel, where I'd met with Thomas Brooke the other night, since we were walking past it. I agreed and told her about that meeting.

Esther's eyes widened. "You're investigating a murder that took place during a wedding?" She declared it "bizarre."

I told her about Celia, the wedding, the corpse, and Celia's charge to me while we were seated and ordered. When I mentioned my father, Esther, who had oohed and ahhed and expressed sympathy, burst into giggles.

"Do you mean you and your father are investigating a murder together? Without bloodshed between you?"

"So far we've done very little of this together. Actually, I think he's done very little."

"He'll surprise you." Esther sounded very sure of that. At boarding school, Esther and I had wanted to find a way to trade fathers. She loved my father's reticence. I adored Sir Henry's enthusiasm.

"Oh, he surprises me all the time. Unfortunately, none of the surprises are good." My father and I had a rocky relationship and had since I was young. It had propelled me into marriage to Reggie and then a job search to pay for my own home once Reggie died.

Esther's look told me she wasn't putting up with my frustration with my father. "Be fair. He's known them, at least the older generation, far longer than you have. That may prove useful."

"The older generation, as you call them, knew about the new will on the evening before the old earl was murdered. One of them could easily have planned the murder overnight and carried it out before breakfast. My father will never consider any of them capable of murder."

At that moment, I looked across the restaurant and saw Lady Beatrice. Dining with a man. Putting her hand over his and leaning in as she spoke to him.

Esther read my expression and turned her head to look. "Who is it?"

"Lady Beatrice, Celia's mother. With a man who is not her husband, although I'd be more shocked if she were with her husband. And they look very friendly."

Esther's eyebrows rose. "Where?"

"Several tables over. She has on a black hat that looks like a beached boat with yards of netting on it, and he is gray haired and distinguished looking."

Esther glanced over again. "That's James Rutledge, the Marquess of Hullworth's brother. He's a well-known barrister."

"A barrister? I need to hear what they're saying."

"Livvy. Is that wise?"

I gave her a big smile. "No."

They were seated near one of the broad pillars that marked the path through the dining room to the hotel. I rose and walked along the path, stopping when I reached the closest pillar and began searching through my handbag. I made sure to stand against the pillar to stay out of everyone's way.

And out of Lady Beatrice's line of sight.

"But James, murder is so permanent. First Father and now Margaret."

My eyes widened and my hands stilled. Had something happened to Aunt Margaret, or was Lady Beatrice planning something?

"The important thing is to make sure you're not implicated," a man's voice said.

"What should we do next?" Lady Beatrice asked. Her voice was a little breathless.

Was this barrister planning the murders or aiding her?

"May I help you, madam?"

I looked up to find the maître d' speaking to me while he stood in full view of Lady Beatrice. "Ah. I found it," I said, pulling my wallet out of my bag. "So silly. I carry too many things in here."

Actually, I had very few things in my bag, but I hoped the man bought my excuse. However, I was certain my cover was blown and it was time to me to return to my chair, hopefully without being noticed by Lady Beatrice.

I slipped my wallet into my bag. As I started to walk away, I heard, "Olivia! What are you doing here?" That stopped me in my tracks.

As I turned my head to reply, I realized the barrister had risen and was standing as if I were a friend and not someone Beatrice had just demanded an explanation from. I pasted on a smile. "Lady Beatrice, what a surprise. I'm meeting a friend for lunch. Are you out shopping— oh, that's right." Lady Beatrice was in mourning apparel for her father.

She'd probably maintain customs for her father longer than I had for my husband. However, if she and this man were in this together... My mourning was at least genuine.

"Olivia, have you heard?" She gasped out her words in tightly controlled sobs. "It's too horrible. Someone tried to kill Margaret last night."

Shock stunned me for a moment. My mouth worked before I could form words. "Good grief. Is she all right?"

"No, she's not all right. She's in hospital," Lady Beatrice snapped at me.

I reached out to support myself on the pillar, shocked at the dreadful news. I couldn't let someone kill Aunt Margaret.

I almost missed Lady Beatrice saying, "I was just

asking James—Lord Rutledge what I should do."

The two sisters never got along. I wasn't sure if I was more surprised by a second attempted murder in the family or Beatrice's seemingly genuine concern for Margaret.

I got the bare facts from her and promised to call at Millhaven House the next day. Then I nodded and left so the well-mannered Lord Rutledge could sit down and continue eating.

When I went back to my seat and told Esther what I'd overheard, her first question was, "What happened to Lady Margaret?"

"Apparently she was fed strychnine. Probably rat poison in her cocoa last night. She's in hospital, not doing well. They don't know if she'll pull through." And no one thought to tell me? I truly was a distant relative to everyone but Aunt Margaret.

"Who could have poisoned her bedtime drink?"

"That's what I'll have to find out."

Esther stared at me for a moment. "That's what you and your father need to find out. Don't do this all on your own, Livvy. Your father is very resourceful. He can help."

I didn't want my father's interference, but this time the attack was against Aunt Margaret. To protect her, I'd accept help from the devil. "Let's talk about something else."

"What have you heard from Captain Redmond? Is he in town?"

My mood, already falling, hit my toes. "He called this past week, so I know he's in Great Britain. He has no idea when he'll be back. He wrote me a very charming letter and enclosed an address where I can write to him."

"Which I'm sure you did."

"Yes. Now, can we talk about something else?"

Esther raised her eyebrows before she started talking about shopping.

* * *

By prearrangement after noon the next day, I met my father outside the hospital closest to Millhaven House. He was carrying a bouquet of flowers. When I looked at him in surprise, he said, "I'm sure Margaret will appreciate them if she's awake."

We followed directions to the ward, an area of unrelieved white that smelled of bleach and something that reminded me of the ghost in Millhaven House. The nursing sister led us to the end of the ward where Aunt Margaret lay in a screened-off bed and then took away the flowers to put them in a vase.

For a moment, I thought Margaret was dead, and regret filled my mind for the loss of a talented poet, my champion as a child, and a life narrowed by her father. Then she shifted in the bed and I breathed a sigh of relief.

My father walked over to the bed and took her hand. "Maggie, it's Ronnie. How are you?"

Ronnie? I'd never heard my father refer to himself that way.

"Terrible. Wish I could go back. Back to before the war. Remember the fun we had at Edward's coronation?" Her voice was so weak I could barely hear her from a few feet away.

"I remember," my father said in a voice full of regret. "We had good times."

"Those days are gone," Aunt Margaret said as the nursing sister came in and took the patient's pulse.

"You must leave. We can't tire out Lady Margaret." She began to hustle us out of the enclosure.

"Of course." My father started down the hall at a rapid pace. I could barely keep up with him.

He didn't slow down until we were on the pavement in front of the entrance. "First the old earl. Now Maggie. We need to stop this madman."

"Where do we start? Tracing her cocoa?"

"Of course." He waved his umbrella to flag down a taxi and we were on our way.

We arrived at Millhaven House to find Charlie and Edwin listening to the wireless in a small parlor tucked away down a hall. When we entered the room, Charlie turned it off. "Thank goodness. We're going mad with boredom. Father decreed that since it's Sunday, we must spend the day with our family. Then all the oldies wandered off. Except for poor Aunt Margaret."

"Do you know how she is?" Edwin asked, sounding sincere in his concern.

"We've just come from the hospital. I think she'll be all right," I told him, trying to sound hopeful. "So tell us who was around the cocoa last night. And why are you both home instead of at school?"

"Mother's decree," Edwin said. "She wanted us to consider the family finances over the weekend. Have our first meeting as heirs to Grandpapa."

"How did it go?"

"Heated and brief." Edwin made a face.

"So the evil potion was in the cocoa? I'll stay away from the stuff while I'm here." Charlie flopped sideways dramatically in his chair. He wasn't taking this seriously.

I turned to Edwin. "Did you have any? Who made it?"

"Charlie and Thomas had already gone out for the evening. I had some, along with Aunt Beatrice, Aunt Margaret, and Uncle Walter."

"When did your brothers go out, and when did you have cocoa?"

My father left the room.

"They both left by nine. Aunt Margaret suggested hot cocoa about ten-thirty, just as I was going up to my room."

"So, what happened?"

"The maid made the cocoa and brought it into the family parlor. I took a mug and went up to my room. Aunt Margaret said she'd forgotten her book and went up to get it. I don't know what happened after that until the ambulance came."

"Did she take her cocoa with her?"

"No. She was going to come back down with her book."

Lady Beatrice and Walter needed to answer some questions. "Thanks. Enjoy your program. And where's Thom?"

"He left early this morning to meet a friend with an aeroplane," Edwin said.

"And we're stuck here with nothing good on," Charlie complained. "It's Sunday. Taste and decency prevail." Then he pretended to strangle himself.

I left the room wondering if I'd been that dreadful when I started university. The honest answer was probably yes. Shaking it off, I went to look for Lady Beatrice.

I didn't hear Walter come up behind me until he said, "Bea and your father went for a walk in the garden."

I jumped and then smiled to cover my silliness. "He's probably asking her what I'm about to ask you. What happened last night after the cocoa arrived?"

"Oh, dear. I'm not sure. Let's see." He studied the far wall for a moment. "Edwin and Margaret both left. Edwin took his cocoa with him. Margaret left hers behind. I waited a little while for Margaret to return. She didn't. I ended up taking my cocoa to my room. Beatrice did the same."

"You both went upstairs at the same time?"

"Yes."

"So Aunt Margaret's cocoa sat in the parlor by itself until she returned?"

"Yes." His eyes widened. "That's when someone poisoned her drink? How awful."

"Where were Lord Humphrey and Lady Amelia?"

Another study of the far wall. "Amelia went to bed early in a snit. The boys won't take direction from her. Humphrey went to his club."

"When did he return?"

"I have no idea. He was here and in his dressing gown when Margaret took sick."

This put us no farther forward than we were after the old earl died, whether or not the two attacks were done by the same person. If they were, then why would the killer change his method of attack?

"Please be careful," I told him. "Someone is coming into your house and attacking your family."

He shook his head. "I can understand Father. Or Humphrey or the boys. They have the title and the money now. But why Margaret? She's a poet. She has no more power or money than I do. That makes no sense."

Why murder a dying man? Or a woman with no money? It made no sense to me, but I was certain someone had a reason.

CHAPTER ELEVEN

When I finally found my father, I led him away from the house to compare what we'd learned. It amounted to the same thing. Aunt Margaret's cocoa was left alone for a time when anyone could have poisoned it unseen by anyone else.

"That doesn't get us any further along," he grumbled.

"I think we need to talk to Ames."

"But he's not here," he exclaimed before glancing around and lowering his voice.

"I have his address. He's in Salisbury, staying with his sister."

"We should be there in less than two hours. Let's go." Without waiting, my father began to stride down the street, signaling for a taxi.

The train trip was comfortable, if boring. Father seemed ready to hop down the aisle. He'd been like that since we saw Aunt Margaret in the hospital.

"Was she an old girlfriend?" I asked.

"Margaret? She was my first love."

Well, that was more than I wanted to hear. I gave him a cheeky reply. "During Victoria's reign?"

He glared at me. "Edward's."

I was astonished to get a straight answer, and even more surprised at how long ago it sounded. "You'd have been hardly more than children then."

"I said she was my first love. She seemed so grown up to me, although she was only a year older." Then he hid behind his newspaper for the rest of the trip.

Once in Salisbury, we found Ames's address not far from the cathedral. It was a stationer's shop, closed for the Sabbath. We stared at the storefront, stymied.

"You'll be wanting the Youngs?" a woman's voice said.

That was the name on the store. "Yes. We're looking for her brother, Mr. Ames," I answered.

The middle-aged woman, dressed in her Sunday best, walked past us as she said, "Ring the bell on the door on the left. They live over the shop."

"Thank you." I rang and waited. It was at least a minute, time for my father to pace up and down the pavement, before the door was opened by Ames.

He looked at me for a moment and blinked before seeing my father. "Sir Ronald. What brings you here?"

"Someone tried to kill Margaret two nights ago. What is going on, Ames?" my father demanded.

The old earl's valet glanced up and down the lane, but no one seemed to be paying us any attention. "I suppose you'd best come in."

We followed him up a long uncarpeted staircase and through a door into their parlor. Amid newspapers, glasses, and ashtrays, Ames, in his shirtsleeves and stocking feet, introduced us to his sister.

"If you've come from the new earl, he's not going back," she told us.

"Beryl, do we have anything to offer our guests?" Ames asked in a timid voice.

I could see the "No" forming on her face. "Actually, Mr. Ames, I wondered if you'd take a walk with us. Our business is delicate." I rushed through my words.

"Of course," he said, putting on his jacket and shoes while Beryl glared at us.

We kept silent until he led us downstairs and into the street.

"I'm sorry if our arrival upset your sister," my father

said.

"Not any more than anything else. If the glass is half full, it will soon be empty. I suspect it's because her feet hurt from standing on them all day for years." He smiled briefly. "What can I do for you?"

"Celia has asked us to make sure the wrong person doesn't hang for the old earl's murder. So I'd like you to tell us, in as much detail as you can, everything that happened from dinner the night before until you found the earl dead."

"Well, Miss Olivia, his lordship was tired by dinnertime from all the business he'd conducted during the day."

"We know about the will, and the ruckus after dinner in his room. Did he conduct other business?"

"Yes. He signed over the deed to an office building here in Salisbury to me. Watkins, the butler, received the deed to a hotel in Exeter, where he's from. Cook got the title to a building with a café in it in Bloomsbury. These were all part of his private wealth and he could give them away as he saw fit, so the lawyer said."

"I wondered why you only received a legacy of fifty pounds after all your years of service," my father murmured so quietly I barely heard him.

"Was this done the same time as the will?" I asked.

"Yes. He timed it so the family was out. His lordship preferred not to have to argue with his family about his decisions. He hadn't the strength for it anymore. Since he knew he'd have a fight coming over the will—" He shrugged.

"Millhaven was known for his secrecy, but he wasn't known for his generosity," my father said.

"He did this for the three of us who've been with him a long time. Since the end of the war, or before it in

Watkins's case."

"Does the family know?"

"Only if they've carefully gone over the books. Only Lord Humphrey would think to do that." He peered at us. "He'll make a good earl."

"Who killed the earl?" I asked.

Ames gave me a troubled look. "I don't know. It had to be someone in the family, or someone with a key. Watkins kept a watch over the ground floor and the doors."

"Even when there's going to be a wedding reception in the garden?" I asked.

"Especially then. After that young fool tried to grab the candlesticks, we were all on our guard."

"Had you organized extra patrols?" my father asked, straightening his shoulders and putting on what I called "the old major" voice.

Ames must have been an old soldier too, because he stood straighter as he faced my father. "When not caring for his lordship, I made rounds of the ground and first floors. Watkins checked and rechecked all the doors, and relocked them when necessary."

"Relocked them?" Something was wrong.

"He told me he'd found one unlocked at three-thirty in the morning. It had been locked at midnight. Then at eight, he found the same door unlocked when he went about opening the ground-floor doors. It had still been locked at seven."

"Which door was it that kept unlocking itself?"

"The side door near the path for the automobiles."

"What time exactly did you find his lordship..." My voice faded off when I saw emotion build in his expression.

"I'd helped him to the facilities a little after six and

then put him back to bed. He was fine then. I dressed and looked in on him before seven. He said he didn't need anything.

"I went downstairs, knowing this would be a busy day for all the staff. Everyone was up and working, so I did my bit, carrying trays of foodstuffs from the storeroom to the kitchen and cases of champagne up from the wine cellar. Then I had breakfast while trying to stay out of Cook's way."

His shoulders shook. "It's all my fault. If I'd been on my usual schedule, no one would have been able to attack his lordship."

"So you helped out and then ate breakfast. Quite rightly. What time did you reach his room?" my father asked.

"I finished my breakfast, but Cook didn't have his lordship's tray ready. That was another ten minutes. I heard the clock chiming eight when I walked upstairs with the tray. I went straight into his room, and as soon as I got a good look at him, I knew something was wrong."

"What did you do?"

"I dropped the tray on a dresser. Made an unholy racket. I ran over to see if I could do anything for him, but it was too late. When I pushed back the covers, I found the knife in his chest and blood everywhere on the sheets."

"Why didn't you call for the police immediately?"

"Lady Beatrice came in, saw what had happened, and told me not to call the police until Miss Celia left on her honeymoon. I was not to ruin her wedding day."

"Did Lady Beatrice often come in to see her father first thing in the morning?" Understanding their routine might help me find the killer.

"She rarely came in to see him at any time. And when

she did, it always ended in a fight. I'd always have to calm his lordship down."

"But you didn't call the police right away at her suggestion."

He looked from one of us to the other. "I knew it wasn't right. His lordship would have wanted his killer caught. I don't think he cared about Miss Celia's wedding at all. Said he felt sorry for Mr. Grayling, that Miss Celia was a flighty bit of trouble."

I'd never cared for the grouchy old man, but Celia loved him. I wondered if she knew how he felt about her. "So you waited until Lady Beatrice was out of the house at the wedding before you called the police."

"Yes, and I paid for that decision. Sunday night, Lady Beatrice came to me with Lord Humphrey and told me there was no longer a position in the house for me. They'd send my references and last quarterly wages wherever I wanted, but I was to leave immediately after the funeral."

I was surprised. "That was quick."

He shrugged. "The household was two smaller than it had been just a few days before. I was the obvious member of staff to leave. But I don't mind telling you, it felt strange. Millhaven House was my home for nearly nineteen years."

We were silent for a minute in the face of his loss. Then I asked, "Did you see anything unusual or out of place when you were up with the old earl at six? Or seven? Or at any other time?"

"I don't know if it was unusual, but—" He glanced at me and then looked at my father. "Do you know how things stood between Lord and Lady Eustace?"

My father shook his head.

I broke the silence between them. "I know Lord

Eustace visited her ladyship after midnight on the day their daughter married and didn't leave until after two in the morning."

My father's eyebrows shot upward.

Ames said, "I saw him later than that. It must have been nearly four. I just assumed he was leaving Lady Eustace's room at that time."

"Are you sure it was Lord Eustace? Lady Beatrice told me he left after two, not an hour or more later."

"Yes. The lighting was weak, but I would recognize Lord Eustace and it was him."

Golly. One thing I didn't want to do was question Lady Beatrice again on her husband's visits. Esther said I'd find my father a help in this investigation. Well, I'd found a way he could help.

"When did you and Bea discuss her husband's— visits?" My father looked a little horrified.

My cheeks felt warm. "The morning of the wedding, Edwin told me a great deal about what was going on at Millhaven House. He'd heard Uncle Humphrey and Uncle Walter arguing with Lord Eustace about his treatment of his wife."

"More like his frequent midnight visits to her of late," the valet said.

"This had been going on for a while?"

"Only in the last few days or perhaps a week before the wedding. And for a short time at midwinter."

I could see on my father's face that he was surprised as he quickly changed the topic. "Did the old earl like his grandsons?"

"Edwin is a sensible lad. His grandfather was very fond of him."

"And the other two grandsons?" This might be my last chance to find out what the victim had thought of his family.

"He hoped they'd turn into something worthwhile when they got older. He blamed their mother for their weakness of will."

"He didn't care for Lady Amelia?" I asked.

"He couldn't stand her and she couldn't stomach him. They ignored each other."

"And his children? You've been around to see them grow into their careers."

"Careers." The valet shook his head. "He was quite proud of the new earl. Lord Humphrey has a good head on his shoulders for mathematics."

"Then why put the three boys in charge of his private fortune?" It made no sense.

"I don't know. I think it was a slap at Lady Amelia. An effort to keep her from having all of the money as well as the title."

"In that case, why not settle some money on his other children?" my father asked.

"He thought the rest of them were wastrels. Two of them never married and dabble in the arts. His lordship thought their lives were a waste of good breeding. And Lady Beatrice. Oh, dear. She drove his lordship to distraction. He'd been after her to move out and live with her husband. I think his lordship wanted to cut off the allowances of all three of his other children or throw them out. He wanted them to learn to stand on their own two feet. But then he'd grumble and say they were too old to change. They upset him."

I was shocked and I saw my father's eyes widen. "Did they know this?"

"Oh, yes. They won't admit it now, but oh, yes. Quite a motive for murder." Ames smiled, showing all his teeth.

I smiled back, while inside I was thinking what a

vindictive man Ames was. "And now we know that there was at least an hour, from seven to eight, when the murder could have occurred. And no one has an alibi for that entire time. Not even Edwin and Charlie or the servants, who we thought were in the clear. Anyone could have been the murderer."

The servants probably had alibis for every moment, but I wanted to shake up Ames. From the frightened look on his face, I'd ruined his feelings of invincibility.

"Had the old earl been in contact with anyone except the family, the staff, and Mr. Craggett lately?" I asked.

"No. His last visitor was two years ago, and the gentleman died three weeks later. He's outlived his friends. His enemies, too, I'd have thought."

* * *

"He's lying," my father said as we took the train back to London.

"Why would he?"

"Anger at being thrown out of his home and job. Being forced to live with his embittered sister. Life with the old man must have been more comfortable."

"Uncle Humphrey was the one who threw him out, but Ames said the old man had good words for his heir. He was good at mathematics." A strange sort of praise.

"I wonder what the police made of his story. I'm sure they thought it was a pack of lies." My father unfolded his newspaper.

"Now that Aunt Margaret has also been attacked—" I didn't get a chance to say any more before my father had a newspaper held up between us.

My father might not want to consider Ames's testimony, but I thought it was important.

Was Aunt Margaret worried she'd be thrown out of Millhaven House because of what her father had said to her? She'd made clear she feared losing her home and her gardens. Now that he was gone, I couldn't see her nephews agreeing unanimously to send her away.

I spent the trip back to London thinking about all that Ames had said. He was furious at the family for throwing him out, so how much of what he had said was the truth?

I'd have to speak to Betsy the maid again, and make certain Watkins was present this time to make sure she talked. She heard and saw a lot in the course of her work.

I was very glad I didn't have servants silently watching me.

When we arrived at the station in London, my father commandeered a taxi for us. His directions, sending us to Millhaven House, surprised me, but I settled in to discover what he had in mind.

Watkins answered the door while looking over his shoulder. I heard shouting.

"Is Lord Humphrey here?" my father asked, barging in and heading toward the noise.

"No, I'm afraid—"

My father didn't wait to hear what the butler had to say.

"Have you heard how Aunt Margaret is doing?" I asked.

"Still with us, Miss Olivia."

I nodded and followed in the direction my father had gone. I found him in the family parlor standing between Lord Eustace and Uncle Walter. Lady Beatrice stood by the fireplace clasping her hands together like a heroine in a gothic novel. Lady Amelia sat at the end of a sofa, her magazine forgotten in her hands.

"Stay out of my business, Brooke."

"For heaven's sake, Eustace, go home and don't come back until you sober up," Uncle Walter said, backing up to stand behind my father.

"I'll see my wife any time I bloody well want."

"I'm sure you will," my father said in a placating tone, "but you don't want her to see you fight with her brother. You're taller and heavier than Brooke. Not a fair fight, and besides, Brooke's always been on your side. Now why don't we—"

"And he's not the one with the money. None of us are," Lady Amelia said with a sneer before she turned her attention back to her magazine.

"Why, you lying bitch—" Eustace turned and headed toward Amelia. "You're married to the weasel—"

"Now, Eustace," my father said, putting a restraining hand on his arm.

At that, Lord Philip Eustace rounded his free arm and punched my father in the nose, sending them both staggering. My father put his hand up to his nose and then grabbed his handkerchief at the sight of blood.

"Oh, Philip," Lady Beatrice snapped, storming toward her husband. He took a couple more steps back, his eyes widening as he watched his wife advance.

Uncle Walter attempted to help my father stop the bleeding, but he shook him off. My father started toward Celia's father, the look in his eyes saying he would repay the blow.

I couldn't imagine my father winning a fight and, despite our differences, I didn't want to see him hurt. I stepped forward, hoping inspiration would strike before my father's fist.

CHAPTER TWELVE

It was up to me to defuse the situation. "Has no one told you about the will, Lord Eustace? It's extraordinary." I hurried forward and took his arm. "Lady Beatrice, could you order us some tea, please?"

"Who the hell are you?" Eustace asked, squinting and trying to get my face to come into focus.

"Celie's friend Livvy. You remember me, Lord Eustace. Now let's sit down with some tea while I tell you about this will of the old earl's. It's quite complicated. I don't think there's ever been anything like it in all of England."

"What? No. Humphrey gets the lot."

"He gets the title and anything entailed, but almost everything isn't entailed. And that's where the old earl got creative."

"How'd he do that?" Now that the bluster had left him, he was beginning to sway on his feet.

"We'll tell you," my father said, taking his other arm. "Is the small red parlor all right?" he asked Beatrice.

She opened the door between the two rooms for us to pass through while giving Watkins an order for tea.

Lady Amelia said, "Make sure he doesn't put those filthy shoes on the sofa," without lifting her head from her reading.

Once my father got Lord Eustace comfortable in the small parlor and I was sure my father was safe, I went back to check on Uncle Walter.

He'd fixed himself a glass of whiskey and a cigarette and was sitting with one bony knee crossed over the other. "I'm fine, Livvy. I don't know what got into Philip."

"A bottle of something, I'm sure," Amelia said.

We all ignored her as Beatrice paced from the fireplace to the window and back. I sat down next to Walter. "What started it?"

"I have no idea."

"I think it was a request for money," Amelia said in an acid tone.

"We all know what you think," Walter said. His usual good humor was gone.

"If you're all going to be in a filthy mood, I'm going upstairs." Amelia dropped her magazine beside her on the sofa and strolled out of the room.

"I thought she became a countess, not the queen," Beatrice said.

"Now, Bea, you know she controls the purse strings through those lads of hers. And she does outrank us. I suppose she should be allowed a little showing off." Walter seemed to relax as soon as his sister-in-law left the room.

"She has no class at all."

Uncle Walter looked at his sister with an amused smile crossing his face. "When did she ever?"

I thought I'd better stop them before one or the other said something unforgivable. "What's the newest on Aunt Margaret?"

"They think she'll pull through. They'll be certain by tomorrow."

"That's good news." I smiled in relief, my gaze moving from Walter to Beatrice. Neither one looked particularly cheered by what they'd told me.

My father came back into the room and silently closed the door behind him. "He's asleep now. What was that about, Brooke?"

"Who knows? He's been drinking."

Beatrice rang the bell and asked for ice for my father's nose before she collapsed into a chair. "Oh, what do you think? Money. It's always about money."

"He wanted a loan?" my father asked.

"That's what he calls it. He never pays it back," Beatrice said. Her voice dripped bitterness.

Walter raised his eyebrows at her. "When are you going to admit he's been living here since Father died?"

"What? Bea," my father said in an outraged tone.

"He's my husband. I have a soft spot for him. And he's quite decent when he's sober. So kind and considerate."

"And when he's not?" my father snapped. I'm sure his nose must have been throbbing. It looked swollen.

"I'm trying to help him adjust to—a better way." Lady Beatrice sounded regal. Or possibly warlike. Lord Eustace and his drinking didn't stand a chance against a formidable opponent like her.

"How long was he really here on the night before Celia's wedding?"

"I told you. He left after two."

"He was seen at nearly four."

"Impossible."

"Nevertheless, he was seen at nearly four. So where was he?"

She shook her head and sat down, scowling at the far wall.

I needed to talk to Lord Eustace, but it wouldn't happen that night.

* * *

The next morning, I was hard at work writing up wedding announcements for the society pages of the *Daily Premier* when I was told to report to Mr. Colinswood's office. I discovered that was a ruse as soon as I arrived. Colinswood sent me up to Sir Henry Benton's office, waving me away with the hand that held his cigarette while jotting a note with the hand that held a pencil.

I hoped he never got them reversed.

"Ah, Olivia, so good to see you. I'm afraid I'm going to have to send you into the lion's den again," Sir Henry greeted me from behind his large desk. His daughter, Esther, sat in a chair on my side of the desk.

It was hard to tell they were related. Sir Henry was short, round, and unpolished, dressed in an impeccably tailored bespoke suit and still appearing rumpled. He was tenacious and pugnacious. Esther was quiet, dark, and slender. She looked like a model in a red wool suit as bright as her lipstick. I guessed she looked like the mother she had lost as a small child.

"It sounds like things have become worse." I sat in the other chair in front of his desk without asking permission. If this were a regular assignment for the newspaper, I wouldn't have dared. But I knew what was coming, and the whole situation was highly irregular.

"Things have become ugly, and our government is being stingy with visas," Sir Henry said. "We need to show that refugees have assets in this country. The government won't let me put up a surety for them. They're afraid the refugees will take jobs away from Englishmen."

"They're afraid they'll overstay their welcome in our country," Esther said, her arms crossed.

I ignored her pout and turned to her father. "Vienna?"

"I'm afraid so."

I shuddered. "What reason do I give for going to Vienna?"

"To interview the woman on the street. To hear the

concerts and view the shops. Your German will take you that far, won't it?"

"That's no problem. Do I need permission from the German government? What are my travel arrangements? Where do I stay? And how do I make contact with Esther's aunt?"

"Her name is Judith. Judith Rothenberger. Her husband's name is Matthias." Esther gave me a weak smile. "They have two children. My cousins, but they're just children."

"Have things become worse since the plebiscite?" I reached out and squeezed Esther's shoulder.

"Things got worse before the plebiscite," she said. "Communication has been sporadic. The head of the Rothschild family in Vienna was arrested on his way out of the country and jailed. Then his bank was seized by the government and my uncle and anyone else who was Jewish lost their jobs. If someone as powerful as a Rothschild can be arrested on trumped-up charges and held for ransom in a German jail for over a month now, what chance does an ordinary person have?"

Esther jumped up from her chair to pace as she continued. "The Nazis have only been in power six or seven weeks, and already there are beatings, lootings of homes and businesses, fires, and ransom demands. Vati gets reports in every day. Things in Vienna are already worse than they are in Berlin, despite years of Nazi control."

I turned to Sir Henry, still blinking over hearing him called "Daddy" in German. A Presbyterian born in Newcastle, he was the one who strode the halls of power. It had been Esther's late mother who'd been Jewish. It was her relatives who were in danger. "Have you talked to Whitehall about easing restrictions on entry visas?"

"Yes," Sir Henry grumbled, "and all we get are platitudes."

"Obviously, you want me to travel soon. How long will it take to get my visa?"

Sir Henry brushed all my concerns away with one hand. "We'll take care of all travel and visa requirements. Telling the German embassy that we want to report on the response of ordinary Austrians to their new government will ensure we'll get their cooperation." His expression darkened. "And someone will no doubt line up interviews when you get there."

I nodded. Someone who might make it difficult for me to meet with Esther's aunt and her family.

"We can't use the same plan as last time. I don't think I dare pick up whatever Esther's aunt gives me as I leave." I'd already passed on to Sir Henry what I learned from German army officer Wilhelm Bernhard when I'd visited Berlin. "I was warned I had made the Gestapo suspicious. They may be watching me this time."

"You'll need to spend a few days, and pick up the assets in the middle of your trip. From then on, you'll need to keep them hidden about your person at all times." Sir Henry was serious.

I, on the other hand, wanted to giggle. "Won't they suspect something when I suddenly arrive at interviews dripping with jewels?"

"Hidden, Olivia, hidden."

That might prove more painful than I wanted to contemplate.

Still scowling, Sir Henry continued, "We'll fly the two of you in and book you into a large commercial hotel. That should make it easier to get in and out of the hotel unobserved."

Two? "Wait. Two of us? Is Esther going with me?"

"It's too dangerous. Jane Seville is going along as your photographer."

Despite the excellent central heating, I shivered. Jane was a friend and I didn't like to lie to friends. "Is Jane willing to go on this trip?"

"Willing, yes. Overjoyed, no."

"Does she know about this secret assignment?"

"No. Only involve her if you find it necessary."

I didn't like that restriction. "It wouldn't be fair to put her in danger without her knowing what she could face."

"No." Sir Henry was adamant. "Only tell her if it becomes necessary. Her innocence is her best defense."

I hoped he was right. I knew I wouldn't like it if a friend kept me in ignorance under dangerous circumstances.

Esther broke into the angry silence that fell between Sir Henry and me. At least it was angry on my part. "Is it all right if Livvy takes a long lunch hour with me?"

"Of course. I'll clear it with Miss Westcott."

By the time I reached our office downstairs, Miss Westcott looked at me with annoyance, but she only nodded when I said I didn't know when I'd be back.

Esther and I met in the lobby. She suggested the Savoy. Her suit was trimmed in a thick, rich fur that was almost as dark as her hair. I looked down at my dark blue dress and gray trench coat and then gazed at her with raised eyebrows.

"My club, then. It'll be quieter, anyway."

"Your club?" I looked at her in amazement. I'd never pictured Esther being a member of an establishment club. But then, she was married to James Powell, who was an influential financier.

"The Ladies' Delphi."

I was impressed at my friend's standing. "Ooh, I've

always wanted to see the inside. I understand it's very classical and posh. You have to be both a scholar and rich."

"It's nothing like that," she protested as we hailed a taxi. "I'll propose you for membership if you like the place."

Once we were on our way, I said, "You've forgotten the second attribute. Rich. I couldn't afford it."

Esther scrunched up her face. "You're right. It is dear."

I couldn't hide my enthusiasm. "But well done, you. I can't imagine a better club to belong to."

When we arrived, I saw the interior was brightly colored with light-toned furniture in the Edwardian fashion mixed with Arts and Crafts style and Art Deco pieces, all sitting on thick carpets to keep down the noise. I vowed to have enough money one day to join.

If the furnishings weren't enough, the food in the dining room and the space between tables to allow for private conversations would have won me over. "Thank you for bringing me here," I said after I tasted my soup.

"They have wonderful lectures here sometimes by really top-notch minds. Your aunt, Margaret Brooke, spoke here only a couple of months ago."

"That's quite an honor." But not surprising. Aunt Margaret was recognized for her brilliant mind.

"She's also a member." Esther went on describing the delights of the club until I said, "Enough. You've convinced me. Now tell me what you wouldn't say in front of your father." I knew there was something.

"I'm pregnant."

My spoon clattered against my bowl. I recovered as quickly as I could. "Oh, congratulations. How are you feeling?"

"Terrible, but I understand that will go away in a few weeks. I hope the fear does, too."

"Esther, you'll be a wonderful mother. And James will be a terrific father. Have you told him?"

She smiled then and her face was radiant. "He's thrilled. And as nervous as I am. Neither one of us know anything about babies."

"I'm sure his mother will be more help than I'd ever be."

Esther reached across the table and squeezed my hand. "I'm sorry. You and Reggie never had children—"

"My one regret. But then, I wouldn't be able to work for your father and I'd have had to move home with my father. I have to remember to look to my blessings."

"You're the second person I've told, right after James. Please be happy for me."

"I am." I had to be honest. "I'm a little jealous, too, but there's plenty of time for me. I don't know if you know her, but Mary Babcock, my favorite of the Whitehall wives, is about to have her first child and they've been trying for six or seven years. I see it as a sign that I just have to be patient." I paused. "And get married."

The last inspired the laugh I hoped it would. "Yes, please marry again first. Your father would be upset otherwise."

"My father would be apoplectic." Then I chanced a guess. "Is this why you're so eager to get your aunt and her children to move over here? To have family close by?"

"Yes. I'm an only child, my father has no close family, and now my mother's family is trapped under Nazi rule. You have to do this, Livvy. You have to get them out of Austria. I want my child to have family around, the way I remember when I was little. Before my mother died."

"I can't get them out, Esther. All I can do is smuggle

out assets and bring them back to England so they can get entry visas."

"I'm so afraid there's no time. We get very little word, but all of it is bad. Beatings, lootings, something called scrubbing parties. We have to get them out now. You have to get them out."

I held up my hands. "All I can do is bring out the goods. The rest will be up to your father."

Esther began to silently sob.

The sight broke my heart. I reached out and squeezed her hand. "I'll see what I can do. And I trust your father can handle the rest."

She smiled at me through her tears, and guilt smacked me in the face. I knew I had to help Esther. She wanted her relatives close by, something my Brooke relatives had but didn't seem to want.

And all I had to do was smuggle jewels past the Nazis. Again.

* * *

For both Esther's and Aunt Margaret's sakes, I had to talk to Celia's father that night. As soon as I got off work, I traveled to the far suburbs to Millhaven House.

Watkins let me in as I asked him, "Is Lord Eustace here?"

"I'm afraid he is, miss. You'll find him in the family parlor."

I was surprised at the butler's honesty, but I decided it would be better if I didn't remark on it. "Thank you."

He opened the door for me to march through and then closed it again. Eustace glanced over from where he was contemplating his shoes, a glass of whiskey in his hand. "Hello, Livvy. I understand I need to apologize to you, too."

I sat down across from him before he rose halfway

from his seat in a show of good manners. Celia's father had always had impeccable manners. His whiskey had a smell like something they'd use in the hospital. Or the morgue. The smell of the ghost. I gave him a hard glare. "I'll settle for the truth."

"The truth is a dangerous commodity."

I ignored his witticism, his good looks faded by age and alcohol, and his title. I needed the truth and I needed it now. "How long have you been living here as a sort of ghost only seen by your wife?"

"I wouldn't put it that way."

"I would."

He folded as quickly as I thought he would. "You mustn't tell anyone."

I stared at him. That wasn't a promise. That could mean anything.

"I've hit hard times lately. I'd been living at my club to cut expenses. I fell behind, and they padlocked the door to my room. Can you imagine? I talked one of the staff there, they've always been fond of me, into unlocking the door so I could get some of my things out."

He took a long swig of whiskey and didn't seem to notice the burn of the alcohol. "I came over here and begged Bea to let me stay here, just until my next quarterly cheques come in. I should be able to pay off the club and straighten out any little misunderstandings then."

I decided the only person he was lying to was himself. "And she said yes."

"She still loves me, poor old girl."

Smug rotter. "Where are you staying in the house?"

"An out of the way guestroom around the corner from Bea's room."

In the women's wing, near where I'd stayed.

Definitely the ghost. "How does the rest of the family feel about you staying here?"

"If they know, they think I just stop in to rekindle the old marital candle."

"Some of them know that you're staying here as a full-time guest under their roof. And it would be good manners toward them, and the rest of the family, to tell them the truth."

"Oh, lordy, how dreary. I can just hear the new countess." He chuckled, and from the sound, I realized he'd had too much to drink to be worth talking to that night.

"Either you tell them, or I will."

"Fine." He waved his glass at me. "Fine."

Blast. I owed it to Aunt Margaret to try to find out if he knew anything. "Did you hear or see anything unusual the night the old earl was murdered?"

"No. I'm afraid I helped myself to the whiskey decanter a bit too often. I went upstairs and went out like a light. Didn't stir except for calls of nature. One nearly caused a collision with Margaret."

"When was that?"

"Who knows? Ask Margaret."

"Promise you'll tell them you're staying here. Otherwise, I'll tell them when I come back, and that will be a lot sooner than your quarterly cheques."

I marched out of the house, knowing I hadn't learned anything useful about the murder or the attack on Aunt Margaret. Hopefully, the police would quickly solve the mystery, because I had something else to attend to.

CHAPTER THIRTEEN

It wasn't until early Thursday that the paperwork was in hand and I took a cab to Croydon Aerodrome. By then Aunt Margaret was home, despite being weak and still having muscle spasms. I warned her to be careful, but she assured me that with my father around, she had nothing to fear. Besides, she'd been a suffragist. Jail in Edwardian times was more dangerous than resting at home.

From Croydon, Jane and I caught the early flight to Paris, our first of several to reach Vienna.

The spring weather wasn't in our favor, bouncing us around in the sky from London to Vienna. Fortunately, Jane hadn't eaten anything that morning since she was sick on every leg of the flight.

Spring seemed farther behind in Vienna than it was in London. I was already chilled by our flights, and the sight of all those swastikas around the airport and on the uniforms of the employees left me shivering.

At least Jane felt better once she was on the ground. We'd just collected our luggage when a smiling blonde woman approached us.

"Mrs. Denis? Miss Seville?" she asked in mildly accented English.

"Yes?"

"I'm Hilde Schmidt. I'm from the Reich Foreign Press office. I'm assigned to help you with your interviews." On her sleeve was an armband with a swastika.

"Ah. The embassy said they would help with introductions." That was diplomatic enough. "Your English is very good. I hope my German matches it."

"Oh, I'm sure it will. Now, where are you staying?"

"The König Arms." At least, I hoped we had reservations there. One of the ladies in the travel bureau used by the newspaper had recommended it because it was quiet, clean, served international businesspeople, and large enough to provide multiple entrances.

"Oh, but that is so impersonal. You must stay at one of the private inns where they will take good care of you." She oozed charm as she took my arm.

I didn't think they had any reason to be suspicious of us, but I was certainly growing suspicious of her. "I like big and impersonal. It's a little foible of mine. I like to travel as a male reporter would. I believe we women should stick up for ourselves." I gave her a determined nod and marched toward the entrance to the airport. Jane followed silently, still looking a little green.

I flagged down a cab and gave him the name and address of our hotel in perfect German before Hilde had a chance to climb in after us.

She gave in with a sigh and squeezed in after Jane. "Did you have a good journey?"

"It was beastly. I was airsick the whole time." Jane shook her head and shut her eyes.

Still determined, Hilde leaned forward to look around Jane while she said to me, "What does your husband think of you traveling without him?" Her question made the cabbie's ears perk up. He also wore a swastika.

"My husband died last autumn."

"Oh, I am sorry." Her surprise and sympathy seemed real.

I decided she'd be my first interview, although I hoped she didn't guess. "Are you married?"

"No. But there is someone who..."

When she hesitated, I said, "Well, go on."

She beamed. "His name is Rolf and he works for the postal authority. He hopes to get a promotion soon so we can get married."

I gave her an automatic congratulation. "Do a lot of young people have the problem of not having enough money to get married?"

"Now, but soon that will not be as much of a problem. The new government is starting to appropriate Jewish assets for Austrian needs. Soon Jewish businesses and banking and riches will be available for the Austrian people."

"Are there many Jewish people in the postal authority?"

"*Nein*. Jews are mostly lawyers and doctors and judges and business owners. The ones with the wealth. But we've put a stop to that." Her tone made it sound like they were preventing people from drowning kittens.

Things didn't sound good for Esther's aunt and uncle.

Up and down the streets, I could see Nazi flags flying from all the public buildings. Occasionally, I spotted a store that had been looted, or had *Juden* whitewashed on the windows. More often, signs in shop windows said in German, *No Jews Allowed*.

Pedestrians either wore Nazi armbands and walked proudly or, lacking an armband, hurried with their heads down.

We checked into the hotel to be greeted with great indifference, which buoyed my confidence that I'd be able to meet Esther's relatives without too much trouble. As it was nearly dinnertime, I asked Hilde if she wished to join us for dinner so we could make our plans for the next day.

Her eyes grew wide. "In the hotel? I do not think I can

afford—"

"No, no. My treat. I'll bill it as a business dinner. The *Daily Premier* will pay." It was part of my slowly evolving scheme. Sir Henry might not know it, but he was paying for Hilde's dinner.

"Are you certain?"

The bellhop with the luggage shifted from one foot to the other, obviously in a hurry to get rid of us.

"Absolutely. We'll go upstairs, freshen up, and meet you here in the lobby in half an hour. In case you want to telephone Rolf and tell him you'll be working late."

She looked relieved. I suspected she had orders to keep an eye on us and decided new arrivals couldn't get into too much trouble in half an hour. "Thank you. I'll go to the phones and call him."

She headed to the phone boxes in a corridor with a great view of the lobby. Once she was inside one and shut the door, I couldn't see her. Good to know where the entrance could be watched from, and where I might make a call if desperate.

I noted the location of the stairs before Jane and I took the elevator two floors up from the lobby with the bellhop. First, we stopped at Jane's room, and then I followed him three doors down the hall.

After I tipped him well for both of us and got rid of him, I checked out my room. It had a good view of the street below and possessed its own minuscule washroom and loo. I partly unpacked in about ten seconds and then went to check out the floor.

There was a back staircase that went down to a door near the loading dock. I went back up and found another that went out a secondary entrance onto an anonymous-looking side street.

After all this running up and down stairs as quickly

and silently as I could, I had to catch my breath before I knocked on Jane's door.

When we finally came downstairs, Hilde was waiting, pacing a step or two in each direction at the side of the lobby.

"Tired of waiting?" I asked brightly.

"No. Rolf says he hopes I will hurry home so he can see me tonight before my mother says it is too late."

"You live with your parents?"

"Yes. Do you?"

"No. I'm still in the flat my husband and I shared. My mother died when I was a little girl, but my father is constantly telling me what to do."

She laughed and took one of our arms in each of hers. "Fathers do that everywhere. Now, they have good food in this hotel."

We headed toward the restaurant. "Good. I'm starved."

"I wish I were," Jane murmured.

After we ordered our meals, we discussed the interviews she had set up for us at shops and businesses. "What church do you go to?" she asked.

"One near my father's house. Oh. You mean what denomination. Church of England. Why do you ask?"

"I wondered if you were Catholic. Most of us are. Well, all good Austrians are."

"And bad Austrians?" I asked with a smile.

"I'm Catholic," Jane told her.

"We have many beautiful churches in Vienna," Hilde said, having apparently ignored my question.

Our soup arrived and she dug in. The soup was heavy and rich, and I ate maybe a third. Jane ate about two sips.

"Oh, dear, don't you like it?" Hilde asked with her wide-eyed, innocent look.

"Too heavy for me, I'm afraid. How does this match up to your mother's cooking?"

"It is almost as good."

"Then your mother must be an outstanding cook."

"Would you like to meet her? You could interview her for your story."

"That would be very nice. Who else have you lined up for me to interview? I'd like to know their age and marital status, whether they are mothers or not, whether they are working outside the home. I'd like a mix. That way our readers will find someone they can identify with, whatever their station in life."

Hilde was at first upset because I said her sample was too similar, but after some discussion, she finally came up with some women who varied from one another. I suspected they were all Nazi supporters.

"Do any of them work at night?"

"No. It's mostly men who work at night in factories and power plants."

"Tell me a little about life since Austria became part of Germany. Is there a curfew?"

"No. Of course not."

"So at night you still have restaurants open? Theaters? Movie houses?"

"Yes. Lots of people go out in the evening. If it is nice out, we like to stroll around the city center. We have a beautiful city center."

"I hope to photograph it," Jane said, finally showing some interest. I was glad to see her coloring was improving.

"Oh, you will. We're going to meet several women at a building downtown for interviews. It's only a few streets from here."

"Then we'll walk from here in the morning. Do you

want to join us for breakfast, or will that be too early for you?"

Her face fell. "I suppose I should meet you."

"Don't worry about it. You don't need to, unless your boss said you need to entertain us the whole time while we're here."

She bit her lower lip and nodded.

"Well, we don't need entertaining. We'll probably go straight to bed after dinner tonight, and sometime tomorrow morning we have to check in at our embassy. Travel is very wearying." I gave her a tired smile and hoped she found us boring.

"I know I'll go straight to bed. I was sick every leg of our journey," Jane said, glaring at me as if it were all my fault.

"How about if I meet you here at eleven tomorrow? It should give you time to visit your embassy," Hilde suggested.

Our meeting arranged, I paid for dinner and said good night to her in the lobby. Then Jane and I went up in the elevator and said good night before going to our rooms. I looked out my window and spotted someone I thought was Hilde hurrying away. I made notes in my reporter's notebook about Hilde for my article and after half an hour went back to the lobby.

I glanced around as I went to the desk and asked if there were any messages for me. There weren't, and there didn't seem to be anyone interested in me. Confident no one was watching, I slipped a map of the tram routes off a table by the hotel desk. I started back toward the elevator before veering over to the phone boxes in the corridor.

A woman answered the phone on the second ring. "Judith Rothenberger?" I asked.

"Ye-es." She sounded wary.

"Sir Henry sends his love. My name is Olivia Denis," I said in German.

"Oh, thank goodness. You've arrived to save us." The relief in her voice reached through the telephone line.

Her words stunned me for a moment. I'd never thought of myself as a savior, only a courier. "I don't know about that. I am here to help you. I'll visit on Sunday morning. Is that all right?"

"Are they watching you?"

"I have a minder from the Foreign Press Office. She'll not be following me on Sunday morning. What's the best way to get to your home?"

She gave me the address, directions, and information on the tramlines. She told me her district was mixed Jewish and gentile, so getting a tram or a taxi to her area would be easy. It would be smarter, she said, not to take the taxi to her door. "There is a Catholic church about two streets away at a tram stop on the main street. Walk from there."

I didn't sleep well that night. I took a bath to relax me, but I couldn't get the temperature just right. The bed was lumpy. I was afraid that I'd oversleep and not hear my alarm clock. I finally rose before the alarm went off and dressed in a green wool dress and jacket with navy pumps, purse, and a tucked-crown hat.

Before I left, I left some German coins seemingly scattered on the dresser. If anyone came in with thieving or mischief on their minds, they'd be sure to at least move the coins if not take them.

When I met Jane in the restaurant for breakfast, she was dressed, as always, in brown and rust. She wore a smart turban for a hat so she wouldn't have a brim to get in the way of her camera. Once we finished breakfast, we headed for the British embassy.

The line for visas to enter Britain wrapped around the building.

We found the entrance for British citizens to use and went inside to speak to the cultural secretary. He was a roly-poly sort in his forties who apparently enjoyed Viennese pastries. He knew my father and had heard about Reggie's death. After a few words of condolence and the most basic of scrawled notes serving as our registration at the embassy, he started a nonstop litany of complaints concerning how his desk was undervalued. The Germans didn't want to do any cultural exchanges from Vienna, and the Austrians were following their lead.

"Soon," he moaned, "this will only be a consulate."

"Who's handling all these people looking for visas?" I asked to stop the flood of woe.

"We're all having to do our bit. They even make me help when they get overloaded. Imagine. Making a diplomat help with visas for a bunch of Jews." He shuddered. "The man in charge is Peter Thornhill."

"Oh, I know Peter. He and Reggie were office mates when we first married." That was the first piece of good news I'd had since we arrived in Vienna. Peter was conscientious and fair minded.

"Come on. I'll see if we can break him loose from his paperwork." The cultural secretary led us down corridors and back offices until we found Peter Thornhill carrying a stack of paper two feet high.

"Never ends, does it?" the secretary said. "I understand you know Mrs. Denis."

"Livvy!" He dropped the papers on a nearby desk, grabbing the top to keep them from flying. "It's been ages. I was so sorry to hear about Reggie. But what are you doing here?"

"I write for the *Daily Premier* now. Since my German is passable, they sent me over to write about the change in governments from the point of view of Austrian women."

"Golly. You wouldn't think it was popular from this stack."

"Are those all exit visas?"

"Entry visa requests. About a week's worth. We're drowning in paperwork."

"All Jewish?"

"Mostly. Some socialists and communists. Former politicians and military officers."

I noticed Jane's ears perk up. I knew she had socialist sympathies. "How many will you be able to fill?"

"Not nearly enough. Just a small fraction."

I introduced Jane. She and Peter found a common interest in photography and discussed it until the cultural secretary, now bored, wandered off.

Once he was gone, I asked, "If the owner of a London newspaper had relatives here, theoretically speaking, and goods were transported out of the country that would support them in England until the current situation changed, what would be the best way to get entry visas for these hypothetical relatives?"

Peter nodded and tapped his fingers on the stack of papers. "I'd expect this theoretical newspaper owner would have friends in the Home Office. Once the Home Office issued a directive, a notice would be sent by diplomatic pouch to this office. Then we would issue them. A phone call from the newspaper could alert these imaginary relatives to come to the embassy, pick up their visas, and if I were them, head directly to the train station."

"Do they need to come here together in person as a

group?" I was aware as I spoke that Jane was carefully listening to us.

"Yes. There's too big a demand to just hand out entry visas in batches. Plus, our entry visas aren't any good without exit visas. We have to check every last one of them. Match exit visas to passports to faces to our entry visas."

"Formidable amount of paperwork," I said, "and it can't be any fun for you."

He sighed. "I'm going to need a very long rest after I leave here."

"Thanks for your help, Peter. There are a great number of people relying on you. It can't be easy."

He studied me for a moment while he chewed on his lower lip. "Let me know when the visa requests are in transit from the Home Office. Send me a telegram saying your feature article is in the newspaper. And have your boss contact his relatives. They must be in contact somehow. Give them my name and have them say they've received the newspaper article."

I was surprised at the stealth a British diplomat would employ. "Isn't that awfully cloak and dagger?"

"You have no idea what we're up against, do you? This used to be a happy place. Politically unstable, but the arts, music, and literature flourished. And then the Nazis came in and it's like joy died. Everyone's looking over their shoulder. Everyone hates their neighbor. All of a sudden, they want war."

Then Peter lowered his voice to a whisper. "If you're planning something, let me warn you. It's dangerous. This has become a city filled with hate."

He invited us to have luncheon with him and some other embassy staffers in the private room of a restaurant on Sunday. We accepted gladly. If things were as bad as Peter indicated, I'd be glad to spend time with embassy personnel, especially since by Sunday afternoon I'd be loaded down with the jewelry I would smuggle.

When we walked outside, the massive line applying for visas seemed to have grown.

CHAPTER FOURTEEN

Once we were a street away from the embassy, Jane said, her voice dripping with accusation, "Sir Henry promised we'd return Monday."

"We'll leave Monday. Do you want to take the train rather than fly back? It'll take longer."

She gave me a grim smile. "We'll leave Monday by train."

When we reached the hotel, I saw Hilde talking to a pinch-faced man.

I walked over to her as the man hurried away. His furtive glance, coupled with a leer, put me on guard. "Who was that?"

"I don't know."

"What did he want?"

"I don't think it's important," she said. Her dismissive tone annoyed me.

I put some steel into my voice. "Well, I do. He looked like the type to harass young ladies."

"He's harmless. He wanted directions to City Hall."

I didn't believe her, but I let it go. "Are you ready to show us around your city center and start the interviews?"

"Yes, but where is Miss Seville?"

At that moment, Jane walked out of the lift carrying her camera bag with her equipment and we set off.

Once at the government building in the city center, I worked quickly from practice. I listened to women—young, old, fat, thin, married, unmarried—as they all told me the same thing. Life in Austria was much better under the new government. It was wonderful to be reunited with Germany. I didn't point out they'd never been united in the first place.

In two hours, my notebook was bursting with notes in English from a dozen interviews and Jane had her scenic photographs.

I suggested we find a café away from the city center for our lunch. I told Hilde that of course I was paying, which again brightened her outlook considerably. She took us by tram to a spot on the north side of the city along what I thought of as a high street, lined with shops and cafes.

Down a side street, a crowd of men and women were shouting and shoving, all facing the center of a circle. Hilde glanced over and said, "We'll go this way. It is better."

My reporter instincts took over and I started toward the group, Jane on my heels as she pulled out her camera.

Hilde grabbed my arm. "No. They don't want you to see this."

"See what?" I found I was dragging Hilde forward with me.

"It is a scrubbing party. They are cleaning the pavement. Removing the pro-independence slogans. That is all."

I could see swastika armbands on many in the group, and I spotted two SS officer caps near the center of the throng above the heads of the crowd. On the other side of the street, people rushed past, their faces averted. I pushed in until I could see.

Jane followed, her camera ready.

On the pavement were three middle-aged men in suits, on their hands and knees, scrubbing the pavement. They had buckets of soapy water and wooden brushes, and their hands looked red and sore from chapping. The knees of their suit trousers were soaked and probably ruined. Above the jeering, I heard a harsh voice say in German, "Work harder, Jews. You'll never clean away the filth without effort."

Hilde shoved in front of me and blocked Jane's view. She grabbed Jane's camera bag and dragged her backward, pushing me along. My spot was immediately filled with men, women, and even children whose faces showed eagerness. I could smell the blood lust.

I felt soiled.

Jane, recognizing a missed opportunity, was furious and tried to push back in.

Hilde held on to the camera bag and snapped, "One more step and I'll break your camera."

"You break my camera and you'll pay," Jane snarled, clutching it to her chest. "You don't have enough money to replace it, so don't make threats." Their argument didn't attract attention since the crowd was faced the other way watching the men's humiliation, and Hilde and Jane spoke in English with their voices lowered.

"I am empowered by the German government to make certain you do not take back bad impressions of my homeland. I was told to use any means necessary."

"But to break her camera?" I asked in amazement.

"What do I care about her camera? And don't think your complaints to my bosses will go anywhere. I'm a member of the National Socialist Party." She lifted her head and gave us a cold stare.

In that moment, I could picture her in that crowd, taunting the poor unfortunates. I tried to get one more view of the men, but all I saw was a solid wall of jeering bodies.

Hilde led us away. "It is regrettable you saw that."

"But I did. And I'm shocked," I said.

"Stay away from my camera," Jane said, her face flushed and her eyes narrowed in fury as Hilde approached her.

"Why are you shocked? For years the Jews ran everything. Had everything. And we were their servants. No longer. Now we will get what should be ours by right. This is our country." Hilde was deliberately ignoring Jane's warning as she took her arm.

Jane jerked her arm away, but she walked along beside us.

"What we can see and take photographs of is decided by someone higher up? You are following their directives?" I asked.

"Of course our leaders decide what reporters get in and what stories they can cover. I wouldn't be your guide if I didn't agree completely with their goals." She walked smartly along the pavement, her arm linked in mine until we reached the café.

I didn't say anything and let Hilde order for us. Once the waitress had left, I said very quietly, "But they were humiliating those men. What was their crime?"

She shrugged. "They're Jews. You'll like the soup here. And the bread is the freshest in Vienna."

"Hilde—"

"No." She put up a hand. "I don't tell you how to run England. Don't say a thing, either of you. Since the vote last month, you are now a guest of the nation of Germany. Of the Third Reich. Please act like a guest."

There wasn't much I could say to that. I was here to accomplish a mission and get a story at the same time. But I would let people know when I returned to London what I had seen.

I gritted my teeth and said, "You're right. I shall try to act like a guest. Okay, Jane?" I pleaded with my eyes.

Jane studied me for a minute. She must have guessed there was something more to our journey, because she nodded but remained silent.

I took a deep breath. "So what is on our itinerary for this afternoon?"

We followed her directions until it was time to go back to the hotel to dress for dinner and the opera. We finally got rid of her in the lobby and then went upstairs.

"When do I find out what is really going on?" Jane asked in the corridor.

"Would you care to window shop? All the shops are closed now and the pavement should be fairly empty."

She nodded.

The main shopping streets were nearly deserted as Jane and I walked along, elbows linked. Jane looked around and then murmured, "We shouldn't have to worry about someone listening to us. Tell me. Now."

Sir Henry had said to tell her if necessary. "Sir Henry has given me a secondary assignment to carry out while I'm here. You don't have to get involved if you don't want to. Sunday morning I'm going to mass at a particular church at a distance from here."

Jane nodded.

"Afterward, I will walk two streets over to a flat to pick up some merchandise. I will have to carry this merchandise on my person at all times until we reach London. I hope to leave Austria Monday morning without attracting any notice and get these goods back to London safely."

"Is this merchandise heavy?" We stopped to examine the contents of a dress shop window.

"No, but it's very expensive and there's a lot of it. And it must remain hidden. As must the people we get it from."

"They're willing to give it to us?"

"Yes. We take it to Sir Henry, and he uses it to get them visas."

"Jews," Jane said with a note of disgust.

"Yes. Sir Henry's family," I added with firmness.

"But he's Christian." Jane was clearly puzzled.

"His late wife, Esther's mother, was Jewish."

She nodded, weighing this new information.

We continued down the street to the corner. I spelled out our timetable and was telling her about the church at the tram stop when we heard male voices followed by glass breaking.

Jane moved forward to get a better view up the side street. "They're looting a shop. It's still light out."

"See the policeman down at the next corner with his back to them?"

"Yes. Is he deaf? Why doesn't he do anything?"

"Because it's a Jewish shop and what they're doing is not only allowed, but encouraged."

Her eyes flashed with righteous indignation. "That's stealing. That is so very wrong. And these people are supposed to be Catholics." I couldn't tell which upset her more, the looting or the fact that Catholics had chosen to break the law.

I kept my elbow locked with hers. "That's why I need to get assets out for Sir Henry's relatives so they can get visas and escape."

"Sir Henry can't use his own money? He's got a pile." I'd long suspected Jane was what my father called a union rabble-rouser.

"No. The British government won't allow it. They must have their own assets physically located in our country before the visas will be issued. The government doesn't want refugees to take jobs away from the native

English."

"They have a point."

Before Jane could begin a lecture on socialist economics, I said, "Let's go before we find ourselves in trouble." I steered her back the way we'd come.

"You mean more trouble? Like at lunchtime?"

"Yes."

"At least I don't have my camera with me." I couldn't tell if she thought that was a good or a bad thing.

We were almost back to the hotel before she said, "What the Nazis are doing is wrong. Hateful. Count me in."

"Thank you."

She considered for a minute longer. "Are you worried our rooms are bugged?"

"It's a possibility, and we don't want any slipups."

"Slipups?" Jane gazed at me, her eyebrows raised.

"Caught carrying whatever we'll be asked to take to England with us."

"Could it be dangerous?"

I remembered my trip back from Berlin the previous autumn. "Yes."

* * *

The Wagner opera that night was beautifully done and warmly received by the audience, and the following day went more smoothly for us. We didn't see anything Hilde didn't want us to see. I managed some good interviews and Jane was happy with her photographs.

We went shopping. Jane found colorful candies to take back as presents for her nieces and nephews. I found a tiny knitted sweater for Mary Babcock's anxiously awaited arrival.

After we had a late lunch, we went to the park to hear an outdoor concert. The warm Saturday afternoon brought city residents to the park in throngs. Hilde introduced us, rather proudly, as English journalists she was showing around Vienna to some neighbors she bumped into.

Jane saw the opportunity to take some lovely photographs of the park before the concert, so we started walking. We had seen most of the park when we tried to pass a group of tall, good-looking young men. Despite their civilian clothes, it was obvious they were German soldiers. They surrounded us and made vaguely suggestive comments in German. I didn't think they meant any harm, and Hilde was openly flirting, but Jane began to shrink in fear while clutching her camera.

Hilde's threat the day before had left its mark.

I started to translate their comments in English so Jane would know there was nothing to worry about, but that seemed to egg the young men on. They became physically more assertive, tightening the circle around the three of us, which made Jane begin to panic.

I told them to leave us alone in German, which they laughed at and crowded closer to us, teased by Hilde. I told her to stop. I told them to stop. In the distance, I heard the band tuning up and told the young men that we had to get back to the concert. They laughed.

Jane was starting to shake, and I didn't feel very safe.

Then one of them put a hand on her camera. She gave a little cry and tried to pull it away, but he kept a grip on the strap, taunting her and laughing.

Suddenly, a voice snapped out a command. The one with his hand on her camera strap dropped his grip as if he'd been burned. The whole group stopped laughing and backed up, facing in one direction as they stood at attention.

I turned around and blinked. Standing behind us was

Oberst Bernhard. The helpful, frightening German officer I'd met while trying to find Reggie's killer. The man with the penetrating dark brown eyes.

He told the young men to be on their way and then said, "Frau Denis. I never expected to see you in Vienna."

"Oberst Bernhard, how nice to see you again. I'm afraid their exuberance frightened Jane, since she speaks no German." Then I switched to English. "Miss Jane Seville, this is Oberst Wilhelm Bernhard. I met him last year while he was posted to the German embassy in London."

"How do you do?" he said in heavily accented English and bowed over her hand.

Jane quickly overcame her shock and smiled at his continental manners. "Pleased to meet you, Oberst."

I switched to German then. "And Fraulein Hilde Schmidt, our Reich Foreign Press Office assistant, this is Oberst Bernhard of the Reich army. Oberst, Fraulein Schmidt."

Hilde gushed what a pleasure it was to meet a distinguished member of Austria's liberators. The oberst, in turn, was very cold and correct in his reply.

Then he switched to English and said, "Frau Denis, Fraulein Seville, are you going to the concert?"

"Yes."

I must have sounded eager since he said, "May I escort you? I enjoy band music."

I discovered I did, too, sitting under the spring sun among contented adults with children running and playing a distance away. The oberst and I exchanged smiles and small comments as might be heard among friends. Hilde watched us closely and made certain to add her comments to everything, even the ones the oberst made in English so Jane could understand.

I could tell he was getting annoyed.

When the concert finished, he said in English, "Do you have any plans for dinner tonight?"

I looked at Jane. "Well, no."

"Good. Let us go find a traditional Austrian restaurant. It will be better than your hotel, and certainly better than the mess hall." When we looked uncertain, he said, "Please. I hate to eat alone."

I smiled. "Gladly. Are you ready, Jane?"

She glanced around uneasily, still shaken by her experience with the young soldiers. "Yes."

Hilde said, "I'd love to join you."

Bernhard glared at her as he might a private who'd failed at his task and said, "No. I'm sorry. Another night, perhaps. Tonight, I want to relive good times with old friends."

She slunk back a step.

"Have a good day tomorrow, Hilde," I said in German. "We're going to church and then dinner with British embassy people, and we have to leave Monday morning. It was nice working with you."

"Thank you for your help, Hilde, and your translations," Jane said in English. "We've had a lovely couple of days."

"I'll stop by the hotel Monday morning in case there are any last-minute things to be done," she assured us.

"You don't need to, but it would be nice to say a proper good-bye. Enjoy your day off with your family," I told her and turned back to Bernhard.

Bernhard and Jane started a discussion of the terrors of air flight. After a minute, I heard Hilde walk away.

We found a family restaurant and were taken to a booth where we wouldn't be overheard over the boisterous voices around us. After we'd ordered, I told him about changes to London since he'd left before Christmas, and he told me he'd enjoyed skiing in Austria last winter. I realized that was before Austria had been taken over by Germany, and knew without him saying a word that he was part of the reconnaissance team.

That was hardly a surprise. Bernhard was a high-ranking officer, and I suspected a well-regarded one. But that led me to another realization. He could well have been in London to study our military, our defenses, and our political will.

I asked about his children, and he told me stories of their Christmas. We carried on our conversation in English so Jane could join in, and I could tell Bernhard was struggling to find the right words.

I switched to German. "Did you bring your children with you, Oberst?"

"They are safe where they are." There was a note of finality in his tone.

Taking a chance, I asked, "Oberst, what brings you to Vienna?" in German.

His dark eyes seemed to see through me. Did they see my worries? "What brings you here?"

"I'm doing a newspaper article on women's lives as they've changed under the new government. And you?"

"My division was sent here last month to maintain order. We haven't had much to do. The Austrians have been happy to see us. Which makes my life very pleasant."

"I'm glad." I liked Oberst Bernhard despite the fact he was German. A Nazi, maybe, but I suspected in name only.

"Your accent is better," he told me.

"I've had to use German for everything here. It hasn't been as big a struggle as I expected."

"I'm glad," he said, his eyes twinkling. "How are you

choosing your women for your article?"

"You met Hilde Schmidt. She lined up some interviews for me. We visited some shops, the palaces, and listened to concerts."

"Sounds like a very wise choice." Bernhard smiled at me over his beer stein.

"And you recommend that I practice wisdom in this assignment for the newspaper." I smiled back, certain he was giving me a warning.

"And in your assignment for Sir Henry."

I felt my smile melt off my face. My words struggled out of my strangled throat as I asked, "How do you know?"

"I do now. Before I was only guessing. I had no trouble finding out what you were doing in Berlin."

I felt the room heat up like a sauna. "Am I being followed this time?"

He shook his head.

Finally, I swallowed and said quietly, "It's all legal. They have exit visas."

"Then the problem isn't us. It's your government. You have nothing to fear."

I knew better.

CHAPTER FIFTEEN

We fell silent as our food arrived, plates piled high with sausages, cabbage, and potatoes.

Once the waiter left, I spoke quietly. "They wouldn't have to leave if—" I stopped, warned by the look on Oberst Bernhard's face.

"Be careful around Hilde."

"You know her?"

"I know her type. There are more of them in Austria than in all of Germany. When do you return?"

"Monday morning."

He smiled at Jane and said in English, "I imagine you return by train through Switzerland. The scenery is beautiful and there is no need to fight air sickness."

She smiled. "Two good reasons. I hope to take some photographs."

"For your newspaper?"

"And for myself."

He lowered his voice and leaned forward, looking deeply into my eyes. "I, too, will leave in a few days."

"Are you saying Sir Henry's assignment should keep this in mind?"

"Yes."

I remembered the worry in Judith Rothenberger's voice. And then an image of those poor men, forced to scrub the pavement in their business clothes while people jeered at them, came and robbed me of my appetite.

And then I saw the pinch-faced man from the hotel lobby enter the restaurant, glance over at us with Oberst Bernhard and then leave.

The oberst noticed I'd stopped eating. "Isn't it good?"

"It is. It's just—oh, dear."

He smiled at me. "Tell me what is wrong."

"Have you seen a scrubbing party, I think they're called?"

He set down his fork. "Fraulein Schmidt let you see that? Idiot." The scorn in his voice for Hilde was substantial.

"No. She tried to get me to go another way, but I was curious." I wanted to be fair to her.

"There are times when curiosity is not good."

Suddenly, I had to know. The Oberst Bernhard I'd known in London was a German, might be a Nazi, could have killed dozens of people, but I couldn't shake the belief he was basically decent. "How do you deal with it?"

"This is new to me, too, since I came to Austria. I understand these attitudes among the people now are spreading back to Germany."

"But how do you—?"

"I go another way."

"It's not right."

He gave me a sharp look. "You are a guest in our country. Don't ask the wrong questions. It's not healthy, and you have a job to do."

I studied his face for a moment. He was talking about my secret assignment for Sir Henry, not my story for the women's pages. I was certain he wanted me to do what he would not, or could not. He wanted me to save people. People who had nothing to do with military security or tactics. People he had nothing against. People he wouldn't face on the battlefield in the war he had told me was coming.

A war he had warned me of when we first met.

Despite what he knew, he wouldn't turn me in. For

that, I was grateful.

* * *

The next morning, we rode the tram to St. Mary's, the Catholic church that was my landmark in finding the Rothenbergers' building. The church loomed large and stone-faced in a small park by the road. All around us, gaily dressed people greeted each other, lingering outside in the early morning light. I followed Jane into the church and copied her movements as closely as I could.

In the candlelight and increasing sunshine that chased away the cold, dim atmosphere, I could see the interior of the old church was decorated in vibrant colors. The service was in Latin and I was lost, but Jane followed without effort. Still, I felt safe, invisible within the crowd tightly packed into the sanctuary.

I wanted to linger, knowing we'd soon put ourselves in danger.

When the service was over, we went outside. I saw the pointy-faced man who had spoken to Hilde at the hotel now was lingering by the tram stop. A cold breath of air slid under my coat, making my heart skitter while he studied the worshipers.

Someone wanted us watched closely. The sooner we got out of Austria, the better.

"Let's walk around the park before we head to dinner," I said to Jane in English, pulling her down a path so a large bush stood between us and the man.

She nodded and we started down a side street that I knew didn't lead directly to the Rothenbergers' flat. After a few minutes, with the rat-faced man nowhere to be seen, we turned down another street and eventually ended up at their building. The brick five-story building blended in well with the others. Here I didn't see any whitewashed signs or notices forbidding Jews plastered on any doorways.

The front door of the building was unlocked and the concierge was nowhere in sight, probably still at church or busy with her Sunday dinner preparations. We entered unnoticed. We took the stairs up and stopped in front of a door marked 2R. I knocked, not certain of our reception.

Then I heard a child's giggle.

The door immediately swung open and a man stood there in his shirt, vest, trousers, and stocking feet. "*Ja?*"

"Matthias Rothenberger? Sir Henry has sent us," I said in German.

"I was afraid you wouldn't find us. That you wouldn't come." He nearly pulled us into the flat and quickly shut and locked the door.

I'd acted the same way after Reggie had been killed and our flat ransacked. "Of course we came. What's going on?"

A little dark-haired girl skipped around us, giggling. Matthias patted her on the head and said, "Liesbeth, go back and play with the other children."

She gripped his hand for a moment, fear flashing across her face as she looked at us, before she skipped down the hallway and through a doorway.

"Have you seen the signs saying Jews aren't allowed in this park or that shop? The broken shop windows?" A woman came up to us in a heavy sweater and wool skirt and slippers. She looked younger than Esther's other aunt whom I met in Berlin, possibly under forty, but the two women looked enough alike that I knew they were sisters. And they both looked like Esther.

"We've seen some looting and a scrubbing party. We've seen some of the danger. Are you Esther's Aunt Judith?"

"Yes."

"You have passports and exit visas?"

"Yes, but we had to register. Everyone does to obtain exit visas. This means the Nazis know where we live. Then before the annexation vote, they took over the bank and arrested Baron von Rothschild. That was nearly a month ago."

"If he's not safe with all his money, none of us are," her husband said. "And with his arrest, all of us are out of a job."

"You worked for the Rothschild bank?"

"*Ja*. And the rumor is that he can only get out of prison by paying a huge fine. Really, it is ransom. And so, we removed all our savings from the bank. We needed it to pay the tax to get exit visas."

"They are glad to give us exit visas. They want to take our money and get rid of us. The problem is getting visas to go to England. To go where we have family and can start again." Judith hugged herself as if she were cold.

"Do you know what Sir Henry wants me to do?"

"Yes. Ruth has told me how you helped her and her son."

"I haven't helped her." I wished I could. "She won't leave until your parents go with her."

Judith's lips formed a grim smile. "My father will never leave, and my mother will not leave without him. My sister will not leave as long as they need her. They are fools."

Her words told me she wanted to leave, but one big question remained. "Do you trust us to carry your assets to England to Sir Henry? He's the one who will try to use them to get visas for the four of you."

"We trust you, yes. Ruth did, and she is glad she did." Then Matthias held my gaze as he said, "We have to. It has been decreed throughout the Jewish community that we will have to submit an inventory of all property with a value of more than five thousand Reichsmarks. Either we hand everything over to you, or the Nazis will grab it all. We'd rather take our chances with you."

"Where is your suitcase?" Judith asked.

"My suitcase?" That would be too obvious. How would we ever get through customs carrying a suitcase full of smuggled goods? Or hide it from the prying eyes of Gestapo informers working at the hotel?

"You'll need a suitcase to carry it all."

"We can't. We have to hide everything on our persons, both while we're here and then when we leave for England."

Jane watched our exchange without understanding our words. Her skepticism was written on her face. Apparently she had guessed things weren't going smoothly.

"Didn't you tell Esther?" Matthias asked his wife.

"I tried to. I have to be so circumspect in letters or telegrams. The Nazis probably read everything we send or receive." Judith looked slightly frantic.

I probably looked confused. I know I felt confused, and I understood every word we'd spoken. "Tell her what? And why would I need a suitcase that I can't conceal?"

Husband and wife looked at each other. Then Matthias said, "There is something you do not know."

Judith added, "There are others who need your help, too. Come with me."

I followed them down the hall and through the first doorway, Jane on my heels.

As soon as he opened the door, I thought there must be a mistake. The room held a dozen people, sitting and staring intently at us. Looking at us with hopeful faces.

On a table in the middle of the room were piles of gold and jewels. More value than I could imagine. More weight than I could carry.

I stared back. Behind me, Jane gasped. The people around the room didn't say a word.

"What's going on, Livvy?" Jane murmured.

"It appears our job is larger than I was led to believe."

People I didn't know had piled up riches on the table for us to take, trusting us to do the right thing. And in a corner children sat, trusting these adults to keep them safe. Expecting me to help bring them to freedom. Faced with their desperation, I had to do something.

I couldn't turn my back. I couldn't fail them.

As I stood there, trying to adjust to the size of this mission, a woman sobbed, "We want to leave, too. Just like Judith."

This woman was warmly dressed like Judith but wore smart shoes. She looked younger than Judith but her coloring was very pale. She kept twisting her fingers together as her lower lip quivered. And her eyes were wet with tears.

"I should introduce you," Matthias said. He walked into the parlor and laid a gentle hand on the woman's shoulder. "This is my little sister, Lilith, and her husband, Joseph. Joseph Gruen. He's a physician," Matthias told me.

"No longer. I can no longer treat anyone not a Jew," the man sitting next to the sobbing woman said, giving me a brittle smile. He was stocky and balding, with a deep voice. "Last year, I treated many Austrian children in my practice. I never asked about their faith."

Matthias moved on. "This is my older brother, Isaak Rothenberger. He is a world-famous poet. You perhaps know of him?"

He was an older version of Matthias, tall and slim, with gray hair and a neatly trimmed beard. He looked at me expectantly, with the same hope I saw on Lady Margaret's face when she was introduced to someone new. All poets hope you've heard of and enjoyed their work. "I'm sure Margaret Brooke has. She's an English poet and a close friend of my father's."

"Lady Margaret Brooke? Yes, we have written back and forth about poetry and language for years. She is a brilliant woman."

"I'll tell her you said that."

Isaak then welcomed Jane in heavily accented, flowery English and told her how much he appreciated what she was doing to help them.

Then he introduced his sons, Nathan, a boy of about fifteen, and Solomon, who appeared to be my age, and his fiancée, Gabriella, a very pretty, terrified-looking woman of about twenty.

I looked around the comfortable room with thick carpets and well-padded furniture. The view out the window faced down the street where I'd come, now bright with morning sunlight. It was hard to believe things were so bad these people were offering me their wealth to help them leave everything else behind.

"Gabriella has already been assaulted by Austrian thugs," Solomon spit out. "They had been waiting for her to leave her house again, so we smuggled her out in the early morning. She's been hiding here, knowing it's not safe for her to go home."

I looked into her eyes and saw pain. Worse, I saw shame, and that made me angry. No young woman deserved this.

I quickly translated for Jane, whose face showed more compassion than I expected to see.

"Obviously, the police are no help in this situation," Judith said. "She desperately needs your help to get out of Vienna."

A short woman with gray-streaked hair said, "And I am Gabriella's mother, Deborah Morgenstern." She looked at her daughter and then gave me a fierce glance.

"Who are the children?" I asked. Their wide-eyed, furtive glances urged me to get more involved in this insane mission.

Matthias called them. When five dark-haired, solemn, big-eyed children came to him, he said, "These are my children, Liesbeth and Joen." He gestured to the other three in turn. "And Lilith's children, Laila, Benjamin, and Aaron."

"We all need to leave. Please, ask Henry to get us all out. We need fourteen visas," Judith said in English.

"The little girl, Liesbeth, reminds me of my niece, Marianne. I'll help," Jane said, still glancing around the room.

"You have to get us out. Take us with you," Lilith cried out in German. Her hands reached out to clutch me. She was too far away to touch me, but I stepped back in alarm. Her husband put an arm around her and shushed her.

"I'm afraid to leave the building. Judith and Joseph have to do my shopping. We must leave Vienna now," she continued, panic in her voice, tears running down her face.

"All I can do is get your assets to England so Sir Henry can get you the visas." I was feeling overwhelmed with the task they wanted to place on my shoulders. All I was supposed to do was smuggle jewels, not people, and not all of these riches.

"Lilith knows," Judith told me. "That is why we

brought you our gold and jewels to send to England."

Deborah Morgenstern, on the other hand, announced she was certain we were as evil as the Nazis and were going to steal her savings. She announced she wanted to use her jewels to bribe an official to get them out safety. She wanted to hire a guard to get her daughter Gabriella out.

Gabriella Morgenstern faced her mother and told her she was leaving and she wouldn't go with anyone but Solomon. She had nothing to put in, but she wanted to go with the group. Solomon Rothenberger put his arm around her and said they would go. He and his father would put in her share if her mother did not.

This was all in rapid-fire German. Jane shot me a glance, hoping I'd explain this fervent exchange of words. I nodded, probably looking a little confused and not helping Jane at all. There was no way to quickly explain the shouting between mother and daughter.

The group argued about what jewelry and how many coins we should take with us and how much they should keep for bribes. Jane watched everything, not understanding the words but following the intense facial expressions and frantic tones of voice.

I gave Jane a quick explanation, saying I'd tell her more later.

The children sat huddled together on the floor, watching us in silence. Did they know we were discussing their future?

I suspected the older ones understood. They met my glance with grave faces while a girl held the youngest, who was squirming to get off her lap. The younger children watched with wide eyes while Lilith Gruen wept.

I needed to inject a dose of realism as their

discussion veered farther from the practical. "I was told I was moving things for four, not fourteen. We can only take what we can hide. Sir Henry will have to change his plans with whoever he deals with at the Home Office."

"It doesn't matter. Nothing matters. We're doomed," Lilith sobbed.

"Oh, will you be quiet?" Deborah Morgenstern snapped.

Lilith subsided into quiet sobs while aiming dark looks at the other woman.

I'd heard enough fighting. "Do you still want us to take your assets to England to Sir Henry for entry visas or not?"

"Judith and I do," Matthias answered. Isaak and Joseph Gruen nodded.

"And the others?"

"It's hard to have faith when the world is going mad," Solomon said. "But I want to get to England so I can fight the Germans and know Gabriella is safe."

"Jane," I said in English, "let's see how much we can carry."

Then we got into the business of whose gold and jewels was whose and what they would part with. I would wear Matthias's belt that contained gold pieces; Jane would wear Joseph Gruen's. We put the jewels and jewelry at the bottom of our purses. I had Isaak's and Matthias's. Jane had Joseph's large bounty and what little Mrs. Morgenstern was willing to part with.

After Jane and I had hidden everything we were to carry, I said, "Judith, stay in touch with Sir Henry." I gave them the information I was given by Peter Thornhill on what they'd hear and what they should say and do when they got the message that the entry visas had arrived. Then we wished each other luck and Jane and I left.

"Did that go well?" Jane asked as we walked down the street.

"Most of it. The mother of the good-looking young woman, Gabriella, doesn't trust us, but Gabriella is determined to travel with her fiancé and his family. Once we're in France, I'll feel safe telling you everything. Until then, I need you to trust me."

I took a deep breath. "I know you don't approve, Jane, but please, keep quiet."

CHAPTER SIXTEEN

Jane grabbed my arm to stop me. "I saw the looks on the faces of those children. They are so frightened. And that one little girl reminds me of my younger niece. I'll trust you and Sir Henry for the sake of those children."

As we approached the tram stop, I noticed the man who kept popping up around Vienna was now standing as if waiting for a tram. A tram pulled up and some older people got off and headed into the church.

The man continued to linger until we climbed onto the tram and sat down. At the last second, he hopped aboard and sat across from us. He looked us over from head to toe while Jane glanced at me with one eyebrow raised.

"Perhaps he doesn't like Englishwomen," I said in English.

He continued to stare at us with an expressionless face.

We rode the tram straight to the restaurant where members of the British embassy had hired a private room for their Sunday luncheon. I scarcely breathed, terrified of the man and his constant stare.

When we alighted, the pointy-faced man stopped in front of the closed offices across the street, but I suspected he would come in to ask questions about us as soon as we were seated.

I knew that diplomats were always diplomats, but Jane was amazed that we could talk all afternoon without anyone saying anything remotely controversial or mentioning a detail that would incriminate them. Nevertheless, we had a lively time speaking English with a host of mostly unattached young men far from home.

They wanted to hear about the latest West End plays, any new nightspots opening up, and whether we kept up with the Ascot races, the Henley regatta, and cricket test matches. Anything to remind them of home in an increasingly hostile city.

We told them every scrap of sporting and entertainment news we could think of.

As the afternoon turned into evening, Jane and I returned to the hotel. We decided without discussing it that staying in for the evening would be the safest thing to do.

And in the morning, we'd catch a train out of there.

As soon as we walked by the desk, a man in hotel livery behind the desk called to me, "Frau Denis, I have a telegram for you."

Thanking him, I took it and walked in the direction of the elevator. It read

GET BACK HERE THEY'VE ARRESTED THOMAS
FATHER

"What's happened?" Jane asked. I showed her the telegram and then translated. Changing direction, I went to the phone boxes.

It took a few minutes, but I finally heard an English operator putting through my call on the scratchy-sounding line. "Father. It's me, Livvy."

"What are you doing in Vienna? Sir Henry won't tell me a thing. He—"

"I'm doing a piece on the lives of Austrian women. Why did they arrest Thomas?"

"For killing his grandfather. Everything's in shambles. Margaret—" crackle, crackle "—the worse." More crackling and then "Walter." Finally, a ghostly voice said, "Get back here." His command came through clearly, even though I could barely hear over the static.

"Tomorrow."

The line, bad to begin with, grew louder with static. I hung up. At least my father knew I'd received his message and wouldn't try to reach me through the overburdened British embassy.

"What's happened?" Jane asked when I came out of the phone box.

"Do you have an hour?"

I received a pained look. Jane may have taken my words for a joke, but I was serious. A short time in jail wouldn't hurt Thomas, and I planned to find the real killer and have Thomas released as soon as possible. My worry was the words "Margaret" and "worse." I needed to get back as soon as possible to learn about Aunt Margaret's condition, and I wouldn't rest until I learned how she was faring. Until I knew she was safe.

Jane and I went up to my room where I proceeded to tell her all I knew about the Brookes and the murder.

* * *

The next morning, we said farewell to Hilde at the hotel, to her relief and ours. All went well until we reached the train station. We bought our tickets under the indifferent gaze of a railway clerk and then headed toward the barrier where customs and immigration awaited.

A cluster of émigrés was ahead of us, getting orders such as "Only one suitcase," "You can't take shoes out of the country," and "This photograph doesn't look like you." Their suitcases were pawed through and they faced the indignities of being bullied into paying extra "fees" to the officials.

Slowly, singly and in families, red-faced and shaken, they were allowed to pass.

This was petty corruption on the same level as I'd seen years before in the Balkans while traveling with my father. At least in the Balkans, they were equally corrupt with everyone who spoke their language.

There were three officials that day, a scrawny youth who didn't open his mouth, an older, saggy-skinned man who leered at all the women, and their leader, a beefy man with a potbelly who made the demands and collected the "fees."

If this was the best Austria could provide, they were in serious trouble. I suspected they were here because of their party loyalty or because some well-connected relatives thought to put them somewhere out of the way.

The family ahead of us, a father, mother, two young children, and a baby, huddled together. The children clung to their parents who trembled every time one of the children made a sound. The heavy-set customs official looked at their papers and then his mates, winked, and said, "The baby doesn't have its papers. He'll have to stay behind."

"Surely she does not have to have separate papers," the father exclaimed.

"She is on my papers. She is only a baby," the mother begged.

"You'll have to leave her behind, Jew."

"No." The woman appeared to be in agony.

"Then stay here. It's all the same to me."

I was furious and I could hear Jane, who could guess what was happening, making growling noises in her throat. We couldn't risk being searched, because this crew would at best take the jewels from our handbags. At worst, we'd never be heard from again.

I remembered the oberst's words about being a guest in what was now Nazi Germany. But using a baby in a sadistic game was more than I could stand.

When I could bear the mother's terrified tears and the guards' threats no longer, I stepped forward.

"Do you have entry visas?" I asked the father in German.

"Yes," he told me. "My cousin Noah is in England. We have papers to join him."

Relief surged through me. I might be able to bluff my way through. "We are British diplomats," I said to the officials in German, my gesture including Jane. "These people are under our protection, traveling to our country. Let them through."

"You? A woman?"

I did my best imitation of Lady Beatrice with my nose in the air. "Many countries employ women in their embassies. We are diplomats."

"This is not Britain. This is Germany. You have no say here, Frau." He leaned toward me, smirking.

I hated smirks. "One call to my embassy, and your bosses will be out here. They'll want to know about all the fees you've been putting in your pockets and how you've been managing your station. They might even want their share. Do you really want that to happen?"

"I've done nothing wrong." He was all bluster.

"Shall we get your superiors out here and see if they agree with you?"

Sweat beaded up around the line of his cap, but he didn't move an inch.

I stared at him, not moving either.

"Take the baby," the guard barked to his fellows.

As the older guard made a half-hearted attempt, the mother shrieked, "No."

My heart leaped into my mouth. I was sure something was about to go wrong and I didn't want those oafs to find out about our smuggling. Not declaring gold and jewels and not paying the fees was punishable by imprisonment.

I had to get home. Something else must have happened to Aunt Margaret. And Esther's relatives were counting on me to get their savings through to England.

But I couldn't stand by and see a defenseless infant harmed.

An evil grin crossed the beefy man's face. "Then pay me."

Oh, how I wanted to slap that smile off his face. "How much of a bribe do you want?"

He mentioned an exorbitant amount.

I gave him a dry look and shook my head slightly.

He shrugged.

I leaned forward to put my face in front of his bad breath and double chins and said in perfect German, "That baby is going onto the train with its family. Now how much do you want? And remember, if I don't like your answer, I'll find your supervisor."

"Frau Denis."

I turned around to see Oberst Bernhard, in full uniform, striding toward me. "Oberst, you're just in time." I've never been happier to see anyone.

The guards sprang to attention, but not before Bernhard had seen the confrontation between me and the official.

"What is the problem?" He used a tone of voice that I'm sure made underlings quake. It certainly made me nervous.

The official tugged at his uniform to hide the gaps where the fabric strained and said, "You know this woman?"

Bernhard gave me a hard look and said, "*Ja.*"

"She wanted to know the exit fee for this Jew baby." The customs official used an ingratiating voice.

Oberst looked at me in shock. "Why do you want to know?"

"He wasn't going to let the baby get on the train with its family," I said in an aggrieved tone. "How anyone can treat an infant—"

Bernhard stared hard at the official, who now was sweating profusely. Then the oberst switched to English as he said to me, "Tell me what you are doing." He did not look pleased.

"I said Jane and I are British embassy officials."

"What?" He let loose an English oath I didn't know he knew.

"They are letting the rest of the family through, but not the baby. They've been taking bribes from everyone else, so I thought if I couldn't get him to relent, I'd pay the bribe and get the baby through—"

The oberst turned to Jane. "Talk some sense into her."

"I think she's right. Something had to be done." She crossed her arms.

The oberst let out a ferocious oath in German as he turned to the official. "Are you satisfied with the paperwork so we can get that baby on the train and out of my city?" His voice rose with each word as he leaned forward.

The guard, leaning far back out of the oberst's reach with a startled expression, nodded. Then I turned to the parents. "Go. Now."

The father gathered up their stamped documents and their battered suitcases. The family, still open-mouthed, hurried in a many-footed glob to the train and climbed aboard.

With the oberst standing there, Jane and I had no problem crossing the barrier. Our passports were stamped in moments without a mention of any bribes.

As we walked toward the train, Bernhard looked at our tickets. "First-class sleeper. Very nice."

"The joys of traveling for work."

He pulled me aside where we couldn't be seen by the customs officials. "I couldn't have you leave without saying good-bye. Now I'm wondering what would have happened if I hadn't come to see you off."

"I don't know. I'm glad, for myself and for that family, I didn't have to find out."

"Let me guess. They are going to England."

"Yes."

"Fitting somehow. Have a safe journey."

"Will I?"

"Yes." He sounded certain. I felt relieved.

"And you?"

"I'm off on Wednesday."

The conductor helped Jane board and turned to me.

"Good-bye, Oberst." I smiled at him. "I wish you a safe journey. Thank you for your help. I won't soon forget it. Or you."

"Good-bye, Frau." He kissed the back of my hand. "I've found you unforgettable. And reckless. Please, never come back."

I knew the last was a rebuke and a warning. Red-faced, I climbed aboard and joined Jane in our compartment. From there, I watched Bernhard as he stood facing us with his arms crossed. I opened a window and waved as the train pulled out of the station. At the last moment, he gave me a nod and a smile.

Then I began to read a book I'd brought along and Jane started knitting. Before long we were rumbling through the Austrian countryside, mountain vistas filling our view out the window.

For the first seating of dinner, we sat at a table with two nuns. They blessed the food and then ate in silence. It suited me and my nervousness well. Jane was fascinated by the view out the window, which entertained her during the entire meal.

I kept thinking of Oberst Bernhard's help when he and I had crossed the border out of Germany the last time. Austria was part of Germany now, and he wouldn't be there when we made the border crossing into Switzerland.

Twilight lingered above the mountains when we reached the border. Unlike the guards and the soldiers on the Berlin to Amsterdam train, they showed no interest in me. They also didn't appear to have a member of the Gestapo on the train with them.

Once they handed back our papers and walked on, I felt like lead weights had been lifted off my head and chest. As soon as we were rolling along in Switzerland, I fell asleep sitting up.

Jane took pity on me and didn't ask any questions until we had crossed the border into France in the early morning and were headed toward Lyon. Tucked into our tiny room, she climbed down to my bottom bunk. I then filled her in on why we'd gone to Vienna and the families we were trying to help.

When I finished, she asked, "How long have you been working on these special assignments for Sir Henry?"

"Since last autumn when I came to work at the *Daily Premier.*"

"You have more nerve than I gave you credit for," she said and smiled.

"I'm sorry I had to drag you into this without telling

you first. Sir Henry left it to me to explain this as necessary."

Guilt must have shown on my face because Jane said, "Now that it's over, I'm glad I was chosen to help. I suppose I can't tell anyone."

"No one must know."

* * *

From the Charing Cross rail station that evening, Jane and I took a taxi to Sir Henry's house. As Esther was introduced to Jane, she hugged her. "We can't thank you enough."

"I didn't do much. Livvy gets all the credit. I just followed her lead."

Jane and Esther both turned and stared at me. "With Livvy, that's sometimes the best thing to do," Esther said.

As soon as we reached the front parlor and were certain no servants were present, I emptied out the contents of my bag on a table. Jane then did the same on another table.

"We need to keep the valuables of the various families straight," Jane said. "And I need to get this belt holding gold off before it digs any further into my sides."

Esther showed us into a bedroom, where we quickly slipped off the straps containing gold from under our clothes. When we took them back into the parlor, Esther ran her fingers over the jewels and gold. "Various families? What's going on? That's more than enough for four visas."

"What about fourteen?"

"Fourteen?" Sir Henry echoed, entering and shaking our hands.

"Judith's husband's brother and sister and their families." I told them about our after-church visit and their desperation. Then I told them about the scrubbing party and the customs officers holding a baby hostage. My disgust poured out in my voice.

Esther paled and her eyes were moist as I finished my tale. Turning to her father, she said, "We have to get them all out."

He held up his hands. "I'm not sure I can wheedle that many out of the Home Office."

"Surely there's enough value here to support fourteen people, five of them children and another still a schoolboy, until the adults are allowed to find work." Esther sounded desperate for them. As well she might.

Sir Henry looked at his daughter. "I've explained this to you. The policy decisions belong to Sir Samuel Hoare of the Home Office, but the actual visas are handed out by a diplomat at the embassy in Vienna. And the government's position is that Jewish refugees will come here temporarily until they move on to a permanent home in another country. Therefore, they don't need temporary jobs; they just need enough money to support themselves until they relocate."

"I don't care what their policy is," Esther said, wrapping her arms around herself. "If we need fourteen visas then we must get fourteen visas."

There was no sense in my saying how much I agreed with her. Sir Henry would get enough pressure from her.

I told him that Peter Thornhill was in charge of visas and about my conversation with him.

Sir Henry said, "Let me talk to my contacts," with a great deal of weariness in his voice.

Esther must have heard it, too, because she gave her father a hug. "I know you can do it."

Jane and I left the valuables with Sir Henry and went outside to take the taxis Sir Henry's footman called for us. Before we climbed in to the vehicles, I thanked Jane for her help.

"If I ever find myself in a jam, I now know to call you," she said and grinned.

I took the cab to the house I grew up in to find my father was home. "How is Aunt Margaret?" I asked as soon as I entered.

"Go sit in the parlor," he said. "I'll bring in brandies."

"She's that badly off?"

He didn't answer me.

"Father. What's wrong? Did she die?" My heart beat rapidly. She was my favorite in Millhaven House. I didn't want to lose Aunt Margaret.

There was no reply. I heard his footsteps enter the study and return a minute later. I sat and he handed me a brandy snifter.

"Now," my father said in full interrogation voice as he sat across from me, "why were you in Vienna?"

CHAPTER SEVENTEEN

"I was working on a story for the newspaper," I told my father. "What about Aunt Margaret?"

"In Vi—!" He lowered his voice. "Are you mad? They've just become part of Germany. Don't tell me Sir Henry Benton has promoted you to foreign correspondent."

"No. I was doing a women's feature on how the ladies of Vienna like their new situation. Now, what about—"

"Doesn't that depend on whether they're Nazis?"

"Oh, the government made certain I only met Nazis. No women of ill repute, no dissidents, no Jews. But I did manage to meet a friend and fellow poet of Aunt Margaret's. Isaak Rothenberger. Sir Henry is trying to get him out. How is Aunt Margaret?" I was ready to start screaming at him to get an answer. Probably the way my father felt in trying to get a reason for my trip to Vienna.

My father's mouth, which had dropped open, snapped shut. "She was doing better until Thomas was arrested. And now Walter is ill as well. It's like the whole family is under a cloud."

"Have you figured out who killed the old earl?"

"You've been gone less than a week and you expect me to have discovered the identity of the murderer?" My father sounded exasperated.

"No. Of course not." It had been a wild hope. "Why did they arrest Thomas?"

"His lack of an alibi mixed with his lack of common sense. Every time that boy opens his mouth—" He slammed down his snifter. "And he admitted to the police that he and his grandfather didn't get on because of the man's tight hold on the purse strings."

"Means, motive, and opportunity." I knew they were wrong, but I couldn't fault the police for making their assumption.

"And his mother refuses to cooperate with us. She says this is all our fault."

That sounded like Amelia. "I suppose we'd better go over to Millhaven House tomorrow after work. Are Margaret and Walter both at home?"

"Yes. Walter saw his doctor, who is incredibly tight-lipped. He did assure me that Walter was not poisoned, nor did he suffer a murderous attack. Margaret was home when she suffered a relapse Saturday after Thomas was arrested. The doctor was not surprised. He said she'd been pushing herself too hard working on her poetry and in her garden."

"I'm sure she'll be glad to hear her friend will soon be in London."

"Who? This poet Rothenberger?"

"Yes."

His eyes narrowed as his voice dropped. "And how do you know this?"

I couldn't tell him the truth. He'd have my passport pulled or start a row with Sir Henry and get me fired. "Gossip in the embassy in Vienna."

"See anyone we know?"

I filled him in with the staff members I'd seen and how they were doing. That seemed to be enough to keep him from asking too many more questions about my travel.

* * *

After a long day at the *Daily Premier* working on my story about the women of Vienna and filling in my expense report, I met my father for the trip out to

Millhaven House. One of the joys of traveling with him was a taxi ride I didn't have to pay for.

My father once again had flowers for Aunt Margaret. I felt guilty that I didn't have anything for either of the patients.

When we arrived, Watkins answered the door.

"Is anyone home, Watkins?" my father asked, walking in and handing his hat, gloves, and umbrella to the butler.

"Both Lady Margaret and Mr. Walter are here, Sir Ronald. Lord Millhaven is still at the Treasury. The younger two lads are at school. Lord and Lady Eustace have gone out."

"And Lady Amelia?" I asked, noting the omission.

"Is not receiving visitors, Mrs. Denis."

"Or at least not receiving us." I gave the old butler a smile and followed my father, who I knew would want to see Aunt Margaret first.

We were escorted up to her room without my father having to say a word.

When Watkins knocked on the door, we received an "Enter." We opened the door to find Aunt Margaret sitting propped up in bed, with her hair neatly pinned up and wearing a pink silk bed jacket. "Oh, Ronald, I'm so glad you returned today."

"Of course. I said I would," my father replied, pulling over a side chair.

"You look better, Aunt Margaret," I said. "And I'm glad no one else has been attacked."

"So am I. But to have Thomas in jail? No. It's impossible. Thomas wouldn't hurt a flea." She reached out and took one of my hands. "You must find out what happened and rescue that poor boy from the gallows."

"Do you have any ideas?"

"No. I'm sure it was no one in the family."

We fell silent for a moment before I told her, "A friend of yours is moving to England. Isaak Rothenberger."

"Isaak is escaping the Nazis? Oh, that is good news. What about his sons?"

"They're coming with him."

"Excellent. When will they get here?"

"I don't know. They're scheduled to get entry visas to England, but I don't know when."

"I hope it's soon. Austria a part of Germany? It makes no sense. The world has gone mad. I must write to him."

I gently pulled my hand away. "That might not be a good idea until they are actually out of German hands."

She paused for a moment before she said, "The situation is perilous?"

"Yes."

My father shot me a look that told me how much he feared for my safety while traveling. I appreciated his concern, but I didn't want him interfering with my work for the *Daily Premier*, or my work for Sir Henry.

"Perilous for them," I added.

"All right. I won't write to Isaak until you tell me it's safe. But I will pen a note to Thomas. You'll take it to him for me, won't you?"

She sounded so desperate I immediately agreed. "Tell me why you don't believe Thomas is a killer. Surely, all of us are capable for the right reason."

"Yes. For the right reason," Margaret said. "Thomas hasn't found a reason yet that he would kill for. Although he's the oldest, he's perhaps the most unformed of Humphrey's children."

"You think he's a weakling?" my father said, sounding slightly outraged on Thomas's behalf.

"Oh, no. Not a weakling. Merely unformed. Still a boy in a man's body. His day will come. I'm sure of it."

We talked for a few more minutes while Aunt Margaret composed a note to Thomas. Then she sent us away, saying she was tired.

Father led the way to Walter's room and knocked on the door. "Who is it?"

"Sir Ronald Harper."

My father never dropped the "sir" before his name, even with close friends. Fortunately, he didn't see me roll my eyes.

"Come in."

"Olivia is with me."

"All the better."

We walked in to find Walter sketching, a cigarette burning in a half-full ashtray. He was casually dressed in trousers, a shirt, a sweater vest, and slippers. He set down his pencil and pad to pick up his cigarette and gestured toward the other chairs in the room.

"Sit down. This is wonderful. Company."

"You haven't felt well enough to go out lately?" I asked, taking a chair.

"No. Doctor says this is going to drag on for a bit and to get used to being an invalid while it lasts."

"What's the diagnosis, Walter?" my father asked.

"Influenza with a topping of pneumonia."

"Beastly stuff."

We were all silent for a moment. That sounded like what my mother had died of at the end of the war. I thought of her. I had no idea what my father or Uncle Walter were thinking of.

"What do you think of Thomas being arrested for your father's murder?" I asked.

"Ridiculous," he said with heat and then had a

coughing fit into his handkerchief. When he'd caught his breath again, he said, "The grandchildren all liked their grandfather. It was my generation that couldn't abide the old tyrant."

"Do you think whoever killed the old earl poisoned your sister?"

He shook his head. "Why? He had money and power. She doesn't. There would have to be two different motives, and how many people have two different motives to murder two people in the same family?"

That was a point I hadn't considered. Aunt Margaret could be in danger from someone other than her father's killer. Had his death freed someone to act on their hatred of Margaret? Or was there a single thread wound around both their lives?

I'd have to ask Aunt Margaret.

"Who did it, Walter? You know these people better than anyone," my father said.

"Oh, now you're flattering me. I don't know them any better than you do. Less, in fact. They're my family. I don't see them when I look at them anymore. Haven't in years."

"Have you started looking at them since your father was killed?" I asked.

He turned to smile broadly at me, and his shirt twisted around his frail body. I realized with a start just how much weight he had lost. "We've all been watching each other very closely since the old man was murdered."

"What do you think? What if you were figuring the odds on them as if they were in a race?" my father asked, leaning forward in his chair.

"I'd put myself fairly high up on the list. Thwarted as the younger son most of my life. And then that new will. Putting three young men in charge of the money, two of whom will likely never be earl. Not even putting me on their advisory committee. Undervalued as a brain. Not valued as an artist." When he started to cough violently, I noticed how flushed his cheeks had become as he spoke of his role.

When he stopped coughing, he took a sip of water and caught his breath. "I'd consider Humphrey a nonstarter. He gets a good salary from Treasury and he's never really wanted the title. His wife, now, I'd cast her as Lady Macbeth."

"Pushing her husband forward?" I asked.

"No, not Humphrey. She's pushing herself into the role of countess and her sons as holders of the purse strings."

"What about the boys themselves?" my father asked.

"What about them? I can't see it. They're sane. Normal. They're out for a good time. Edwin's still at Harrow. They don't want the bother of all those business decisions yet."

"And Celia?" I asked. "Or her parents?"

"Celia's getting on with her life away from here. She loved the old man and he loved her. No. And Bea is all bluster. She doesn't have the courage or the brains to kill someone and hide what she did. Philip—Lord Eustace— is a weak man. He doesn't have the bottle to kill someone, unless he was in the bottle, and then he'd make such a hash of it the trail would lead right to him. No, I'd put them far down the running."

"And Margaret?"

"She's strong willed and bright enough. But she wouldn't have. Besides, she was the second victim, or very nearly. It has to be someone from outside."

But none of us could come up with a single suspect.

My father brought Walter news of mutual friends and they spent a few minutes discussing politics. I sat back and studied Walter. For all his claims of not noticing his family, he had a clear picture of their characters.

But was he right?

And what about Ames's claim that the old man didn't like Celia? That might move her up the list if Aunt Margaret hadn't been poisoned after Celia was out of the country.

Unless Uncle Walter was right and each victim had their own attacker.

* * *

The next day, I was back to my old schedule of covering teas in aid of good works and writing wedding announcements for the *Daily Premier.* My wordy tale of all I'd seen and all the people I'd talked to, including the unauthorized view of a scrubbing party and the tormenting of a young refugee family, had been turned in the day before. Now editors would decide what, and how much, to run along with Jane's photos.

The one person I'd not mentioned in my story was the helpful Oberst Bernhard. I left out dinner with Bernhard and his role in getting the baby along with her family across the barrier to the train. He did not appear in my article, but he played a large part in my memories of Vienna.

Now, as I spoke to a mother of the bride about either placing her notice now or holding off until she had a photograph to add to the piece, I found half of my mind wondering if my father had successfully applied to Thomas's solicitor to get us into the prison. I needed to find a killer to protect Aunt Margaret.

I received a telephone call to meet my father at his office in Whitehall after work. Or as he put it, "When you finish whatever you might be doing for the day."

He still wouldn't acknowledge that his daughter was

a reporter, even the socially more acceptable role of society reporter.

We met and took a taxi to the prison, where we were told the rules—no touching, no exchanging anything, including cigarettes, staying on our own side of the table, and remaining seated throughout the interview. Then we were sent into a cool, brightly lit room with brick walls, a stone floor, and painfully hard chairs on either side of a table. A window allowed a guard to see our every movement, but the glass presumably blocked our voices.

A half-minute after we sat down, Thomas came in, hesitated while he stared at us, and then finally came over and sat down. "Why are you here?" His sneer was almost believable.

"We know you wouldn't kill your grandfather. We're certain you didn't poison your aunt," I told him.

He glared at me, the sneer still on his face. "Tell it to the police. They're sure I did it." He lit a cigarette and his hands shook.

"You can stop acting tough with us. We know you didn't do it and we're here to help."

"How?"

Drat. That was the question. I wished I had a better answer than "I don't know yet, but there has to be clues to the identity of the killer. You weren't in the house when the killing or the poisoning took place, were you?"

"No, but I don't have an alibi either. The police think I sneaked back in and did the deed." He grimaced.

"Didn't you go out with Charlie the evening Aunt Margaret was poisoned?"

"I left the house with him, but we split up pretty quickly. I'd heard Pierre Lonteau was supposed to be staying at the Savoy and I went there to try to meet him. I hung around the bar and the lobby for a while, but I didn't spot him. I finally left a note for him at the desk and went out to meet my friends."

"Lonteau the aviator?" my father asked.

"Yes. I wanted his advice on how to start a career as a pilot."

"Did you see anyone you knew? Talk to anyone who might remember you?" I asked.

"No. No one."

"What time did you meet your friends?"

"Nearly midnight."

No alibi for the time Margaret was poisoned. "This is as useless an alibi as walking around the new housing estate before the wedding." I tapped my fingers on the table. "There must be something."

"Well, you and the police can't find it, and I'm going to hang. It's not fair." He stubbed out his cigarette and wiped his eyes on his sleeve.

I thought I preferred the sneer. "If anyone had any information that might clear you, whether or not they realized it, who would that person be?"

Thomas sat there for a minute looking down at his hands. Then he said, "Charlie. Definitely Charlie. Or maybe Celia."

"Why Charlie? Why Celia?" They had both seemed to be in the clear from the beginning. I stared at Thomas, hoping he'd give me a hint to a new way of looking at this.

"Charlie hasn't given the murder or the poisoning a second's thought. He could have seen all sorts of clues and never bothered to wonder about them. And Celia couldn't wait to get out of here and leave you to figure things out. Seems suspicious, doesn't it? She either knows more than she's letting on or she's more of a silly tart than I'd thought."

"Don't talk about your cousin that way," my father

fumed, half-rising from his chair and then thinking better of it when the guard tapped on the glass.

"I thought you wanted my opinion." Thomas leaned back in his wooden hard chair and crossed his arms.

"I do," I told him. "Somewhere, someone knows something that will prove your innocence, or someone else's guilt. When was the first time you saw Celia that morning?"

"Seven. I was just getting up and she was going down to breakfast. I made a comment about her wedding night and she called me disgusting."

"Do you think she or her mother had anything to do with the disappearance of the countess's necklace?" my father asked.

"Did you have anything to do with the vanishing necklace?" I asked.

Thomas sat upright. "No. I didn't steal it. I wouldn't. Celia or Aunt Bea?" He considered. "I don't know. Celia might steal it for her mother, but she doesn't need it herself. She has Robert to buy jewels for her."

A guard came in and said Thomas had other visitors.

"Who?" he asked.

"Your mother."

"Oh, Lord. Sneak out the back way. She's looking to skin you both alive." The prisoner did not look happy about his new visitor.

We rose, said we'd be in touch, and left the room to find Lady Amelia outside in the hallway. She scrunched up her face at seeing us and snapped, "What are you doing here?"

"Trying to find the real killer of your late father-in-law."

"Well, look elsewhere. Thomas didn't do it. And don't come near him or any of the rest of my family again." She shoved by us and stalked inside the interview room, tossing her fur stole over her shoulder. "Darling. How is my brave boy?"

Past her shoulder, I could see a look of dismay on Thomas's face as they shut the door.

CHAPTER EIGHTEEN

The next day, Friday, was the last chance for Sir Henry to do anything about the visas until Monday. I hoped I'd hear something, but instead I spent the morning rewriting announcements sent in by proud mothers who'd gone to finishing school rather than university. I probably had the same reaction to their writing that Miss Westcott had had to mine when I started on the paper, but at least I had gone to university.

Then again, my writing had had to improve if I wanted to keep my job. How many weddings would these mothers write about and send in to the paper? And since I rewrote their announcements, they didn't need this skill.

In the afternoon I followed Jane around an art exhibit, taking notes on who appeared in the photos and grabbing a few quotes to go with the basic information I would include on hours and location.

On the way back, Jane said, "Any word on our project?"

"Nothing. I'm worried he can't get that many."

She smiled. "Sir Henry? Not able to get something he wants? Not likely. So don't worry."

I wished I could follow her advice.

When we returned, Miss Westcott sent us up to Mr. Colinswood, who in turn sent us up to the top floor to Sir Henry's office. Jane and I both had our fingers crossed.

We were shown in and he said, "Come in and sit down." We took the two chairs in front of his massive, raised desk. I wondered if Jane guessed his feet were on a platform and his chair was set to make him look taller.

"Monday morning, I have an appointment with Sir Samuel Hoare, the home secretary in Chamberlain's cabinet, to request those fourteen entry visas. I have the valuation of the property you brought in, and I'm not sure it's enough. Can you think of anything that might help me get them all admitted? I wish they'd never started this visa program for German and Austrian refugees. Jewish refugees."

"Six of them are children if you include Isaak's younger son, who's about fifteen," I said. "They must need less in food and support since they live with their parents. And they're cute and well behaved. Who can resist cute, well-behaved children?"

"One of the men is a physician, isn't he?" Jane said to me. "That should be useful."

"Yes, and another is a well-known poet, Isaak Rothenberger. He's a good friend of the British writer Lady Margaret Brooke, who is the Earl of Millhaven's sister." If he needed their status painted on thick, I was willing to spread it on with a trowel. They needed to get out of there as soon as possible and for that they needed our aid.

Sir Henry scribbled a note. "All this will help."

"You could say this is a distinguished group. A third man is an associate of Baron von Rothschild. Well, he worked in his bank." Any delay might hurt their chances. That thought made me shudder.

"Close enough." Sir Henry ignored us as he kept writing.

"How hard is it to get entry visas now?"

"Since Austria was absorbed by Germany? The demand is far worse, and it was terrible before. Everyone can see the writing on the wall. Well, everyone but our government. War is inevitable."

Jane muttered something under her breath before saying, "I didn't need to hear that."

"No one does. Nevertheless, it's true."

"Let us know how you do at Whitehall, sir. And tell Esther we're certain you can get those visas." It sounded awfully formal, but I couldn't think of any other way to say what I thought. Not to my employer.

"She's worried, especially now that she's heard her grandfather isn't doing well."

"I'm sorry to hear that." I turned to Jane and said, "I met Esther's grandparents when I made a trip for Sir Henry last autumn."

Jane scowled. "Where do they live?"

"Berlin."

"Right in the thick of it," she murmured.

"I don't need to keep you any longer," Sir Henry said. "Have a good weekend and wish me luck for Monday."

"I'm sure you'll convince Sir Samuel Hoare that he wants to help out."

Sir Henry held me in his stare. "He'd better or I'll let him deal with Esther."

I had to smile at the image of Esther upbraiding Sir Samuel.

Jane and I went downstairs. After I turned in my article, I retrieved my hat, trench coat, and gloves, and headed home on the Underground. I couldn't wait to get back to my flat and peel off my outer clothes and kick off my shoes. I was only halfway through my mail, two advertising circulars and a bill, when I heard a knock on the door.

I looked out the peephole and had to stop myself from jumping up and down. Adam Redmond was back in London.

I threw open the door. "Adam. How are you?"

Our kiss didn't erase the worry lines in his forehead, but it certainly did a lot for my pulse. I didn't want to let him go. When he finally pulled away, he said, "I'm fine, but I've had to vouch for you. I'll tell you about it at dinner, shall I?"

"Please, yes."

I slipped into a slinky long green dress, put on a gold pendant and beige pumps, and was ready before Adam finished reading the sports section in the *Daily Premier*. We walked to the restaurant two blocks away. We'd eaten there often enough that the proprietor greeted us and said, "So glad you are back in town."

Adam gave him a vague smile before scowling at me. I suspected his absence was supposed to be secret. I hadn't told anyone, and I couldn't imagine who would have told Mr. Linkus. He'd been in London for several years, but he was originally from the Baltic area and the threat of war meant everyone was growing more cautious about what they said and to whom.

He showed us to our usual table and we settled in with our menus. By the time the waiter came by, we had settled on cream soup followed by mutton, potatoes, and greens.

I let Adam choose the wine. I'd discovered he had an instinct for a good vintage.

Once we had our wine and no one was within hearing distance in the noisy restaurant, Adam said, "How did he know?"

"I don't know. He might have meant both of us. I haven't been in here without you." Both my father and Esther preferred stylish hotel restaurants beyond my price range. And I was happy to go whenever someone else was paying.

Adam must have seen our soup coming from behind

me, because he gave me a closed-mouth smile and put his napkin on his lap.

We began on our soup and looked around. No one was paying us the slightest attention. "Why did you have to vouch for me?"

"People were curious about your trip to Vienna last weekend."

"Just part of my job." I gave him a smile and ate another spoonful of soup. Then I stopped and looked at him in surprise. "Is that why you were suspicious of what I might have said to Mr. Linkus?"

"People are starting to ask questions about what Sir Henry is up to. Phone calls and telegrams to Berlin and Vienna. Sending his reporters there."

"Reporters besides me?" I wouldn't be surprised to learn Sir Henry was using multiple employees to rescue his late wife's relatives, especially if someone wasn't producing the results he wanted.

"There's Jane Seville."

"She's a photographer."

"And Fred Dale."

That surprised me. "I don't know him. Is he an employee of Sir Henry's?"

"International reporter for the *Daily Premier*. At least he has a good reason to be there. He's reporting on the news."

"I report on the news, too. Just not news you have any interest in," I said in a huffy tone.

All this time, did Sir Henry have someone besides me helping his relatives leave Nazi-held territory? Someone I'd never met. Someone who might be doing the same job as me. Someone doing a better job than me.

Did that mean he wasn't happy with my work? Was he going to lay me off? I felt panic swirl around in my gut.

I needed the money.

"Adam, believe me when I say what I did in Berlin and what Jane and I did in Vienna wouldn't help the Nazis in any way."

"Not carrying letters or messages in with you?"

"No." I stared into his hazel eyes. *Please don't ask what I brought out with me.*

"Just there to report a story."

"Yes."

Adam stared into my eyes. I couldn't believe how cold his gaze was. "Nobody believes that."

I reached across the table for his hand. "I hope you do."

He leaned back in his chair. "I don't know what to believe. Society reporters don't travel to Plymouth, much less Vienna."

I tried to be as honest as I could without divulging any secrets. "I've promised not to mention anything I do for Sir Henry except for my story assignments."

He leaned forward and we gazed into each other's eyes long enough for anyone around us to assume we were lovers. With this secret between us, I wasn't sure where our relationship would go, but I was determined to hold his stare. Finally, he sat up and took my hand. "So there is something more."

"I didn't say that."

"You didn't have to."

At least I hadn't given away any of the details of what I'd done on my travels. I really wasn't any good at keeping secrets from Adam, but I was determined not to give away anything more. I'd promised Sir Henry, and I needed to keep my promise.

"What is it, Livvy? Trading secrets? Carrying messages or money? Smuggling?"

I don't know if a muscle twitched or my breathing changed or how I'd given away what my role was on these trips, but he leaned toward me and said, "That's it, isn't it? You're smuggling something. News? Messages? Records? Artwork—?"

"Oh, I can see me with a huge oil painting in my suitcase. What am I supposed to do? Fold it into quarters and iron it when I get back to England?" I was growing angry now and I wasn't trying to hide it. "We both have parts of our job that we can't share. I'm not asking you where you've been lately—"

"You know I can't tell you."

"—So don't expect me to tell you everything." I narrowed my eyes as I held his gaze.

"But you work for a newspaper."

I glared at him. "Officially."

He sat perfectly still for a moment. "All right. I can accept that. I'm not sure my superiors will be satisfied."

"They'll just have to be." I set down my spoon and folded my arms over my chest.

We didn't speak again until we'd eaten most of our dinner. Then Adam said, "How was your cousin's wedding? Celia, isn't it?"

He'd met Celia and Robert once or twice. I guessed he was trying to make up with me. "Her grandfather was murdered a couple of hours before the wedding. Caused all sorts of commotion, particularly since it wasn't reported until after the service had begun."

His eyes widened at this breach in procedure. "Why?"

"Her grandfather was an earl. They'd have to observe all the mourning rituals. Since this was the third time they'd set a date, her mother, Lady Beatrice, was afraid they'd never marry."

Adam's eyes widened. "And no one reported the death because her mother said so? She sounds frightening."

"She and her sister, Aunt Margaret, would have made wonderful earls back in the medieval era."

"Take no prisoners?"

I shook my head. "Oh, they'd know what to do with prisoners. They are both not afraid of taking charge and trampling on anything in their way. Aunt Margaret managed to get a university education over the old earl's objections, and then convinced my father to send me to Cambridge."

We went back to eating while I tried to think of a good way to give him the news.

Finally, I set down my fork and blurted out, "Celia is on her honeymoon, so she has my father and me investigating her grandfather's murder. A cousin is in jail, suspected of killing the old earl."

His fork went down with a thunk. "Good Lord. Not another investigation. I found you tied up in the basement of a warehouse the last time."

"Nothing so exciting will happen this time. Father and I are going up to Oxford tomorrow to question one of the other grandchildren. Would you like to come along?"

"It's been ages since I've been there. I have the whole weekend off, so yes, I'd love to. And I have the use of a friend's automobile while he's away and I'm in town. Shall I drive the two of you out there?"

I nearly leaped across the table at him, thrilled with the suggestion. "Are you sure you don't mind?"

"Not at all. It would be a pleasure to drive on nice smooth roads for a change."

By the time the three of us reached Oxford in time for luncheon the next day, Adam was up to speed on our investigation. I, on the other hand, was wondering where he had been driving if he considered some of these roads smooth.

We went to the porters' lodge and asked for Charlie, and a passing student offered to fetch him for us. It sounded to me like the young men didn't want family to see what state their rooms were in.

Charlie arrived ten minutes later, his wet hair slicked down and his eyes bloodshot, but otherwise looking impeccable. He sounded happy to have lunch with us in a pub outside of town along the river.

Adam drove there while Father complained about the heavy motor and foot traffic the whole way. The third time he said "When I was an undergraduate," Charlie and I caught each other's gaze. He made a face and I nearly burst into giggles.

Adam glared over his shoulder at me.

The food and the ale were as good as I remembered from previous visits here with Reggie when we occasionally left London for a day in the country. We didn't mention anything about the murder or his brother Thomas until we were seated in the dark, smoky, noisy interior with our food.

I gazed longingly at the bright sunshine and the tables in the outdoor dining garden, but the men all seemed happy to eat inside.

Then, since my father seemed bent on reminiscing, I interrupted him to say, "We haven't yet asked you any questions about your grandfather's death, Charlie. Did you notice anything strange the day before or the day he died?"

"You know my dear mama doesn't want me talking to you."

"She's angry because your brother was arrested.

She'd be carrying on like this if you were the one who was arrested and we were talking to Thomas. So, what did you see or hear that was out of the ordinary?"

"My cousin getting married."

"You're not being helpful, Charlie." I frowned across the table at him.

"Why should I? You're not the police."

"The police decided Thomas is guilty and they aren't looking any further. Do you want him to hang?"

Charlie took a bite and chewed as he grinned with his mouth closed.

"You want to be earl so much you'd let your brother hang." I glanced at my father, who looked shocked. "Well, I wonder what Lady Amelia will say about that?"

Charlie swallowed hard and gulped down a mouthful of ale. "Hey, I didn't say that."

Furious, I pressed him. "What other conclusion do you think anyone would draw?"

"No. I was joking around because I really don't know anything that will help you. People came and went at the breakfast table, but Edwin and I sat there the whole time. We're the only two with alibis. We're also the only two who didn't see what anyone else was doing."

"What time did you go to bed the night before?"

"We switched the wireless off at ten and then I went to my room and read for a little while. I rose at seven, cleaned up and dressed in that bloody uncomfortable formal suit and that shirt collar that strangles me and went downstairs for breakfast with Thomas. Edwin was already there."

"Went downstairs with Thomas? Where had he been?"

"He walked by me as I came out of my room. I guess he was coming from his room. I didn't ask."

"How did he seem?"

"Annoyed. Grayling's a bit hard to stomach at the best of times. So superior. It rankles Thomas because he's going to be an earl and expects deference from all of us untitled people. He knows he won't get it from Edwin or me, but he thinks Grayling should make an effort."

Charlie's words made me curious about his feelings concerning Celia's new husband. "What do you think of Robert Grayling?"

"He's smug because he's inherited money and a position in a company. We lesser sons," he made his tone ironic, "learn early on that we have to do well in school so we can get good-paying jobs working for people like Robert Grayling."

"But you don't much care for him," Adam said, a faint smile hovering on his talented lips.

I daydreamed about his lips until I dragged my attention back to our conversation. I just caught Charlie saying, "No, I don't. But he's the type of man we all go to work for."

Superficially, they were alike, but would Robert Grayling go as far to save Celia's relatives as Sir Henry was going to save his late wife's? Or would he hire friends of his daughter's as quickly as Sir Henry had hired me?

But my speculations on Robert Grayling's character or Adam's lips weren't getting Thomas out of jail or finding us a killer. "What was the earliest you left your room that morning?"

"Sometime after seven." When I raised my eyebrows, he added, "Seven-twenty, maybe. All right. I went to the loo. And before you ask, I ran into Lord Useless and Aunt Maggie."

"Together?" My father sounded outraged.

"No. Aunt Maggie was just coming out of the bathing

room, fully dressed for a change, and Lord Useless—"

"Eustace." My father kept his voice down with effort.

"—was coming out of the loo. Both of them were doing their best to ignore the other. Say, how long has Lord Use...Celia's father been living in Millhaven House?"

CHAPTER NINETEEN

"What makes you think he is?" Adam asked. He appeared to find the whole conversation ridiculous.

"I don't believe in ghosts. Unless Millhaven House has suddenly become home to one, someone living in a rear guest room during our Easter break would be the best explanation for things disappearing or moving or getting knocked over." Charlie looked at each of us, an amused expression on his face.

I thought of the missing necklace. Did Charlie think Lord Eustace had stolen it? "What's disappeared?"

"According to Father, a great deal of booze. Which would also explain late-night crashes and Aunt Bea not letting anyone into a certain back guest room except Betsy to clean every once in a while. Auntie's been paying her on the side for her discretion in cleaning that room."

Charlie's speculation wouldn't help his brother. I plunged on. "Did either Lady Margaret or Lord Eustace see you the morning of Celia's wedding?"

"No. I stepped back around the corner while they were busy not noticing each other. And by the way Eustace was holding up the wall, I don't think he would have noticed much of anything."

So much for Lady Beatrice's claim that she was aiding his sobriety. "Did you see or hear anything else between then and when you met Thomas going down to breakfast?"

"No. I was in my room the whole time, and I was playing my phonograph records."

We asked about breakfast, dinner the night before, and the whole night. Charlie claimed to be oblivious to everything going on and quite indifferent.

"Any idea what happened to the countess's necklace?"

He shrugged. "Someone pinched it and Mummy is pitching a fit. I'm sure Celia wouldn't because she doesn't need to and Robert would look down on that sort of behavior. Lady Beatrice might, but then Thomas might for the same reason. They both need money."

I guessed the scorn in his voice was for anyone with money worries.

When I asked about his new role in deciding how the Brooke fortune should be spent, he said, "It'll give Edwin and me a chance to keep the money in good investments. I'm not saying either of us know much now, but we're both good students and we don't have a burning desire to squander our inheritance on fast cars and faster aeroplanes."

"You think Thomas would spend the money frivolously?"

"He has no head for finance or anything else. Mummy is furious with him about the flying lessons."

I remembered my talk one evening with Thomas. "What flying lessons?"

"He wants to take flying lessons when he graduates. Mummy's against it, so Father has to be against it, too."

"Surely that would be the earl's decision," my father said.

Charlie gave him a pitying look as if he were senile. "In our house, Mummy is the new earl."

* * *

After we dropped Charlie off at his college, we headed back to London. I was glad Adam's friend drove a traditional sedan instead of a perky convertible so I could hear the conversation he and my father were having in the front seat.

"Why did the police arrest Thomas and not Lord Eustace?"

"Thomas doesn't have an alibi for either attack. Lady Beatrice gave her husband an alibi on both occasions." My father stared at the road, using his gaze to tell us what he thought of Adam's driving and his inflection to say what he thought of Lord Eustace's alibi.

"Remember," I said, leaning forward, "Ames—the old earl's valet—said he saw the old earl alive a little before seven. The next time anyone saw him, a little before eight, he was dead."

"Ye-es," Adam said, listening carefully as we zipped along country roads.

"Well, we know where Philip Eustace, Aunt Margaret, and Charlie were sometime between seven and seven-thirty. But except for the times people were at the breakfast table, nobody has a good alibi. Not really."

"I'd question Lord Eustace again if I were you," Adam said and then glanced at where I leaned between them on the back of their seat.

"Shall we do it now?" my father asked.

"No. I promised to take your daughter out to dinner tonight. I have to report back to my unit by dinnertime tomorrow and it's a long journey," Adam said.

I wanted to whine when I heard his words, but I knew it would accomplish nothing and make me look childish. I wished he would have told me when my father wasn't there. And he wasn't driving.

My father said, "Where shall we go? Perhaps the Ritz, since it's been ages since we've seen you."

"Sorry, sir. This dinner is just for Livvy and me."

I thought he was awfully polite. I wanted to smack my father. Since Adam was driving, perhaps his response was safer for all.

"Shall we try Lord Eustace tomorrow after Sunday lunch? He may be more receptive to our questions then," I said, mimicking Adam's good manners.

"Shall we meet for lunch? Say, one o'clock at my club?" my father asked.

I agreed and then we rehashed everything about the murder until Adam focused on the heavier traffic as we approached London. I leaned back in the rear seat, wishing I could go to sleep.

* * *

The next morning over coffee and toast, I suggested to Adam I see him off at the station. He hemmed and hawed until he finally told me I wasn't supposed to know which station he left from, much less which train he took.

There was something in the way he said it. "I'm not trusted because of my trips, am I?"

"No."

"Adam." We weren't at war with Germany. Yet. I was sent there to cover a story for the newspaper. That was true as far as it went. I'd hate for Adam not to believe my loyalty to king and country.

He held up both hands and spoke quickly. "I trust you. I know you're loyal to Britain. My superiors aren't as sure. But no one is allowed to say good-bye at the station. They don't completely trust anyone. Not even us."

"You really are on a secret mission, aren't you?"

He winked at me, which was no answer at all.

After Adam left with a fond farewell on both our parts, I dressed in a new spring blue suit and met my father at his club. The food there was always good, if traditional. Soup followed by fish, followed by roast with vegetables, and ended with a pudding. After this heavy lunch, we caught a cab to Millhaven House. I'd rather have taken a walk.

Watkins opened the door for us, and at our question, said, "Lord Eustace is in the study with the earl. If you'd care to wait in the parlor, I'll let them know you're here."

We found the parlor empty of Brookes. I was so used to the room being full of people every time I was there that I found the silence odd. Then I realized it was more than the silence that was strange, it was the lack of bickering.

Never having had siblings, I'd always wanted some. My desire had made me surprised to hear arguments between brothers and sisters when I was younger. And any time I'd been here before, Celia and her cousins had also made use of this room for their disagreements.

Aunt Margaret was the first one into the room. "I didn't know you had called. Ronnie, how are you?" She came toward him, the vigor missing in her stride. At least she was on her feet.

"Maggie, my dear, it's so good to see you." My father had leaped up and met her halfway to kiss her cheek.

"We've come to talk to Lord Eustace. We understand he's in with the earl," I said, half as a question.

"Once Humphrey gets done with him, he won't want to talk to you or anybody," Aunt Margaret said, collapsing into a chair.

"Uncle Humphrey is tired of him living here?"

She gave me a dry look. "He's tired of him hiding out here, not admitting to anyone that he's here or that he's broke or that his drinking is out of control. Humphrey is looking for honesty, and I don't think Philip recognizes it anymore."

"You don't think your sister has much chance of straightening out her husband?" I was curious. They were Celia's parents and she saw them as wonderful, sympathetic people. I'd seen them the same way throughout my childhood.

"None. If she were going to do so, she'd have done it twenty years ago when there was some hope that he'd turn out to the good. What worries me is whether he killed Father and poisoned me."

"Why would he do that?" My father sounded shocked.

"Think about it, Ronnie. Father told him he was worthless to his face just a few days before Father…" she sighed, "was murdered. He knows I saw him near Father's room that morning at the approximate time. And then I was poisoned."

"You think he did it?" I was surprised, and maybe a little worried that Celia had me investigating because she also thought her father was the killer.

I watched her cold, pale brown eyes as she turned to stare at me. "It certainly wasn't Thomas. The boy's a young fool, but he's not malicious. He's definitely not a killer."

"While I most certainly am."

We all swiveled to stare at Lord Philip Eustace.

"Eustace," my father said, "no one believes—"

"Of course they do. I served on the front during the war. I learned all about killing. If you're looking for a murderer, look at an ex-service member. Why would we fear the hangman after we faced the barbed wire and the trenches? After we spent day after day eluding death for years. Years! And then came home to unending pain." He sounded close to tears.

"We were hoping you saw or heard something that might help us identify the killer." I thought it better to ignore his outburst. I patted my hand on the sofa cushion next to where I sat.

He came over and dropped onto the sofa, putting as much space between us as possible. "I don't see how I can help. Maggie always says I'm unreliable."

"It's Lady Margaret to you," she sneered in a tone I associated with angry fellows teaching wayward undergraduates at a women's college. I wasn't used to hearing it from her.

"Celia doesn't think you're unreliable, so I don't either. Now, what did you see or hear in the hours before Celia's wedding?" I hoped he saw something useful.

"After the argument with Humphrey and Walter about me seeing my wife, I was tired so I went to the rear guest room. Yes, where I've been staying. I lay down and slept for an hour or two until the pain woke me up. Then—" he stopped, looking very uncomfortable.

"Then what?" Did he really have the key to this murder?

"It wouldn't be very gallant of me to say anything, what with me hiding out here. And no one would believe me."

"Why?" I was staring at him.

"Good grief, man, Thomas's life is on the line," my father said.

He lit a cigarette with trembling hands. "I was headed toward the loo when I heard footsteps. I peeked out and saw Amelia, fully dressed, coming up from the main floor. I waited until she went into her room and then I went to the loo."

"Fully clothed?" I found that comment intriguing. "What was she wearing?"

"Heels. Stockings. I could see her legs shine in the butler's lamp at the top of the stairs. A dark coat and hat. And oh, yes. Her hat had horns."

Lady Margaret made a scoffing noise.

"Horns? Can you describe this hat?" I might be able to find this hat, if it existed, as a sort of proof to his story.

"Well, it was a sort of cap with a small brim the whole way around and something sticking up on each side. Made me think of horns, since it was Amelia, although they weren't shaped like horns. Just feathers or bows or something." He shrugged.

"Really, Philip." Lady Margaret sounded annoyed more than anything.

I wasn't. His description sounded like something I could track down. "Anything else?"

"Dark gloves. She was carrying them in one hand with her purse so her other hand was free. The same way Bea does."

My father had enough of listening to fashion descriptions. "Did you see where she came from on the ground floor?"

"No, I didn't see her until she was on the stairs. That's all I know. And then the next time, I nearly ran into Lady Margaret. I'm sure she's already told you about that."

"What time did all these meetings take place?" I asked.

"Lord Eustace and I met in the hall well after seven-thirty. I'm sure because I heard the men setting up for the wedding reception out in the garden before I came out of my room." Aunt Margaret glared at Lord Eustace.

"If you say so." He shrugged. "I didn't hear them until a little later, but I wasn't listening for them." He started to get up, probably to fix himself a drink, looked at all our grim faces, and sat back down.

I thought it was the smartest move he could have made. "What about when you saw Lady Amelia?"

"It was still full dark out. Beyond that, I couldn't say."

"You don't wear a watch?" my father asked.

"No. I—I had to pawn it."

"Just how bad are your financial losses?" My father was willing to press on where I hadn't the stomach to tread.

"There are days when I don't think I'll ever get my head above water again. Poor investments. Bad luck. The high cost of being a peer." I heard the snobbish undercurrent in his last words as he looked at my father. Daring him to question a man of higher status.

He annoyed me enough for me to ask, "You don't believe you'd be in this mess if you weren't a peer?"

He shook his head. "It's not that. Nothing's been right since the war. The carnage. The constant pain. The friends lost. No heir. The—" He closed his eyes as his face began to crumble. "Excuse me."

He jumped up and ran from the room.

I looked at my father, wondering if I'd done something wrong.

"He's probably gone off to some hidden stash of drink. Oh, that isn't entirely fair. He hasn't been right since he returned from the war. His wound wouldn't heal properly and no doubt he had shell shock. We thought he got better, time after time, but perhaps he never has." Aunt Margaret sounded annoyed. "Doesn't he realize how lucky he is that he came back? That he didn't end up buried on the continent?"

"No, I don't think he ever got better," my father said in a vague tone, still staring at the door as if he hadn't heard Aunt Margaret's last words.

"And now we have to ask Lady Amelia where she was coming from at something after three in the morning." I glanced from my father to Aunt Margaret, wondering if either of them could guess at where she'd been.

"I think that's enough family secrets for one day,

don't you?" She slowly rose and walked out of the room, her head held high.

According to Charlie and Lord Eustace, Aunt Margaret had come out of the bathing room before seven-thirty, but she put it at later. The workers started setting up for the wedding reception at seven-thirty. Had she forgotten, or were Charlie and his uncle in league against her?

I didn't believe either choice. I was about to rise when Humphrey walked in.

My father said, "We've just been talking with Philip. Didn't realize it was as bad as all that."

"Yes, his drinking is completely out of control. It's ruining his life."

"It's more than that, Humphrey. He's still suffering from shell shock and pain from his wound."

Disbelief settled on the new earl's face. "That's impossible. The war's been over twenty years this autumn."

"I've heard of a few other cases. Men who came back suffering from war wounds and shell shock, who tried for years to keep everything under control and are now falling apart. Lewis, for one—" My father walked over and stood beside Uncle Humphrey.

Humphrey gasped before he said in a quiet voice, "He killed himself not six months ago."

"Yes."

I didn't know the person they were talking about, but Uncle Humphrey and my father sounded shattered.

The new earl shook his head. "Oh, no. Eustace just needs to pull himself together."

"He needs our help. All of us. Bea's been trying, hasn't she?" My father put a hand on his shoulder.

Uncle Humphrey nodded.

"You're the head of the family now. You're going to have to help her help him."

The new earl jerked away from my father. "And what are you going to do?"

"Help you help him any way I can. I was in the trenches, too. It still gives me nightmares. Don't be too hard on him."

I had no idea my father still had nightmares from the war. I stared at him, slightly open mouthed.

Humphrey walked to the door. "I spent time there, too. I don't want to talk about it. Ever. Now, was there anything else?"

I looked at my father, wanting to ask about Lady Amelia's midnight journey. He shook his head.

We said good-bye and left. My father seemed even less inclined to talk than I did. I couldn't imagine what horrors my father and Celia's father must have gone through in the war. I thought of what I'd seen in Austria and decided I didn't want my generation to find out.

CHAPTER TWENTY

It was the season for typing. We were being inundated with engagement, wedding, and birth announcements, and I was growing weary trying not to word everything exactly the same way. At least Miss Westcott didn't continuously red pencil my work anymore.

At lunchtime, I telephoned Millhaven House and asked to speak to Lady Beatrice. She came on a minute later, breathing as if she were hurrying. "Hello?"

"Lady Beatrice, this is Olivia Denis. Have you heard from Celia lately?"

"Oh." Her disappointment leaked out of the telephone receiver. "Yes. Their ship docks at Southampton tomorrow night. We're having a welcome home dinner Wednesday evening. We'd like you and your father to attend."

"Speaking for myself, I'd love to. I'll pass on your invitation to my father, who I'm sure will attend if he can. But I was calling to speak to you, Lady Beatrice. Can we meet privately this evening? Dinner?"

"Dinner at the Savoy sounds heavenly. You don't know how long it's been since I've had dinner in a hotel restaurant. Full mourning can be so tedious. But then, you should know, shouldn't you."

A not-so-gentle dig about my failure to keep full mourning for my late husband for more than a weekend at a time, and often not even that. And then to decide that we'd eat at the Savoy, when it would no doubt fall to me to pay for this dinner, made me grumble. "We'll meet at the Savoy at eight, shall we? It'll make a change from eating at the Dryesdale for luncheon with the Marquess of Hullworth's brother."

I tried to hide my annoyance at her attitude behind my stuffy tone, but the reference to another meal in a hotel restaurant since her father's death should have told her I wasn't impressed.

After I called my father and invited him to dinner that night and to Celia's dinner on Wednesday, I went back to work and took out my anger at Lady Beatrice's superior tone on the typewriter keyboard. The keys were stiff, and by the end of the day, I was in a better mood.

I went back to the flat after work and put on my navy blue, bias-cut gown. I decided to accessorize with a white shawl, long gloves, and a wisp of an evening hair decoration I'd bought at the *Daily Premier's* expense for attending an embassy party the past autumn. I was very fond of that outfit.

Then I caught a cab to the Savoy and found I was the second to arrive. Lady Beatrice was there armored in full mourning minus the veil, accentuated with jet and diamond jewelry.

"I invited my father to join us. He should be here shortly," I said by way of a greeting. His old-fashioned manners assured that he'd pick up the tab for dinner. I couldn't afford the Savoy on my salary.

"Oh, good. I've always found your father's presence to be so calming."

I always thought of his presence as leaden.

We were seated and, by mutual agreement, ordered a bottle of red wine. Once the wine steward had poured and left us, I said, "I heard my father speak highly of your assistance to your husband last night. Do you see his problems the same way my father does, as due to his old wound?"

For a moment, she looked like she would get up and walk out. Then she took a sip of wine and said, "Yes. I suppose you're too young to remember all the soldiers who came back with shell shock and tremors and lung diseases. And the wounds. The horrible wounds."

"I don't, but my father remembers. He was there."

"He's lucky in a way. Your mother died and you had no one but him. He had to get through his misery, hold down a job, and take care of you. He conquered what the war did to him. Philip knew Celia and I would be looked after by my family, so he never had that worry driving him. I suppose it made him weak."

I was about to deny her comments about my father when I realized I didn't know. Had all of our problems begun in my childhood due to my father suffering from shell shock? The fact that I couldn't see it, then or now, didn't make it untrue.

I dragged my mind back to the problems at Millhaven House. "How long has your husband been living in the house?"

"There were two or three weeks in midwinter when he had no money and no place to stay. Then an investment paid off and he went back to living at his club. At least, that's what he told me. Then he ran out of money again and had to move back in."

"When was this?"

"A few days before Celia's wedding. He was so embarrassed. He hid as much as possible or stayed out. We didn't want Celia to know. She'd worry. And we couldn't have Humphrey and Amelia find out. They'd have rubbed it in. Embarrassed us and Celia at her wedding."

I couldn't believe anyone would be that cruel. "They wouldn't have done that to Celia on her wedding day.

Her father's drinking isn't her doing."

"Amelia would. She hates Celia. If she'd known, she'd have made a terrible uproar before and after the wedding. We were on pins and needles, hoping no one spotted Philip and said anything to ruin Celia's big day. And instead, the day was destroyed when someone murdered Father."

"Not quite." I stared at Lady Beatrice. "You made sure the wedding went ahead before the police were called. Most of the guests didn't learn about the murder until it appeared in the papers."

Lady Beatrice's nose went up. "I wouldn't let the king disrupt Celia's wedding day when it finally arrived. I certainly wouldn't let a murderer destroy her happiness."

"If you were trying to hide Lord Eustace's presence in the house, wouldn't it be easier just to share your room with him?"

Her look said I was a creature from another universe. "I realize your generation sees nothing wrong with a husband and wife sharing a bedroom, but my generation sees that as unforgivably middle class. Besides, we'd gone our separate ways years ago. This is not the time to pretend things have changed between us."

"Of course, if you were staying in separate rooms, that ruins your alibi and that of Lord Eustace for the morning of Celia's wedding." I gave her a big smile, satisfied that I'd punctured her snobbishness.

She glared at me.

I pressed my advantage. "I suppose Lord Eustace's drinking made hiding him in Millhaven House difficult."

"He told me he'd stop drinking if I let him stay in the house. He promised. And then he broke his promise.

More than once. Amelia has been after Humphrey to throw him out since she learned he was staying there."

"When was that?"

"A week or so ago. Humphrey finally told her."

"Why?" I was beginning to think telling Amelia anything was a poor decision.

"Because my brother is nearly as big a fool as my husband." Lady Beatrice looked up then and pasted on a welcoming smile at odds with her words. "Sir Ronald, it's so good of you to have dinner with us."

"I was almost afraid I wouldn't be able to get away." My father gave me the same peck on the cheek as he did Lady Beatrice. As he sat down, he said to me, "Have you asked her where Lady Amelia went in the middle of the night before Celia's wedding?"

Surprise was quickly replaced by anger on Lady Beatrice's face. "She sneaked out while we were all abed? The little hussy." The look on her face told me her husband hadn't mentioned this to her. "How did you learn that Amelia went out the night before Celia's wedding?"

"From Philip," my father said.

"No one will ever believe it if Philip is your only witness," Lady Beatrice said. I couldn't tell if the anger I detected was directed at her husband or her sister-in-law.

"I believe him. But I think I'd better know more about this before I question her," I said. Somebody must know what Lady Amelia was up to. Every idea I came up with seemed more ludicrous than the last.

"What time was this?" Lady Beatrice now sounded determined.

"After three and while it was still dark. She came upstairs dressed in heels, hat, and gloves. Oh, and he could see she was wearing stockings, so her dress would have been street length and not an evening gown."

"Not a party." Lady Beatrice tapped her fingernail on the tablecloth. "It would have to be a private meeting. And as much as I dislike her, I can't picture her having an affair. Does Humphrey know?"

We stopped our discussion while we ordered.

When the waiter had left, I said, "Would she have taken the car or gone on foot?"

"Oh, the car. She's obnoxiously proud of it." Lady Beatrice said this with a little sniff I suspected was due to jealousy.

"Did you hear it start or return?"

"No, but the garage is on the side of the house where Walter and the boys sleep."

I planned to follow up with them. "I can't think of a single person who would hold a professional meeting at that hour except a reporter or a clergyman." I glanced at Lady Beatrice. "Do you know of any reporters or clergymen she's been seeing lately?"

"No."

"Any lovers?"

"Olivia." My father sounded horrified.

Lady Beatrice shook her head.

"How well do you know Lady Amelia's background?" my father asked. "I must have known when they first married, but I've not paid any attention to her for years."

Good for you, Father.

"They're very respectable. Her grandfather was made a lord by Victoria. Her sister is a marchioness. One brother is a bishop; another is a judge."

"Hmph," my father grumbled. "No black sheep in that family she'd need to meet in the middle of the night."

"And I suppose Philip couldn't give you any helpful details?"

When I shook my head, she said, "I'm not surprised. That was the night he broke his promise to me about his drinking. He was so upset about Celia being married here, out of my family's home, at my family's church. He said it was like he wasn't her father."

"Oh, Bea, don't pay any attention to what he says in that condition. I think the hopelessness is made worse by the pain from his wound," my father told her, reaching across the table and patting her hand.

"Do you think there's any hope?"

"Yes. Of course, a lot depends on whether the doctors can do anything for him. They've made advances since the war. Perhaps someone on Harley Street can help. Do you want me to talk to Humphrey about having Philip stay at Millhaven House indefinitely to take some worry off of his shoulders?"

She clutched his hand. "Do you think that would work?"

"It can't hurt. Millhaven House is still far enough out in the suburbs to provide fresh air and quiet." My father extracted his hand while the waiter placed our soup bowls on the table.

We ate in silence for a while before Lady Beatrice said, "Will you come back to the house with me tonight to talk to Humphrey?"

My father glanced at me. "Why not?" I asked. "This way I can talk to Uncle Walter and find out what he knows about Amelia's midnight travels."

We finished dinner and caught a cab to Millhaven House. "Why didn't you drive in?" I asked Lady Beatrice.

"I don't have a car. The only one at the house

belongs to Humphrey and Amelia now, and Amelia does not share."

While my father chatted with Lady Beatrice about mutual friends the whole way out to Millhaven House, I wondered what Walter could tell us.

We strolled up to the front door, where my father summoned Watkins with a push of the doorbell. Lady Beatrice asked, "Where are my brothers?" as she handed off her coat.

"The earl is in the study with your husband, and Mr. Brooke is in his room."

My father nodded to Watkins as he and Lady Beatrice hurried off to the study.

"Would it be all right if I go up to see Uncle Walter?" I asked the butler.

"Let me see if he is entertaining visitors tonight." I followed Watkins up the stairs and waited in the hallway while he knocked and walked in. He came out a minute later and nodded.

I knocked and walked in. "Hello, Uncle Walter."

"Hullo, Livvy." His clothes hung on him and he seemed to have picked up a tan. Strange. He hadn't traveled to any beaches, here or in the south of France, and certainly not since I saw him last. He was propped up in bed with a book, which he set aside. "I'm glad to see you. Pull up a chair and tell me all the gossip from Fleet Street."

I laughed. "I work on the society pages."

"That's where the best gossip is found." As he lit a cigarette, I realized there were a few burn marks on his covers. He must be spending a lot of time in bed, or smoking a lot. Or both.

I pulled up a chair and sat. "Why don't you tell me when the car was taken out and returned the night before Celia's wedding?"

"For the society pages?" came out in a cloud of smoke.

"To clear away the puzzles so we can discover who really killed your father. It wasn't Thomas."

"I know the boy wouldn't do it. But I really don't think I should tattle on the person who took out the car."

"It was Amelia."

His eyes widened. "You know?"

"Yes. I need to know the times."

He watched his smoke rings rise toward the ceiling. "She left after her last phone call that evening. After midnight. And she returned at four."

"Who was she calling? Could you hear what she said?"

He took a bit of tobacco off his tongue and shrugged.

Who had she telephoned? It might be vitally important, or a waste of time. I could ask the police to check the phone records for this house on that night and learn what numbers were called, but they'd never tell me the answers. Or maybe Sir Henry had contacts who could find out for me.

"If she was out until four, she was probably still asleep until eight. That leaves her out." I was so sure that was another piece of knowledge Amelia was saving for herself.

"Out of what?"

"Being the person who heard Lady Beatrice and Ames in your father's room before breakfast. I thought it was her."

"Still wondering about that?" he asked me.

"Yes."

He stubbed out his cigarette. "I was in the hall. On

my way to the necessary. I thought from what I heard that he'd had a fatal heart attack. No sense ruining Celia's big day for an old man's natural death."

"You'd been told by the doctors to expect his death."

He nodded and then said, "Where's your father?"

"He and Lady Beatrice are talking to Uncle Humphrey about having Lord Eustace stay here in relative peace and quiet while she tries to help him heal from his war wounds."

He scrunched up his face. "After twenty years? I wish them luck. I don't think it'll happen."

"Why not?" I'd seen Lady Beatrice force school matrons, university fellows, her family, and complete strangers to do her bidding. My money, if I had any to bet, was on Lady Beatrice.

"His wound is in the abdomen. It's rotted him from the inside out. It's affected his brain, made him feel less than a man. It's kept him from fathering a son to continue his title. Philip has to be ready to fight, and fight hard, to reach a stalemate with a wound that has taken so much from him."

I felt sorry for Lord Eustace. "And you don't think he's ready?"

"I've not seen any sign of it so far."

We gossiped about famous people for a few minutes until I saw I was tiring him. I promised to come back soon with more gossip and went downstairs to look for my father.

When I reached the ground-floor hallway, I found Aunt Margaret standing outside the study door. "I think we'll be able to go in soon," I told her, trying to ignore the strident voices filtering out to us.

She stared at me, her pince-nez hanging on a cord around her neck. "They sound annoyed. What happened?"

I always tried to be honest with Aunt Margaret. Except for those few times when I wasn't. Well, one time in particular, and I still regretted my stupidity. "My father and Lady Beatrice came here to talk to Uncle Humphrey about treatment options for Lord Eustace. I have no idea what could have angered them."

"Treatment options," she scoffed. "Lock him away somewhere without alcohol. If he survives, he might stay sober."

"My father thinks it's a symptom of pain from his war wound." I sounded stuffy, but I didn't like Aunt Margaret talking about Celia's father in that tone of voice. He'd served his country. If we had another war, would Adam come back as damaged?

I froze. That was my fear. I didn't want Adam to turn into Lord Eustace. I didn't even want him to turn into my father.

Lady Margaret didn't notice my reaction. "Lack of will. All too common in men. Well, shall we break up the disagreement?"

She'd have said "disagreement" if we'd opened the door to bloodshed, drawn sabers, and fire. As it was, she knocked and opened the door to the earl and Lady Beatrice leaning toward each other red-faced, shouting, while my father stood aside with his arms crossed. Seeing us, Lord Eustace stormed out of the room and nearly knocked me over.

"Is Philip going for a drink? I think I'll join him," Aunt Margaret said and followed him down the hall.

I glared at her retreating back, angry at her casual attitude over his illness, before I walked in and said, "Are you ready to go, Father? Has everything been settled?"

"Nothing's been settled. Think about it, Humphrey." My father stormed from the room and I trailed behind.

We went into the parlor where Aunt Margaret sat on the sofa with a glass of sherry and Lord Eustace stood by the fireplace with a half-full glass of deep amber liquid. From the color I knew he hadn't touched the soda bottle.

"What the hell are you doing, Philip?" my father said, striding toward him. "Beatrice goes to bat for you, and you come out here and have another drink."

"It's my life." He lifted the drink to his lips, but I don't think he drank much before my father knocked it out of his hand. The glass shattered on the stone hearth in front of the fireplace, shooting liquid and shards in all directions.

"Now look what you've done." Eustace moved aggressively toward my father, fists up.

My father showed no signs of backing down. "Look what I've done? You've messed up your life, your marriage, your daughter is furious with you—"

"My daughter? It's your daughter that can't stand you. She complains about you to Celie all the time."

My father frequently annoyed me to the point of insanity, but Celia needed me to spread stories thick and fast if anyone was to have a chance of helping her father. "Is that what Celia told you, or what you want to think? She's angry at the way you've hurt her mother time after time. She believes if you loved the two of them enough, you'd stop drinking."

"I do love them enough. If things didn't keep going wrong. If the nightmares and the pain would go away. If my friends and family," he glared at all of us, "didn't keep telling me what to do."

My father wasn't having any of it. He began to

lecture Lord Eustace while the man dropped into a chair and hid his face in his hands.

"Oh, this is quite too much." Aunt Margaret set down her drink and stalked out of the room, not looking at any of us.

The lecture continued for a few minutes, until Lord Eustace held up a hand and muttered something through clenched teeth.

My father kept talking, but I moved closer. I peered into Lord Eustace's face and knew something was wrong. "Ring for the doctor."

CHAPTER TWENTY-ONE

I rushed over and tried to take off his jacket and tie. He was making faces at me as my father sputtered to a close and came around to look at him. That was all it took for him to shout for Uncle Humphrey and Lady Beatrice.

They came running.

"It's like when Margaret was poisoned," Lady Beatrice said and began to wail.

Humphrey and my father began to get Eustace's tie and collar off. Watkins hurried in and I had him ring for the doctor. Lady Beatrice held her husband's hand as she sobbed. He shook with small convulsions and made gagging noises.

The noise must have alerted Aunt Margaret, who returned. When the doctor arrived, she told him what Eustace had drunk. When the police arrived, they took away the bottle and the fragments of the glass.

The doctor, the ambulance men, and the police moved with practiced precision. The rest of us dithered. In the end, my father and I escorted Lady Beatrice to the hospital, where he and I spent a couple of hours on a hard bench listening to Lady Beatrice sob and complain.

"Celia will be back tomorrow night. No, it's after midnight. Today. I can't have her come back to find her father dead. She idolizes him. Who could do such a thing?"

"Probably your father's killer," I answered after I'd heard the same thing four or five times.

Lady Beatrice burst into fresh sobs and my father glared at me.

"Was Lord Eustace the intended target, or does the

killer want to kill anyone in the family who falls into his trap?" I asked. "When was the last time anyone drank from the bottle Lord Eustace poured from?"

Lady Beatrice quieted and wiped her eyes. Then slowly, in a voice trapped between horror and wonder, she said, "I see what you mean. Philip drank Irish whiskey if it was available when the rest of the family drank Scotch whisky."

"And the family kept a bottle supplied for your husband?" If they didn't like his drinking, it seemed foolish to have his favorite brand available with the rest on the drinks cabinet.

Lady Beatrice must have heard the dismay in my voice because she said, "They were trying to be good hosts."

"They didn't want to help him stop drinking?"

My father glared at my outspokenness and said, "That's enough, Olivia. The important thing is that Philip was deliberately targeted if the poison was in that bottle."

"Strychnine."

I looked at Lady Beatrice. "What?"

"Strychnine. I saw Maggie after she'd been poisoned with it and Philip reacted the same way, but even faster. First, Father was stabbed and then the two poisonings. Someone must want us all dead." Her voice rose in a wail.

There was no point in killing off the whole family. While people gained from the death of the old earl, no one gained by Aunt Margaret or Lord Eustace's deaths.

I blocked out her rambling hysterics, letting my father deal with her while I thought. Celia wasn't present when Aunt Margaret was poisoned. Celia and all three of her cousins were away when Lord Eustace was struck down. Ames the valet wasn't in London when Margaret and Eustace were attacked.

Was the new countess at home when this happened? No one asked where she was, probably because no one wanted to listen to her.

The possibilities dwindled with each attempt.

Unless I thought Watkins or the maids were on some lethal vendetta against their employers, the only possibilities were the new earl, the countess, Lady Beatrice, and Uncle Walter.

I couldn't believe it of any of them.

It must have been two o'clock in the morning when the doctor came out and told Lady Beatrice to go home. Lord Eustace was no longer having convulsions and while she couldn't see him, she could sleep well, knowing his chances of a full recovery were good.

To my father's inquiry, the doctor said Lord Eustace received a little less than a lethal dose, probably because he'd been stopped from drinking a full drink.

Lady Beatrice thanked the doctor while sobbing enough to make anyone walking along the corridor think Lord Eustace had died. We took her home before we took the taxi back to town. I got out at my building, promising to ride back to Millhaven House Wednesday evening with my father.

* * *

The next morning, I took the Underground to work. At either end of my journey, I needed an umbrella to combat the soaking drizzle. Passing cars and buses splashed my heels and stockings. My hair frizzled. Lack of sleep matched my temper to the weather.

I felt guilty when I was called up to Mr. Colinswood's office just before noon. I knocked on the door.

"Shut the door behind you," Mr. Colinswood said, not looking up from the copy he was marking.

I did as he asked and then sat across his desk from him. A cigarette burned in the ashtray among a half-dozen crushed butts. Cheap paper, with corrected typing visible, was spread across the surface and under the ashtray. I wondered how long it would be before the litter caught fire.

The editor looked up at me and grinned. "That was quite a trip you made to Vienna. The information was useful, especially the details we couldn't publish. And Sir Henry told me to tell you his relatives should be on their way on the noon train today."

I felt like I was holding my breath, thinking of those children. "How soon will we know if they all got out safely?"

"Tomorrow or the next day."

Relief made the day seem sunny. I leaned back in my chair. "How did you find out?"

"Your friend Peter Thornhill sent us a message in the diplomatic pouch after he gave them their entry visas and encouraged them to use them immediately. They said they planned to go straight to the train station. Thornhill says they shouldn't face any difficulties leaving. Apparently, the customs officials make a record of their addresses and their homes will be looted in the next day or two."

I remembered dealing with the customs officials in the train station as I left Vienna. "I'll feel better when I hear they've reached London."

Whether I was certain or not, I'd tell Aunt Margaret the good news about her fellow poet, Isaak Rothenberger. She appeared to need some cheering up.

Mr. Colinswood cleared his throat. "That still leaves the other sister and their parents in Berlin. Apparently, Esther has tried and can't get her grandfather to leave for a visit to Paris, much less London."

"She must be worried sick."

"Sir Henry asks that you give her a call."

"I'll do that tonight. Do you have any assignments for me, or am I reporting society matters for the time being?"

He grinned. "You sound like you enjoy sneaking around foreign capitals."

I shook my head. "I didn't like the atmosphere in Vienna. I don't want to go back there." Then I considered the possibilities and added, "But if you ever have an assignment in Paris or the south of France, call on me."

* * *

The next night I was ready when my father called for me. We rode out to Millhaven House by cab, and I could barely suppress my excitement. Sir Henry had received word the fourteen refugees would be in London that evening and had left for the station with Esther to meet them. Aunt Margaret would be happy to hear the news about her friend. And I couldn't wait to hear about South Africa from Celia.

I climbed out of the taxi first when we arrived. As my father paid off the driver, another cab pulled up behind ours. Celia got out and ran over to me. I hugged her, both of us talking at once with damp eyes.

"This is why I wanted you and your father to keep an eye on things while I was on my honeymoon. Both Aunt Margaret and Daddy have nearly been killed. Someone is attacking my family."

I tried to settle her down before her mother heard her and became as hysterical as she'd been the night before. "Come into the garden and I'll tell you what I've learned so far."

She clutched at my arm. "Do you know who is doing this?"

"No, but I've discovered certain things that point to a very small group of people."

"You think one of my relatives is a madman." She let go of me and started to back away.

"No, but one of them is a very clever murderer."

Celia stepped forward and slapped me.

I covered my cheek with my hand, stunned that Celia would strike me. Then I became conscious of the stinging pain and I stepped forward, my hands fisted, eager to strike back.

Fortunately, my father stepped between the two of us and Robert pulled Celia toward the house, demanding to know if she had lost her mind. Otherwise, I would have clobbered her.

Celia didn't say a word as her husband hustled her into the house. Angry and hurting, I walked with my father at a slower pace. I'd almost conquered my tears by the time we reached the door.

If Watkins knew what had happened, he showed no sign that anything was amiss. "Everyone's in the parlor," he said, leading the way.

Lady Beatrice was huddled with her daughter while Robert Grayling stood at a distance, pouring himself a drink. I stared at the bottle, making certain it wasn't Irish whiskey. Then I wondered if dealing with this family was what led Lord Eustace toward heavy drinking in the first place.

Uncle Humphrey walked in from the other doorway, greeting the room in general as he joined Robert at the drinks table and vigorously shook his hand.

Uncle Walter entered a minute later and my father went over to where he'd settled into a chair, asking what he'd like to drink. Apparently, my father had noticed how weak Walter looked. I joined the men at the drinks table and asked my father for a glass of white wine.

He poured it out quickly and I went to sit by Walter's chair. "Are you feeling better today?"

"Yes, thank you. Any new gossip from the society pages?"

I mentioned a friend of his who would soon be opening a show at a prestigious gallery. "Will I like his work?"

"He's modern, but I think you'll find a lot to like about his style. I think he's brilliant, and you should buy one of his pieces. It's bound to be worth a few quid someday."

He spent a few minutes talking about the painter while Aunt Margaret came in, complaining about breaking the long strand of pearls given her by her father for her presentation at court. She came over to me and said, "You look upset and your cheek is red. What's wrong, Livvy?"

"Celia slapped me," I said, glaring across the room at her.

"Good heavens. Why?"

"She asked me to investigate her grandfather's murder, and now she doesn't like what I'm discovering."

In solidarity with me, Aunt Margaret glared at her sister and niece. "If you ask someone to honestly investigate something, you can't object when their search turns up unpleasant things. I never could understand why you allow Celia to order you around. Maybe now you'll stop."

Aunt Margaret went to get a glass of wine and I sighed. She was right. I let Celia order me around as a habit from childhood. She belonged to a large family and I didn't. I was jealous.

And the other reason I had never admitted. Well, no more. Perhaps now was the time for me to confess.

My father was discussing South Africa with Robert when Watkins came in and announced dinner. We all dutifully rose, except Walter, who was snubbing out his cigarette, when Uncle Humphrey said, "Where's Amelia?"

"I suppose the countess wants to make a grand entrance," Lady Beatrice said.

"Oh, really, Humphrey, must we always wait on her?" Aunt Margaret appeared ready to lead the march on the dining room alone if necessary.

"That's the way it's done, Maggie. Must I always point this out to you?" the earl replied.

"That's the way it's done, Humphie, when everyone follows the rules. Amelia keeps us waiting every night."

"Now, that's not fair."

"It's certainly not fair on a night when we're welcoming Celia and Robert back from South Africa," Lady Beatrice said.

The earl sounded as if this was a regular occurrence when he said, "Watkins, could you send someone upstairs and find out how long the countess will be?"

"Of course, Your Lordship." He disappeared, shutting the door behind him.

We stood around in silence, expecting the countess to breeze in at any moment and suggest we go into dinner. Instead, it was Watkins who reentered a few minutes later saying the maid couldn't find the countess.

"Oh, this is absurd," Lady Beatrice said.

"If you can't keep better track of your wife, Humphrey—" Aunt Margaret let the silence linger. "Sir Ronald, will you escort me into the dining room, please?"

My father moved next to her and everyone else fell into place in the line. I came in last with Uncle Walter, behind Celia and Robert, and we all crossed the hall to the dining room.

Even as we sat, ignoring the empty chair at one end of the table, I expected a grand entrance. I was guessing she'd be in a business suit, pumps, and the hat Lord Eustace had seen on her a few hours before the old earl was killed.

Service was slow and conversation was erratic. We were all waiting for the tongue-lashing the earl would get from the countess for starting without her. I was ignoring Celia, who was ignoring me. Robert was watching all of us as if we were a new species of very large, venomous insects.

This was so different from the dinners I remembered from only a few years before. The boys, Celia, and I would be talking and teasing nonstop until their grandfather demanded silence. After that, we rolled our eyes and made faces whenever he wasn't looking. Our parents despaired of us.

During the roast course, I told Aunt Margaret, "Your friend Isaak Rothenberger is out of Vienna and should reach London tonight. He and his family managed to get British entry visas, so you'll soon be able to visit with him."

"Oh, that is good news, Olivia. I'm so pleased for him. How did you find out?"

"His brother is brother-in-law to Sir Henry Benton, my employer. He spoke very highly of you when we met."

"I can't wait to welcome him. His whole family escaped?"

"Yes."

"Thank goodness." Her smile was wrapped around a sigh of relief.

"More Jews to support until we can ship them back," Lady Beatrice said.

When various people made shocked noises, she

added, "That's what Philip says."

"So he's an expert on European matters," Walter said.

"It's more British matters. We have too many on the dole and not enough jobs. What are we going to do with all these people? And how will we get them to blend into our society? To accept our laws and culture?" Humphrey said.

Margaret and Walter exchanged glances. No one wanted to cross the earl after we'd come into dinner without waiting for his missing countess.

The table fell silent as we continued eating.

* * *

The scream came during the pudding.

I was a step ahead of Robert as we rushed outside to find the cause of the scream.

The maid Betsy stood in back of the house by the rubbish bin. She was in bright light near the back door, pointing further out into the garden. Overgrown bushes shadowed the light there, giving us only a murky glow.

At first, all I could make out were a pair of legs with one heeled pump knocked off its foot. As I moved closer, I could see a dinner gown, the skirt hiked up to the knees, no shawl or jewelry, and a blonde head bloodied and battered. I could see enough of the face turned toward us to know it was Amelia. Nearby lay a wood-handled, splattered hoe.

The smell of blood and decay was masked by the spring flowers growing in the surrounding beds. Nothing hid the sightless eye or the blood-red lipstick on the small part I could see of the dead-white face.

Amelia had fallen face down. She'd trusted someone enough to turn her back on them.

Behind me, I heard Celia gasp and moan, and Robert

moved to shield her from the sight. I wished someone would hide such violence from me.

My father took in the hoe, the pushed-up skirts, the heavy blows to the skull, and said, "Obviously a deranged man. Watkins, call the police." He led the stone-faced earl into the house.

Walter and Beatrice didn't move beyond the back door and went inside as soon as they were told what happened, leaving Aunt Margaret and me to stand guard until the police arrived.

"I feel ashamed of the disparaging things I said about her," Aunt Margaret said.

"She was self-centered and petty, but she didn't deserve this," I answered.

"Exactly." She bent down and picked up a crushed white bloom from near the body.

"Why would she come out here while dressing for dinner? She's not the sort to spend time in the garden." I knew the police would ask the same questions I was.

"She saw someone who shouldn't be here? She was very careful of the family's prerogatives."

"Wouldn't she have sent Watkins?"

"Not if the household was readying for a big dinner. She was not afraid of demanding her rights, and she was a determined woman."

"She'd have made a good suffragist," I said, trying not to stare at the body.

"No. Don't say that," Aunt Margaret demanded. "I was a suffragist, and I was willing, like the others, to put up with imprisonment and humiliation to win our rights. Amelia expected hers to be handed to her along with her title."

She stared at the body and shook her head. "She expected everyone else to bow down to her position.

Apparently, she met someone who didn't see her in the same light."

CHAPTER TWENTY-TWO

The first bobby arrived at the murder scene and sent us into the house. I went into the parlor and sat with a brandy in my hand, wishing I lacked either curiosity or an imagination. Lacking one would have kept me from seeing the violent damage to Amelia's head. The other would have kept me from seeing it now.

Unfortunately, the damage to Amelia's skull and the smell of decay reminded me of when I saw Reggie's body in the morgue. One horror was blending into another in my mind until I wanted to wail.

Detective Inspector Guess arrived, told us he would take statements soon, and went back outside.

I was about to fall asleep where I sat in a big, well-stuffed armchair, tucked in with my head leaning against the tall back, when the detective was finally ready to speak to me. I grumbled as I slowly unfolded my limbs and followed a bobby. We went into the small red parlor where a constable sat in a corner with his notepad and Guess sat across from me.

"You look tired," was his first statement.

"So do you."

"Murders are rarely scheduled at convenient times."

His dry humor surprised me so much I nearly laughed aloud.

"I understand you were the first out of the dining room. Why was that?"

"When I hear a blood-curdling scream, I run to see what the problem is. It's usually something simple, like a spider or a wine stain on a favorite dress. Since the countess was missing, I was afraid she'd met with an accident."

"So afraid you arrived first?" His look said he was unlikely to believe any story I told him.

"I didn't have much competition. Celia, Robert, and I were the only three young people at the table, and Celia doesn't run to see who screamed. She does the screaming." Her slap, after she'd asked me to discover who killed her grandfather no matter who the culprit was, hurt, and not just physically.

"Do you know where the hoe would have been kept?"

"There's a shed behind the garage. I imagine it would be found there."

"Is it kept locked?"

"It wasn't when I was a schoolgirl. It might be now."

"Remind me what your connection is to the Brooke family."

He didn't need any reminding. I suspected he wanted to see if I could keep my story straight from one murder to the next. "I've known them since I was young. They're distant cousins. I probably came here with both my parents before my mother died, but I only remember our visits after her death."

I smiled as I decided to tell him, "Aunt Margaret was my father's first love. He and Uncle Humphrey were best friends in school, and Aunt Margaret is only a year or so older than the earl. Since I lacked a mother, she took me in hand and influenced my love of learning."

The inspector took me through what I'd seen and then told me I could go home. I wished him luck.

"This is the fourth murder or attempted murder in a few weeks here. I think the Brooke family needs luck, don't you?" he said.

I looked into his tired eyes. "I think they need a guardian angel."

* * *

I could barely stay awake the next day after a short and restless night's sleep. Corpses—the old earl, Amelia, Reggie—all marched before me whenever I closed my eyes. And then in the afternoon, when I thought I could make it to quitting time without my head hitting my desk as I fell asleep, I received a call to attend a reception at Sir Henry's house with Jane.

What else could I do? I said yes, drank even more coffee, and pinched myself awake when the taxi dropped Jane and me off at Sir Henry's after work.

Esther greeted us at the door in a soft wool dress of pale pink with a waistline that draped off to one side, drawing the eye away from her tummy. However, the way James hovered, there was no doubt in my mind. Their first child was on the way.

We walked into the formal parlor. The Rothenberger clan was all there, talking with Sir Henry and some people my age that I didn't recognize. Seeing the refugees free, especially the children, made me happy I hadn't had to quit working to raise a family. I was proud of my role in bringing them to safety.

They all appeared well scrubbed, in their best clothes, and stunned by the strangeness of everything after their long trip. I was proud to have had a hand in their rescue.

We toasted their freedom with champagne and then helped ourselves to small sandwiches and biscuits. While Jane talked to Matthias and Judith, I found myself standing with Isaak, who explained that this was a milk meal and would have no meat, in consideration of the Jewish dietary laws.

I nodded, trying to remember what Esther had told me.

"Even the plates and the cooking utensils must be kept separate. That is not possible at Sir Henry's home and Esther doesn't keep a kosher kitchen. Judith says her sister didn't, so you can hardly blame her child."

I wasn't going to comment on Esther's kitchen. There was a reason James had hired a cook. "What are you doing about plates and utensils today?"

"We're using a new set that Esther and James have given us as a housewarming present. That is the right word?"

"Yes." How foreign my city must seem to them. "Have you been able to find your way around London?"

"We're going to be living north of the City. In the northeast part of London. I said that right, didn't I?" he asked, sounding certain that he had.

"Yes. Someone has explained the peculiarities of our geography to you?"

"Esther pulled out her *A to Z Atlas and Guide to London and Suburbs.* She showed us where we'll be, where she lives, where Sir Henry lives, how the Underground and buses run. It makes trying to understand where we need to go much easier."

"Where is Esther?" I asked, looking around the crowded parlor.

"Talking to Judith. Between the two of us, I think she may be a mother before long."

"That would be wonderful news." I refused to divulge her confidence until she made the announcement.

I'd received too many confidences lately. Hiding the real reason for my trip to Vienna. Esther's pregnancy. Thomas's desire for work with aeroplanes. Celia's discovery of her grandfather's body before her wedding ceremony.

To take my mind off all these secrets, I said, "Tell me

what happened when your visas finally came through."

Isaak said, "On the evening we received the news from Sir Henry that our entry visas had arrived, we packed our bags and left them at Frau Morgenstern's. Her flat is closest to the train station. Then, first thing in the morning, we all lined up at the British Embassy and asked for your friend, Peter Thornhill. He gave us the visas and told us to leave as soon as we could."

He sighed. "There was room on the noon train to France, but they turned away people behind us. We all got on with our cases and kept very quiet until we crossed the border. Even the children were silent. It was as if we didn't breathe until the train passed the border into Switzerland, the guards were gone, and we were free."

I'd felt that way leaving Vienna, and I'd traveled with a British passport. "I hope you enjoy your time in our country."

"Everyone has been kind. Sir Henry found us two row houses to rent near each other. Solomon and Gabriella have already talked to a rabbi about the wedding."

"So you'll need more room."

He shook his head. "That would be too expensive. They will live with Frau Morgenstern once they marry. Nathan and I will continue to live with Matthias and his family. Frau Morgenstern and Gabriella live with the Gruens now. Lilith is not well, and they're already helping with the cooking and the housework and the children."

"I'm sorry to hear she's ill." I had seen her when I first arrived at Sir Henry's, silent and shivering while around her everyone talked and ate, as carefree as people could be. Hopefully, time and life in London would cure Lilith.

I changed the subject by taking a moment and

writing down Aunt Margaret's address for Isaak, explaining her home was in the far suburbs of London. "Will you visit Lady Margaret Brooke soon? Well, soon after the funeral. She'd love to see you."

He looked at me in confusion.

I tried to make this as bland as possible. "Her family has had some difficulties lately."

"You call a funeral 'difficulties'? You English are more reticent than we expected."

"Her father was murdered a few weeks ago. Then someone tried to kill Aunt Margaret and her brother-in-law. Now her sister-in-law has been murdered."

"Here? In this country?" Shock thickened his accent. "You'd think people would appreciate their good fortune."

"Does anyone ever appreciate how lucky they are?"

He shook his head with a rueful expression. "I suppose not. Do you think she will mind seeing me? After the funeral? I don't want to intrude on her grief. And these are my best clothes. I don't dress like a lord."

I gave him what I hoped was a reassuring smile as I looked at his shabby suit. "She dresses like an academic. I'm sure you two will get along fine."

"When do you suggest I see her?"

"Sunday afternoon, perhaps. The funeral is Saturday."

"Will you come as well? I hate to drop in on a grieving person unannounced. We've had far too much death in Vienna lately. Too much grief."

"I'd be glad to see her as well. But please don't think Aunt Margaret will be in mourning for her sister-in-law. They never liked each other. Still, I'm sure she's sorry the woman is dead."

* * *

I returned home to a ringing telephone. Hoping it was Adam, I ran in and snatched it up.

It was my father.

"I tried to call you earlier. Where were you?"

He can never just say hello. "At a reception. What's wrong?"

"Amelia's children want to see us tomorrow evening at the house."

"Will Thomas be there?"

"Yes. He was released a few days ago and was back in Oxford when his mother was killed. He had nothing to do with this, but he's afraid the police will try to prove him guilty once more."

"Will you be there?" I couldn't be certain my father would show up to a meeting of young people. Even one where he'd been invited. Perhaps he was ensuring I'd go along as a buffer.

"Yes. No one in that family seems to trust anyone else."

"Do you blame them after two murders and two attempts in their family?"

My father's voice snapped over the line. "If the police don't get a handle on this soon, they'll all be dead."

After what had happened, that was my fear, too.

* * *

The three brothers were still alive the next evening when my father and I arrived at the house by taxi. Edwin came around the side of the house as we alighted and said, "Follow me."

My father glared at the grass as if daring it to mar the shine on his shoes as he crossed the lawn following the boy. Then he put down his handkerchief before sitting on one of the old wooden chairs in the summerhouse in his black Westminster suit. I plopped down on the bench next to him and gazed at Thomas and Charlie sitting across from us, expecting them to say something. Since there were no more chairs, Edwin leaned on the back of Charlie's chair.

Fortunately, we were having summer weather early in the season, and in the lengthening daylight the grass was speckled with sunshine scattered by the leafy branches above us.

When no one spoke, I decided I'd have to break the silence. "I'm having a little trouble believing Thomas and Charlie aren't headed out on the town on this lovely Friday night. Or do you plan to go out after this meeting despite the funeral tomorrow?" It was a cruel thing to say, but I was tired of tiptoeing around everyone's feelings. Our reticence was giving someone time to plan more attacks.

"She was our mother." Charlie sounded outraged.

"That's not fair," Thomas added.

"But it is accurate," Edwin said. Then he turned to me. "We talked about this and we agreed. We want to find out who killed our mother and make him stop. What do you need to know, Livvy?"

I was impressed with how grown up the youngest of the brothers sounded. "All three of you sleep on the side of the house closest to the garage. The night before your grandfather was killed, your mother went out after midnight and returned sometime around four in the morning. Do you know where she went?"

"You think Uncle Stephen killed her? Are you mad?" Thomas shouted, jumping up from his seat and pacing across the squeaky summerhouse floor.

"Who's Uncle Stephen?" I asked. My father sat in silence, his arms crossed over his chest.

"Mummy's brother. The barrister," Thomas growled,

surprising me with how much he sounded like his father.

"Why did she go to see him in the middle of the night?"

"That was the night they learned about Grandfather's new will. She called Uncle Stephen and went around to see him after everyone was in bed. She didn't come back until four. I heard the car," Charlie told me.

"How did you find out about her going out?" Edwin asked.

"Your Uncle Philip saw her return."

"Did he tell you this before or after he was poisoned by his favorite tipple?" Thomas asked, scorn dripping from his voice.

An interesting way to look at the attempted murder of Lord Eustace. Especially by someone who'd already come to the attention of the police. "Shortly before."

"Mother wouldn't have poisoned him," Charlie said. "Who else knew he'd seen her?"

"Lady Beatrice and Lady Margaret." Neither of them were my first choice for murderer. "Why was your mother gone so long? She didn't have a copy of the will, did she?"

The three brothers glanced at each other, each looking guiltier than the next. Finally, Edwin said, "Grandfather had a copy locked in the safe in the study. Mummy knew the combination. She took the will out and read it over before she called Uncle Stephen. Then she took it with her when she went to see him."

"This is the same safe where your mother's necklace, the countess's necklace, was stored?"

Three heads, one light, two dark, nodded in unison.

"How many people know the combination of this safe?"

More guilty looks, and then three hands rose. "It's not

just us," Charlie said. "Mother knew, Father knows, Uncle Walter knows, and I think he told Aunt Margaret. Aunt Beatrice knows, and she would have told Celia and Useless. And Ames knew. He would fetch things from it for Grandfather."

This opened a new possibility for the theft of the necklace. I leaned forward, anxious to act if the answer was no. "Did your mother know Ames knew the combination to the safe? Did she have the police search his new home for the necklace?"

"Oh, yes, she knew. No one was immune from her searches. Or rather the searches she sent the police on, including Ames," Thomas said. He sounded bruised from all his recent dealings with the police. Searches, charges, incarceration.

Blast. Another possibility gone. Would nothing ever come clear? "Do you know what your Uncle Stephen said after he read the will?"

Thomas dropped back into his seat. "That it was well-drawn. That it might not be possible to break, even after a long and expensive court battle."

"How did your mother feel about that?"

"She was overjoyed," Charlie said.

"She thought it would be easier to get what she wanted out of us rather than deal with Father," Edwin said.

"What did she want?" I thought it might be a separate residence, although not a divorce. Amelia had made no secret of wanting to be a countess.

The three brothers looked at the floor, the ceiling, each other, anywhere but at me. Finally, Thomas said, "She wanted to throw our aunts and uncle out and sell the house. She wanted to live closer to town."

The silence following his words was filled with an

occasional birdsong or a distant car horn. Then my father spluttered to life. "Sell Millhaven House? Was she mad?"

Edwin looked at him and said, "She'd found a developer to buy the house and grounds. No more summerhouse. No more tennis courts. Aunt Margaret would lose her garden."

"But think of the money she would get for this," Charlie exclaimed.

"Not her. Your father. He's the earl," I said.

"You didn't know Mother," Thomas said.

But she'd destroy the home the Brookes loved. Even if it were for a vast sum of money. Curiosity made me ask, "How would the three of you vote?"

"She's our mother," Charlie said. "It's hard to tell your mother no."

"It would take two of us to vote no. If it were only one, Mother would make his life hell until he agreed to go along with her plan." Thomas glared at his brothers.

"I take it you were against the plan. Were two of you willing to vote no?"

"Not until after she was dead." Edwin sounded miserable. "Thomas was willing to go against her, but I was afraid of her. So was Charlie."

"Well," said my father, breaking his silence, "we have an excellent motive for three people to kill your mother. Except the advisory committee would never have allowed the sale."

"So which one of them did it?" Charlie asked.

I glanced at my father and could tell he didn't want it to be any of them.

"You've forgotten something," I told them. "If the decision wasn't unanimous, the advisory council would have to meet. I know Celia wouldn't vote to throw her mother out, and you've just heard my father. That would have stopped her plan."

"She'd have forced us into a unanimous vote before the advisory council would hear of it," Charlie said. "Millhaven House would have already been sold."

CHAPTER TWENTY-THREE

After that, we sat in the summerhouse as evening turned the sky dark and the air became chilly. The boys reminisced, sliding back in time from last summer's tennis parties to their days in the nursery while I listened, hoping to hear a clue that would point me to a killer.

"You must be freezing out here," Aunt Margaret's voice came from the darkness. "Would anyone like to come in for some cocoa?"

"That sounds wonderful, Maggie," my father said.

"I didn't hear you come out," I said to her. "That must be a handy trick to pull on these three."

"I came out the side door. And these three are more likely to sneak up on me than the other way around." Any bluster in her voice was belied by the smile I spotted as she came closer.

"Uncle Walter told us that if you don't turn on the light in the hall, no light spills out from the open door. And if you're quiet, it's just about foolproof," Edwin told me.

A clever way to sneak up on Amelia in the garden to kill her. I now knew her death would keep the house in the family. A powerful motive.

All three—Margaret, Walter, and Beatrice—who would benefit the most from Amelia's death would have known the trick of sneaking outside undetected since childhood. Sneaking outside to catch Amelia unawares.

Once the cocoa was poured, Aunt Margaret and I went into the library. She sat behind the desk, and as I took a chair opposite, said, "Now that you and Celia have had this falling out, will you please tell me why you've always done her bidding and protected her from unpleasantness?"

"I told you. I'm not part of—"

"Nonsense. What is the real reason?" She gave me a hard stare and I knew nothing less than the truth would do.

"I've been hiding it all these years because you'll hate me." Of that I was sure.

"I could never hate you, Livvy. Parents don't hate children, and you have long been the child I never had."

I studied her. "That's kind of you to say."

"It's only the truth. Now, out with it. You've been asking everyone to reveal their secrets."

I felt something deep inside me sink as she watched me. "I suppose it's time for me to reveal mine."

I took a deep breath and said, "When I was at St. Agnes, we had a poetry competition every year. My entries were always used as examples of what not to do, and I got tired of it. One summer, you wrote a funny little poem for me, and the next school year, I entered it as mine in the competition.

"Everything would have been fine if it had simply kept me from being pointed out as a failure. Instead, it won first prize, and everyone raved over my improvement. That's when Celia saw it and told me she knew who had written it. She said she would tell and get me thrown out of school if I didn't do exactly as she told me.

"After a few years, it became habit to do what she wanted. And I didn't want her to tell. I didn't want you to be disappointed in me."

She reached across the desk and took my hand. "Oh, Livvy. Your father was so proud. He showed me the poem. I recognized it immediately. I've always known."

"And he must know, too. I'm surprised I wasn't whipped for plagiarism. Surely, you were disappointed in me."

"Yes, but I knew you understood the gravity of your error. There was no sense in involving your father." She patted my hand. "I'm proud of the woman you've become. From now on, stop doing as Celia tells you. She can't get you thrown out of St. Agnes now."

No, she couldn't. Once more, Aunt Margaret gave good advice.

"I have a small confession of my own," she said. "When you and Celia found Bea and me arguing over Easter weekend, we weren't fighting with each other. Bea had received confirmation of the details of the new will. The dreadful new will. Oh, we were both furious, but not with each other."

"Why didn't you tell us?"

"Bea had learned in strictest confidence, and we couldn't share it. I'm sorry. That seems rather minor after what's occurred since then, but I thought I ought to tell you. Get rid of one more secret."

* * *

I woke up the next morning, Saturday, to a ringing telephone. Sleepy-eyed, I trudged out into the hall to answer it.

The sound of Adam's voice jolted me awake. "Adam, where are you? Will you be in London soon?"

"I'm in London. I came up yesterday but you never answered your phone, so I went out with some of the lads."

"Blast. I was at Millhaven House again."

"Still no murderer?"

"No, and now we have two murders and two

attempted murders."

"Good grief, Livvy, leave this to the police." The sound of his worry traveled over the telephone lines.

I wasn't going to promise. Not when we were getting so close. Close to what, I couldn't say, but I felt that we'd soon learn the identity of a very careful murderer. "I have to go to the countess's funeral today. Will I see you for dinner?"

"Yes. Would you like to hear a terrific jazz band afterward? Cheer you up?"

We made plans to meet at my flat as soon as I could get away from the Countess of Millhaven's funeral.

* * *

"And wouldn't she have loved being buried with a grand title," my father commented before we climbed out of the taxi at the same church Celia had been married over a month before.

The weather was beautiful until I spotted Detective Inspector Guess among the crowd milling outside the church. Then it felt as if a cloud blocked all the sunlight from Millhaven village and left my mood as gloomy as the proceedings.

The Earl of Millhaven sat with his three sons in the first row. His brother, sisters, and Lady Beatrice's family sat in the second. Amelia's brothers and sisters and their families sat across the aisle. My father and I shared the third row with the Graylings, Celia's in-laws. By luck I sat next to Robert's sister, Annabeth.

Under shelter of music from the grand pipe organ, Annabeth leaned in and whispered, "Robert's not in any danger from whoever's killing off Celia's family, is he?"

"I don't know who is doing it, or why, but I can't imagine any reason for Robert to be in danger," I whispered back.

"Celia's been acting strangely since they returned from South Africa. Snooty. And if anyone mentions her father, she gets all weepy."

"Did she meet any friends of her father, or her family, in South Africa?" It was the only reason I could think for a change in Celia's behavior. Unless she was starting to show her true nature now that she was married. Deep inside, I was still furious at being slapped. And I had no intention of being charitable.

Especially since I had never wanted to investigate these murders. I idolized this family when I was younger, but now my admiration was wearing thin.

"No. She did get a letter from her mother that Robert said upset her terribly. She wanted to come home immediately."

"What did the letter say?" I asked as the choir began the anthem and the procession started.

Annabeth shrugged. "Robert didn't see it," she mouthed.

I spent the entire service wondering what Lady Beatrice wrote to Celia that would upset her so much she wanted to shorten her honeymoon. It couldn't have been her father's poisoning, since they would have sailed for England before that happened.

Could it have been Lord Eustace's encampment at Millhaven House? But why would that have been the reason?

After the service, the entire congregation went to the large family plot in the cemetery behind the church. While everyone else was mourning Lady Amelia or thinking about what foods would be served afterward at the house, I was wondering how to approach Celia without getting slapped again.

As it turned out, once everyone had gathered on the

ground floor of the mansion, Celia sidled up to me and said, "Meet me in the garden." Then she walked past as if she'd done nothing more than say "Hello."

I walked off in the other direction, finally leaving by the side door. I was able to open and close it without making any noise, and arrived in the garden in time to sneak up on Celia.

She jumped when I called her name. "Don't do that. You frightened me."

"Because that was how the Countess of Millhaven was killed? By sneaking up behind her?"

"I don't care how Aunt Amelia was killed. I care about Daddy."

"The person who killed your aunt was probably the person who tried to kill your father. And I think it all has to do with the house."

"Daddy has nothing to do with the house." She turned away from me.

I stared at her back. "He's been living here lately because he's homeless. Your mother told you that in the letter she sent you."

"Why does everybody have to be so hard on him?" came out in petulant tears.

Whew. I guessed right. "Everybody isn't. My father and Uncle Humphrey and your mother are all trying to help him get over the pain from his wound."

She swung around then. "You know about his horrid wound?"

I nodded. "That he's been in a great deal of pain for a long time and it's prevented him from producing an heir to his title."

Celia reddened and turned away. "What does that have to do with Aunt Amelia?"

"You know that your grandfather's will left all the

family decisions to your cousins."

"So?"

"So your Aunt Amelia was forcing your cousins to agree to a sale of Millhaven House and the grounds to a developer. She was going to throw your parents and Aunt Margaret and Uncle Walter out on the street so she could buy a smaller, smarter place closer to town. And have a lot of money left over. For herself."

"The witch." The venom in Celia's words made clear she was willing to belatedly kill Amelia herself.

"You didn't know?"

"No." She held my gaze then. "Throw them out. That's just cruel."

"It is. They've lived here all their lives."

"Especially Uncle Walter."

That caught my attention. "Why especially Uncle Walter?"

"He's dying."

"He said he's recovering, but it's a long, slow process."

"He admitted the truth to Mother. She wrote me that as well."

One more Brooke going to his Maker. "Is there some kind of prize for the member of the family who's the last to survive? A prize I don't know about?"

Celia gave me a dirty look. "Don't be callous, Livvy."

"Then help me, Celia. You asked me to find your grandfather's killer. Lady Amelia's death and the two attempts have to be linked."

"Why? They were by different methods. The physical methods worked. The poisonings didn't." Her voice reeked of skepticism.

"That would mean two different people with a grudge against your family so great they were willing to kill. To risk hanging. I can't see it, can you?"

She shook her head. "Unless the poisonings weren't meant to kill. Perhaps they were just warnings to stay clear of whatever is going on. Perhaps this person gained what they wanted by killing Grandfather and Aunt Amelia."

"The two people most likely to be upset by the theft of the countess's necklace. The jewelry you wore at your wedding."

"I gave it to Mother and she put it back," came back at me like a shot.

"Did you watch her put it away?"

She opened her mouth to snap at me, but then she shut her mouth and shook her head.

"You can do one thing to help your father's alibi," I told her.

"What?"

"I need to see if Lady Amelia had a very particular style of hat your father described."

Her eyes narrowed. "Why?"

"It will prove he saw Lady Amelia when and where he said he did."

"And this will help him?"

I nodded, not wanting to add that it might help his mental state to know he had these details right.

She led the way into the house and up the back staircase to the first floor. From there she led me to the late Lady Millhaven's room. We found her hatboxes in her boudoir.

In the third box was a black narrow-brimmed hat with a large bow on one side and a few feathers on the other. In the dark, they could easily be mistaken for horns. "This is it," I said, turning around. Celia was gone.

I put the hat back in its box on the shelf and turned

around to leave when I heard someone enter the countess's bedroom. I stayed still, trying to hold my breath as I hoped whoever it was didn't find me.

My desire not to be caught warred with my longing to know who else had entered the dead woman's room and why. I peered around the edge of the door and saw Lady Beatrice slip a small bag under the pillows of Lady Amelia's bed.

Then she tiptoed away.

As soon as the door was shut behind her, I came out and started for the door. Then my feet stopped in the middle of the room. My curiosity took control as my legs carried me over to the bedside. I reached under the pillows and came up with a small green velvet cloth sack.

I opened the drawstring and dumped the contents into my hand.

The countess's necklace.

I dumped the necklace back into the bag and found black soil left on my hand. Dusting off the dirt, I shoved the bag under the pillows and hurried from the room, hoping no one would catch me.

My luck held as I went down the back staircase. Then I dashed around the corner into the red parlor and skidded to a halt. Lord Eustace and Celia were huddled in conversation not three feet away, while the others in the room paid us no attention.

"It's too bad you didn't stay with me, Celia," I told her in a low voice. "I saw where your mother hid the countess's necklace."

There were other mourners in the room, none of whom I knew. I hoped Celia wouldn't make an outburst. I didn't want to involve anyone else in this sordid theft.

"She wouldn't have stolen it." Celia turned to walk away from me.

I reached out and stopped her with a grip on her arm. "She did, and I'm going to call the police."

"Outside," Lord Eustace said. He grabbed my shoulder. The pinch made me drop Celia's arm and stopped any cry in my throat. He made it look as if he were marching me from the room in a friendly embrace.

"No," I gasped. I tried to pull away and failed. I didn't smell any liquor on him, and somehow that made him more dangerous.

"Outside. Celie, go find your mother and bring her to the summerhouse." He hustled me down the hall to the back door. He was so quick we didn't see anyone to arouse their suspicions, and I was so busy trying not to get run over by his quick steps I didn't think to cry out.

Once we were outside and on our way to the summerhouse, Lord Eustace said, "Bea didn't take that necklace. I found it in the guest room I've been using."

I stopped fighting him, curious to hear what tale he would tell me. "When did you find it?"

"This morning before the funeral, but it could have been there a day. No longer than that."

He shoved me into the summerhouse ahead of him. "How do you know so precisely?"

He grumbled out his words. "I have a bottle hidden in the top of the wardrobe behind the winter blankets. The last time I—looked at it was the evening before last. This morning I was going to throw the bottle away, but then I found the necklace. I panicked and took it to Bea."

"It's true," Lady Beatrice said as she and Celia walked in and joined us. "I had no idea you were in Amelia's room, Olivia."

Her actions made no sense. "Why hide it in Lady Millhaven's room? Why not turn it in to the police? Or your brother?"

"Humphrey has enough on his plate right now. It may not be nice of me, but I'd like to make it appear as if Amelia had it all the time. Then hopefully the whole idea of selling this place will go away."

I wanted to put her mind at rest. Particularly if it stopped any more murders. "I think any deal for the property has already fallen through. None of the boys want to sell. They say their mother was pushing them to agree."

"She never liked any of us. She hated living in the wilderness, as she called it." Celia crossed her arms. "I think you should leave now."

We stared at each other. I knew we'd never be friends again. Maybe we never were. "This isn't your house, Celia. It's your cousins' house. Perhaps you want to tell them to ask me to leave. And explain why."

Scorn made her features ugly. "None of us ever wanted you here. Ever. We laughed at you behind your back. But I thought you might be useful. You couldn't even manage that."

I jerked back as if she'd slapped me again. *We laughed at you.* I turned to leave and found Robert Grayling in the doorway staring at his wife. I couldn't tell if he was angry or horrified from his scowling expression.

"Robert, make sure the police know the countess's necklace has been located. Otherwise it's insurance fraud, and you don't want to start your married life under a cloud," I said as I stalked past him.

He murmured, "Which one of them stole it?"

I glanced at his cold eyes and knew he'd seen through Celia. "Her father claims he found it. Her mother was seen hiding it. I don't know who stole it."

He dismissed me with a nod. I strode away, glad to leave the Eustaces in his keeping.

CHAPTER TWENTY-FOUR

I hurried toward the house as my heels sank down into the grass and dirt. I didn't look down at the damage. I only wanted to leave this cursed house.

I went inside and quickly found my father. "Let's go." I kept my voice down.

He looked startled, but he spoke quietly. "We can't just leave."

"Yes, we can. We can come back tomorrow." I was beginning to hate the idea of bringing Mr. Rothenberger into this den of snakes.

No, that wasn't fair to Aunt Margaret or Uncle Walter.

"Where have you been? What are you so upset about? And why is the backside of your nice black dress dusty?" My father scowled, puzzled.

I brushed the back of my skirt with one black-gloved hand and then smacked my gloves together to get the dust off them. "I just had a talk in the summerhouse with Celia and her parents. Celia wants me to leave and never come back. You, too, probably."

"I don't feel that way, and neither do my brothers," Edwin said in a quiet voice as he joined us. "Since the house is ours under Grandfather's will, I want you to know you'll always be welcome for trying to find his killer. And Mummy's."

"Thank you. And so you know, the countess's necklace has been found placed under the pillows on your mother's bed. You might want to get your brothers and retrieve it."

Edwin studied my face for a moment. "You know

who put the necklace there?"

He was definitely the smartest of the three boys. I'd have to tell him everything later. "Lady Beatrice, but I don't think she stole it. Please, get the combination to the safe changed."

At that moment, Mrs. Gibbons, the widow who had clung to my father at Celia's wedding, came up to us. "Ronald, Olivia, I'm so glad I finally caught up with you. How are you?" she said as she maneuvered close to my father and took his arm.

Edwin backed up a couple of steps to get out of her way, gave me a smile, and left.

"Oh, Mrs. Gibbons, I'm sorry we can't stay, but we're late for another appointment. Perhaps some other time?" I said, grabbing my father's other arm. "Come on, Father. We can't be late."

He detached himself from the woman with a regretful expression and hurried away as quickly as possible through the crowd. We were lucky. As we reached the street, a taxi finished dropping people off at the church. We waved the driver down and escaped Millhaven House.

"I suppose you have an explanation," my father said as we headed back toward town.

"I doubted you wanted to be present at the finding of the countess's necklace."

He raised his eyebrows.

"I'm meeting Adam at my flat, so I might as well tell you now. Lord Eustace said he found the necklace and gave it to his wife. She hid it under the pillows on the countess's bed. I saw her do it and told Celia, who'd been with me until a moment before her mother appeared."

"I hope someone reports this to the insurance company." It was a sign of my father's shock that he didn't question my meeting Adam at my flat.

"I hope so, too. I reminded Robert about insurance fraud after Celia let me know our help was no longer desired."

With a huff, my father said, "I would think they'd want all the help they can get before someone else dies."

We sat in silence until my father said in full investigatory mode, "So Redmond is back in town."

* * *

My father didn't know it, but Adam had a key to my flat and was waiting for me when I got home from the funeral. He took one look at my face and said, "Someone you'll miss?" as he pulled me into an embrace.

Neither of us spoke for a while. When we both caught our breath, I said, "No. I've known her most of my life and never liked her. She was the countess who was daughter-in-law to the old earl who was murdered a few weeks ago. She was also murdered."

He pulled me tighter to him. "Blast it, Livvy. Stay away from them. Leave it to the police."

I felt safer in his embrace than I had in days. "Gladly. I discovered Celia's parents hiding the family heirloom that was stolen after Celia's wedding. They said they just found it and were putting it in the countess's bedroom since it was the countess's necklace they recovered."

"Good grief. First they stole this woman's necklace and then someone stole her life."

"Not necessarily. The necklace belonged to the Countess of Millhaven. It wasn't hers until her father-in-law died, and now it will belong to her husband's next wife or her son's wife when he marries."

"I'm afraid there's no jeweled heirloom in my family," he said, nuzzling my neck. He didn't seem to be in any hurry to let me go.

And that was fine with me.

* * *

We went out to dinner and met friends to go dancing to the music of a jazz band, and then lazed about the flat the next morning. Adam didn't have to report back to his secret assignment until Monday evening.

I was determined to enjoy every minute with him that I could. "Why don't we go out to Sunday lunch before I have to go back to Millhaven House?"

He put down the Sunday edition of the *Daily Premier*. "No."

"I have to go. I'm taking a poet who escaped from Vienna to see Lady Margaret. They've been corresponding for years. I promised."

"No. I mean, we're going to Millhaven House. I won't let you go back to that madhouse without me."

"You just don't want to miss out on all the fun," I said lightly. Truly, it hadn't been fun to go out there since I had been dragged into solving a murder. And I'd feel safer if Adam were along.

"That's it. I don't want you going out and having fun while you leave me behind to sit alone in your flat." His wry smile made my heart flutter.

But that wouldn't do me any good when he left. I hardened my tone. "Wonderful. Where would you like to eat?"

The telephone rang before he gave me his answer.

When I answered, my father's voice said, "Olivia. I thought we'd have lunch together and then go out to Millhaven House. You have that poet to escort and I want to check on Humphrey and Philip. Make sure they haven't killed each other."

"Fine. Where will we dine? Adam will be eating with us and then going along to Millhaven House."

"Why on earth would he want to do that?" His tone made it clear he couldn't imagine why anyone would want to travel to that house of murder and mourning.

"I think he secretly hopes to recruit Lady Beatrice for the army."

I heard a snicker a moment before Adam wrapped his arms around me.

"Hmph. Ask Adam to meet us at the Dryesdale at one."

"I will. Thank you."

"One o'clock." My father disconnected the call.

"The Dryesdale," Adam said when I'd hung up the receiver. "I'd better get cleaned up and presentable."

"My father is taking this investigation very seriously. Uncle Humphrey, the new earl, and he have been close friends since their first day at school. Lady Margaret was my father's first love. Don't laugh," I added when I saw Adam's eyes crinkle at the corners.

"I wouldn't dream of it. I look forward to seeing her again. Being someone's first love is a serious position. Almost as much as someone's all-time love." His expression turned serious.

I knew we could no longer avoid having this talk. "I know that's the direction we're headed in, and it frightens me." I moved closer to him, clutching his shoulders.

"Why?" came out as a sigh.

"You're always dropping in and out of my life."

He captured my gaze. "Be honest with me, Livvy."

"There's a madman in Germany who's determined to start a war and you're in the army. I don't want to lose you. If anything should happen to you, I don't think I could bear it."

He kissed my nose. "I don't want you to lose me,

either. But I refuse to not live my life or ignore my feelings for you because of what Herr Hitler may or may not do."

"And then there's Lord Eustace."

Adam drew back, a puzzled look on his face.

"What do you know about shell shock and pain from old wounds?" I asked him, watching his face.

He nodded as if he understood what I was thinking. "That a lot of men returned from the trenches suffering from shell shock. Maybe most of them in one form or another. I also know gunshot and mortar wounds can leave lifelong pain and injury. And avoiding injury is a matter of luck, not skill."

"My father thinks Lord Eustace is still suffering from both twenty years later."

"I've heard talk of some cases of shell shock that have lasted the rest of the man's life. It certainly lingers with soldiers for years. It's not like whooping cough, gone in a week or two. And there's nothing that can be done for those who survived gunshots or shrapnel mortar fire." Then he pulled me close. "I don't think I'm the type to end up with shell shock, but there's no way to know. We have to live our lives and hope for the best."

"I do hope for the best. So why do I worry so much about you?"

He kissed me then. "Because you love me so much."

I thought of what I'd seen in Vienna and shivered at our prospects for the future. Since there was no sense in worrying Adam, I pinned on a bright smile and said, "We don't want to be late. Go get ready for lunch."

We ate off delicate china on fine white linens in an airy, light-filled room. As always at the Dryesdale, the food was delicious. Even though we dined out last night, this would be the tastiest meal of my week. Adam appeared to be in heaven, savoring every bite. The wine was from a favorite French vineyard, well-chilled and fragrant.

A pianist was playing classical concertos on a large, white grand piano. The waiters were all impeccably dressed. The diners wore fashionable day wear. The women's hats held my attention, and a few of them made me jealous. Adam, with his broad shoulders and handsome face, was the best-looking man in the room.

Everything was perfect. And yet, I couldn't escape my feeling of impending doom.

My father, never the most perceptive of men, finally asked if I felt all right.

"I'm afraid your daughter doesn't want to discuss the future with me until we know what Germany has planned. And when we know, she might put me off even longer," Adam said and took another sip of wine.

"Olivia, it will be years before we know what that madman has in store for us. And by then, cooler heads may have taken over the reins." I knew Adam wouldn't be my father's first choice for me, but he found marriage to Adam and possible grandchildren preferable to his daughter working for a newspaper.

"I think it's seeing Mr. Rothenberger again this afternoon. And going back to Millhaven House where there have been four vicious attacks, two of them fatal. I feel like something is going to happen soon. Today. It's as if the whole world is about to fall apart."

Adam stared into my eyes. "You do have it bad, this mood of yours. I'm sorry, darling."

I took another sip of wine. "It'll be gone in a day or two. Unfortunately, you'll be back to work by then. Please forgive me for ruining your leave."

He shook his head as he took my hand. "You can't

ruin it, as long as I get to spend time with you."

My father, with his perfect timing, said, "Where exactly are you based, Redmond?"

* * *

We met Isaak Rothenberger at King's Cross station since it was convenient to him and an obvious landmark to a new arrival. I introduced him to Adam and my father, and I found his heavily accented English already improved after his short time in England.

"Have you told them how much you helped us escape?" Isaak asked me.

"That is a secret," I told him as I felt my eyes widen.

"Olivia, what have you been up to?" my father asked in a cautious voice, as if afraid to hear the answer.

"That question ranks right up there with where Adam is based," I said.

Adam raised his eyebrows but he didn't say anything. He and my father exchanged looks, and I knew one or the other would be questioning me someday soon.

"Well, Mr. Rothenberger," I said, taking his arm, "let's take a taxi out to Millhaven House."

"A real English taxi? Oh, this will be a treat," he said, letting me lead us to the taxis. We all piled into one, gave the driver the address, and rode off.

Isaak commented on various sites as we passed. Shops, traffic lights, automobiles, pedestrians, parks—all were fodder for his questions and comments.

"You've not seen this part of London yet?" my father asked.

"No. This is a huge city. A magnificent city."

"Margaret Brooke's house was deep in the Surrey countryside a hundred years ago. Now the area is part of the suburbs," I told him.

"It sounds very grand."

"Oh, it is," my father hastened to tell Isaak. "Her father, and now her brother, are earls. They once were surrounded by huge landholdings. Now their farmland is away from the town, but the house sits on extensive grounds."

"They sold closer-in land for housing estates," I told him.

Isaak nodded, but I suspected we'd confused him.

"How long have you and Aunt Margaret been corresponding?" I asked.

"I wrote her when her first volume of poetry was published. Fifteen years ago now? Yes, 1923. I have always been a great admirer."

"I didn't realize she hadn't been published before then. She's written poetry as long as I can remember. She used to write verses to amuse my cousin Celia and me." That memory stung in view of yesterday's falling-out with Celia and my admission to Aunt Margaret of plagiarism.

"Two years ago, when I was having trouble getting published because of the Nazis, she told me she had a publishing contract before the one that led to her first book." Isaak shook his head. "It was during the war. First, her father went to the publisher and made him cancel her contract. Then he told her she was a failure because she was writing poetry and not married. He said the only thing she was good for was producing babies. And then George died."

I looked at Isaak, confusion on my face. "Who's George?"

"Her fiancé," my father said. "He was killed in the fighting. In 1915."

"I always despised the old earl," I said with heat. Now we had another war coming and Adam was in the army.

No wonder Aunt Margaret worried for me.

But what would she advise? Marry him now or wait?

CHAPTER TWENTY-FIVE

When we finally pulled up in front of Millhaven House, Isaak's first words of amazement were in German as he climbed out of the taxi and stared at the enormous Georgian building. "Lady Margaret really lives here?" he asked in English.

"Yes," I assured him.

"I cannot go inside. I'm not dressed for a palace. She will be ashamed to let me in."

"You've written to Aunt Margaret for how many years?" I asked. "Has she ever written you anything that makes you think you'd be less than welcome?"

He shook his head, still staring at the edifice.

I looped my arm around his. "Come on."

Watkins answered the door and told a cowering Isaak that we were expected. We followed him to the library where Aunt Margaret rose from behind her desk to greet us.

My father said he was looking for Humphrey and left behind Watkins.

Aunt Margaret and Isaak greeted each other warmly, as if they'd known each other forever. Perhaps they had, at least in their correspondence. She also clasped Adam's hand and told him how glad she was to see him again and that she wished him much safety and happiness in his future.

As she ordered tea for the four of us, Adam glanced at me with a surprised look. I could only give him a faint smile as heat rose on my cheeks. Aunt Margaret had given away that I'd said aloud how much I cared for him.

After a few minutes and a cup of tea, I said, "Are the

boys here?"

"They're around somewhere," Aunt Margaret said and continued her academic discussion about poetry with Isaak.

I gestured with my head to Adam. We made quiet farewell noises and left the room.

At Watkins's direction, we walked toward the tennis court, where an occasional *thwup* gave away Edwin's and Charlie's presence. Thomas lay on a bench nearby and stared at the sky, if indeed he was looking at anything.

Charlie waved to us and then served the tennis ball as Edwin turned to see who was coming up behind him. The ball narrowly missed him, bounced a couple of times, and then rolled along the grass. Adam fielded the ball and tossed it back to Edwin.

Edwin walked over to us, followed by Thomas, and since they'd been away at school when Adam was here before, I introduced them. Charlie shouted something about the match, but then he wandered over as well.

"We've taken care of the necklace for Father," Edwin said. "Mr. Craggett has it now and is dealing with the insurance company."

"What did you say to Robert? After you left, I heard him tell Celia they wouldn't be visiting her relatives again anytime soon. That she was his wife and she needed to act like it," Thomas said.

"Robert overheard a conversation between Celia, her parents, and me about the necklace. None of us were on our best behavior." Well, at least they weren't. I'd tried to stick to the facts.

Thomas dominated the conversation once he found out Adam was in the army. Adam answered his general questions until Thomas made clear his interest in flying.

"You just have exams before you graduate?" Adam

said, scowling slightly.

Thomas nodded.

"Done any flying?"

"I have a classmate with an aeroplane. I've taken some lessons with him."

"There's a chap you may want to meet if you're truly interested in flying. I'll get his number and give it to Livvy. Give her a call later on this week," Adam said and glanced at me.

"I will. Thank you." Thomas seemed to come alive, shaking Adam's hand and smacking him on the back.

"Finish your exams first. And do a good job. That'll have a bearing on whether this fellow will take you on," Adam said, grinning.

Isaak and Aunt Margaret came out to the tennis court, Isaak exclaiming over everything he saw. "You do not know how lucky you are in England. I hear lots of complaints, but what do you have to complain about?"

"Our mother was just murdered. Right over there," Charlie said and pointed to an area of the large flower garden at a distance from the tennis court.

"It is very sad, and I am sorry, young man. But the English police will hunt for this murderer. Perhaps that will give you some solace."

"I wish it would," Charlie mumbled.

"There are many crimes in Vienna where the police will not hunt for the criminals, even if they see the crime committed right in front of them." Isaak sounded depressed by the government of his former home. "You are lucky you are here, safe, among your family."

"Safe? Ha," Charlie said and turned to me. "Where did you find her, Livvy? Where was my mother?"

His anguish spilled out in his words.

Poor kid. I started to walk along the garden paths to

the spot I remembered from that awful night.

"Careful, don't step on my—" Lady Margaret shouted something in Latin. I had no idea what plant she was talking about. I veered away from anything flowering.

I had to circle around before I reached the spot traipsed over by the police. The plants there were damaged and the flowers trampled.

And then as I looked toward the house in the bright afternoon sunlight, I spotted something shiny at the edge of the garden under a big, leafy plant. I carefully stepped over to the spot, bent over, and picked it up.

How did that get there?

I rolled the beautiful white pearl in my hand. I pictured Lady Amelia's body as I'd seen it that night. She hadn't been wearing pearls or any other jewelry. There were no pearls around her body. But someone had mentioned pearls while we waited for her.

Who was it?

"What do you have there?" Charlie asked. He now stood where I'd seen his mother's body lay a few days before.

"A bug. And I don't have it anymore," I said, slipping the pearl into my purse as I pulled out a handkerchief and wiped my hands.

Adam, who'd walked over and had seen what I found, watched me carefully but didn't say anything.

Thomas and Edwin walked over to the edge of the trampled area but didn't step on what had been the location of the corpse. Edwin's face twisted up before he shoved his racquet at Thomas and sprinted inside.

"Guess I'd better see what I can do for him. Father's useless right now." Then Thomas paused. "Thank you, Adam. I look forward to meeting your friend."

I watched him stride toward the house and enter by

the back door.

Charlie came over to us. "So much for our tennis match."

"Are you that keen on tennis?" I asked.

"No. It just keeps me from thinking. What if I'd come home from school for a few days? Maybe I could have stopped the attack." Amelia's middle son made lanky strides toward the house with the tennis balls and his racquet clutched in his hands.

"I was younger than they are when my mother died," Aunt Margaret said as she and Isaak made their way to where Adam and I stood. "They're upset now, of course, but it will be the making of them."

I'd lost my mother when I was young and saw no benefit to it at all. "How can that be the making of them?"

"Amelia crushed their initiative and any idea that hard work might be good for them. Now they'll be able to grow into men."

"So you believe that hard times, terrible times, build character in our young people?" Isaak asked.

"Only when their mother was such an awful person." Lady Margaret spoke as if she were handing down wisdom from the mountaintop. "It's unfortunate, and painful for them now, but in the end, they'll be better off."

Isaak shook his head. "Our young people are already facing horrors. Some will survive unscathed, but most will be damaged. Many will perish. I'd rather they develop character the usual way. It may take a little longer, but more will survive."

"Oh, Isaak," Aunt Margaret said. "I didn't mean war or Nazis or anything so unspeakably terrible. I mean their mother prevented them from attempting new concepts or activities. And so they missed the usual knocks any young person may receive growing up."

"Of course, my dear Lady Margaret. And now I need to return home. My family relies on me to translate. It has been a pleasure to meet a poet of such eminence. I hope I may visit again." He bowed over her hand.

Aunt Margaret smiled. "I believe I was the one to meet a great poet today. Thank you so much for visiting us. And please, come back soon."

They went through this for a few minutes as they walked around the side of the house toward the road.

Adam pulled me aside. "What did you find?"

"A pearl."

"That doesn't mean anything."

"Probably not." But I remembered who had complained of a broken pearl necklace the night Amelia died. And the dirt on the countess's necklace. "Will you make sure Aunt Margaret stays downstairs for a few minutes? I want to check something."

"Livvy—"

I went in the back door and up the back stairs. I heard Adam come in the door a moment later and then my father called to him. His footsteps continued down the hall.

I didn't have time to figure out what the shouting was about on the ground floor between my father and Lord Eustace if I were to check Aunt Margaret's pearls undetected. I hurried to her room and knocked before I opened the door.

No Aunt Margaret. No family member. No upstairs maid.

I went over to her dressing table and started going through her jewelry cases, one at a time. Finally, I opened one and had to catch the exquisite white pearls from cascading out of their case onto the floor. Most were still held by their knots onto the broken string, but one was clearly missing at the break.

I opened my purse and fished out the pearl I found in the garden. It matched the color and size of the others.

"My father gave me that long string of pearls when I was presented at court. To King Edward and Queen Alexandra. Aren't they marvelous? Each one a thing of beauty. But what I wanted was a university education. He wouldn't hear of it."

Aunt Margaret. My heart hit my stomach on the way to my feet.

"How—how did it get broken?" I turned to face her.

"How do you think? Miss High and Mighty Amelia caught her hand in it when she shoved me." Aunt Margaret stepped inside the door and shut it. I knew how much those old, heavy wooden doors blocked out sound.

"She shoved you? Lady Amelia shoved you?" I blinked. "I didn't think she ever stirred herself enough to be overtly rude."

"The rest of the world heard her snide comments and cruel dismissals, but the family had the pleasure of seeing the worst of her." She stayed where she was. "You found the pearl I must have missed when my necklace broke."

"Yes. In the garden."

"Put it in with the others. Thank you."

She was between me and the door. I did as she said, putting the pearl, now sweaty from my hand, in the box.

Once I closed and set down the jewelry case, I took two steps toward her. "She was going to sell this house and throw you out."

"She threatened to. Money does funny things to people." She sounded bitter.

"And yet the old earl rewrote his will in an attempt to stop her from doing exactly that." It was what Aunt Margaret would call a plausible deduction. I hoped she bought it.

I could tell by her frown and the puzzled look in her eyes that this idea had never occurred to her. "What do you mean?"

"Your father had taken the measure of Lady Amelia. All those votes and advisory committee meetings? It was just to keep Amelia from talking Humphrey into selling the house or sailing to South America or anything else she decided to do. I believe your father knew what she was capable of." I took a couple more steps toward the door. I hoped I wasn't giving the odious old man more credit than he deserved.

"We all knew what she was capable of. But if my father guessed at her true nature, it would have been the first time he realized what any woman was capable of. He never gave me credit for what I could do." Aunt Margaret stood motionless, watching me.

"He sounds like my father," I said with a rueful grin.

Fury glowed in Aunt Margaret's eyes. "Your father is a gentleman. He's a kind, dear man. Don't you speak badly of him."

"I'm not. I wouldn't. But he has no idea what I am capable of." Another two steps. "Did you ever surprise your father with your ability? He must have been pleased when you graduated from university. Or when you became a published author."

Her eyes looked past the walls of her room. "Traveling into town every day for years to attend classes, only to take the train and then the omnibus to get home in time to dress for dinner. And he couldn't be bothered to make the trip once, to see me graduate. And my poetry? Mere doggerel, he said. Did you know he had my first publishing contract voided?"

"Isaak Rothenberger told me. I'm sure your father is

paying for it now, wherever he is."

"He didn't know how to be proud of a daughter, or anyone with artistic talent, and so he deserves to be burning in hell." Her voice was cold and vindictive.

Margaret had been instrumental in getting my father to let me go to university and to see me graduate. "Thank you for persuading my father to send me to university."

"It was the least I could do. You're a very bright girl. I'm very proud of you."

I moved next to her. "Unfortunately, I'm bright enough to know you killed your father and Amelia. Why, Aunt Margaret?" I heard anguish in my tone. Did she?

She smiled. I didn't expect that reaction to my accusation. "You're far ahead of the police, but I would expect you to be. You know how to pay attention and to draw logical deductions."

"Not that far ahead of the police." I didn't want her to think that killing me would hide her guilt.

"You're wrong, of course, but tell me, how did you come to such a conclusion?"

I hoped if we talked long enough, someone would come looking for us. "You were seen coming from the bathing room during the hour your father was killed, and there was no indication that you had taken a bath. You could have needed to wash your father's blood off you. Once Lord Eustace mentioned the time he saw you, he was poisoned. No doubt in an effort to silence him, but my father knocked the glass containing the strychnine out of his hand so he didn't get a fatal dose."

She didn't say a word. All she did was watch me with that neutral face university tutors use for oral exams.

I took a breath and continued. "And then Lady Amelia—sorry, Lady Millhaven—told you she had twisted her sons' arms and would be selling the house.

You'd have to move. Give up your garden." That raised a question in my mind. "How did you get her out into the garden right before dinner?"

"I told her I found a better offer for the house and grounds."

"She believed that?" I knew Margaret didn't have business connections. I would have been skeptical.

"She did after I said I wanted half of the difference between the two offers." She shook her head. "That seemed to make the offer valid in her eyes. Amelia was always blinded by money and the lifestyle it could buy her."

"And no one thought anything of you doing a bit of weeding with a hoe that afternoon."

"Of course not, Livvy. There's always more to do in the gardens than I and the gardener have time for." She shook her head in sorrow. "No one noticed anything or had any suspicions until you started asking questions." I saw her hand reach behind her to the dresser that was styled with carved designs on the drawer fronts.

"Aunt Margaret, I really started digging into this investigation, not because of Celia's request, but because someone poisoned you. I wanted to keep you safe."

"I thank you for that, but are you certain you're right about my father's killer? Are you sure it wasn't Amelia?" She pinned me in place with her gaze.

Really? Could I be so wrong about someone I'd been close to all my life? And if I was wrong, would Aunt Margaret ever forgive me?

CHAPTER TWENTY-SIX

"What?" I'd eliminated Amelia when she was murdered. No, before that, when I realized how much use she was making of the new will. She wasn't angry at her father-in-law. She knew he was dying. She could wait for nature to do the rest.

"Amelia went out in the middle of the night to confer with her brother the barrister. When she came home, she looked for her first opportunity to kill Father. When Ames went downstairs to have breakfast, she went in and stabbed the old man. She was tired of waiting to be countess, and with the new will signed, there was never a better time."

"Do you mean she poisoned you and Lord Eustace?"

"Yes. I saw her meeting with the property developer and warned her that I would stop the sale by letting everyone know what she was doing. I was poisoned that night."

"Why would she poison Lord Eustace?"

"With your father and Bea trying to—cure him is the wrong word—help him regain his balance in the quiet of Millhaven House, Amelia must have guessed Humphrey would stop the boys from agreeing to a sale. She wanted the house sold, not turned into a convalescent home for Lord Eustace and Walter."

"I suppose you killed Lady Millhaven in self-defense."

"Of course it was self-defense." I didn't like the way she didn't look me in the eye when she said those words.

"Convenient that the murderer is dead."

"It can't be proven, and she can't confess now." Aunt Margaret gazed straight at me. There was something hard and cold in her pale brown eyes.

Her eyes had once been warm, at least when she looked at me. When had she taken on this chilly expression? I remembered her pinched look the day of Celia's wedding. The day of her father's murder. And after that, but I hadn't paid enough attention.

I weighed what she told me, thinking of how it affected everyone else in the family. This was going to hurt everyone, no matter which story anyone believed. Margaret or Amelia as killer?

Then I remembered a conversation I had with Amelia. "She knew your father was dying when he wrote the new will. She knew she didn't have long to wait before she became countess and the boys took charge of the money. Her boys."

"She was impatient."

"No one would believe that. She's waited all these years to become countess, married to a man she doesn't like. She wouldn't rush the old man's death by a couple of months now. Why bother?"

"Very good, Livvy. I've always said you have a creative mind." She sounded as if she were grading an oral argument for a degree.

"I want to believe it was Lady Amelia, but I can't. Give me a reason to believe the killer isn't you." There was sorrow in my voice again.

"It's far too late for that, don't you think?" She sounded so sad. So resigned.

"Why did you poison yourself?"

"To throw suspicion away from me."

"But you could have made a fatal mistake in the amount of strychnine." I was in anguish. This woman had practically raised me. How could she be a murderer?

She gave me a sad smile. "I don't think I would have

minded."

"Why didn't you talk to my father? He could have made Humphrey stop Amelia from selling Millhaven House."

"He couldn't have. No one had any power where Amelia was concerned." She smiled then, looking at the floor. "So what shall we do? I'd hoped to wait until Walter dies before this comes out." She sounded calm. Pleasant, even.

"How long does Walter have?"

"A few months." Her eyes welled up. "He's my baby brother, Livvy."

I didn't have a baby brother, but I thought I understood her pain. "You want to wait so he's not upset before he dies?"

"To let Walter have a peaceful passing, have my new volume of poetry published, and see my garden through to autumn. Leave it in good shape for someone else."

I wished it were that easy. "What if the police figure everything out before then?"

"They won't." She gave me a proud smile. "They aren't as clever as you. Or me."

As much as I wanted to, I knew it was wrong. "I'm sorry, Aunt Margaret. I can't."

"I'm sorry, too. I've failed to live up to your standards."

"I wish things were different. For both of us." Tears were starting to form as I asked, "Did you steal the countess's necklace and bury it to help Walter—"

I never saw the blow coming.

Pain rattled my brain as I fell. Then darkness swallowed me.

It felt like ages before I clawed my way up into the light. Something gooey blinded one eye and covered half my face.

All I could think was that I had to go after Aunt Margaret. I struggled to sit and then pulled myself up on the glass doorknob to stand. Panic pushed me on. I had to reach Aunt Margaret.

By leaning on the wall, I stumbled my way down the hall toward the main staircase. I turned the corner and saw her by the stairs. I couldn't register anything more than someone was in the shadows at the far end of the hall coming toward us.

I had to protect her. Stop her. Save her. "Aunt Margaret." My voice sounded far away.

She turned toward me at the top of the stairs. "Livvy. Let me go."

Still looking at me, she set her foot half on the top step and half off. I saw her grab for the railing as she started to fall sideways down the staircase.

And then in what felt like the slowing of time, she vanished. I heard thumps and crashes as I hurried to the top of the staircase. Edwin came out of the darkness from the other hallway and put an arm around me to help me down the stairs. "Somebody help," he shouted as I clung to the banister.

There were more thuds as we slowly made our way down the long staircase. It wasn't until we turned the corner that I saw Margaret sprawled at the bottom on the tiles, blood pooling around her head.

Someone screamed.

Suddenly, Adam was running up the stairs toward me. He picked me up in his arms and carried me the rest of the way down the stairs. "Hang in there, Livvy. Please."

My father was somewhere nearby saying, "Pull her skirt down," while Uncle Humphrey was shouting, "Call an ambulance."

Somewhere, someone still screamed.

My brain finally unscrambled enough for my eyes to focus on Adam's gorgeous hazel ones peering into the one I could see out of. Then, "How many fingers am I holding up?"

After a couple of false starts with no sound coming out, I finally managed to whisper, "Two."

"I need water and some towels to find out how bad her injuries are," Adam called out, and a moment later, Watkins was there, saying, "Set her down, sir."

Adam lay me down on the cold tiles, my head and shoulders elevated against his chest. I felt like every bone in my body had broken and turned into liquid. I'd try to figure out how they could do both when I felt better. Right then, I was concentrating on staying awake and trying to ignore the pounding in my head.

"Aunt Margaret—" I needed to tell him what I'd heard. But all I saw in my memory was the sadness in her eyes and the feeling that something was wrong.

"They've called an ambulance."

"Wha—?" I tried to take in more air. "What?" This wasn't one of my better efforts at conversation.

"Lady Margaret seems to be paralyzed from her fall," Edwin said.

"Oh, dear heavens." I shoved at Adam until he moved out of the way.

I scooted across the marble tiles to Margaret's side. Blood leaked from her mouth. "Aunt Margaret. Why?"

I had to bend over her to hear her say, "I'll leave that to you, dear Livvy."

"You must get well. Please, Aunt Margaret." Love, remorse, something forced the words out of my mouth. "I love you."

She lay unmoving, sound barely making it past her

lips. "It's in your hands. Look in the library. Dear Livvy." She smiled at me, looking again like the woman who'd argued with my father to convince him to send me to university. Gone was the frightened, bitter woman I'd seen recently.

Before I was gently moved aside, I thought I heard one more word from Aunt Margaret. "Love."

The doctor, the ambulance, and the police arrived for her. Adam picked me up and carried me into the family parlor and then hovered, watching me and searching for the source of the blood he'd washed out of my eye. The boys were sent in to join me and huddled alone in individual chairs as far apart as they could get.

We sat in silence, listening to clipped pieces of conversation between the various professionals outside the room. Adam could probably have translated their phrases into something that made sense, but he sat staring at me.

"You want a drink?" Thomas said, heading for the brandy.

Adam shook his head.

That seemed strange. Adam was so pale I'd have thought he fell down the stairs.

"I'll take one," I whispered.

"No," Adam said, holding up a hand to Thomas. "Nothing to eat or drink for a while, not until we're sure you're all right."

"I'm fine." My voice was barely audible over the booming drums in my head.

"I'd like somebody else's opinion on that. Preferably somebody who knows what they're doing. Preferably before I go back in the morning." He wore his "Don't argue with me" face.

"Fine. We'll go to the hospital. I want to find out how

Aunt Margaret is."

I went out into the hall leaning on Adam's arm to find my father and Uncle Humphrey talking in low voices. Everyone else had gone.

My father said, "What happened?" in an angry voice.

Uncle Humphrey took my father's arm and said, "Not now." Then he walked toward the family parlor, where his sons stood in the doorway.

"I want to take Livvy to the hospital and have her checked out," Adam said.

"And I want to find out how Aunt Margaret is."

My father gave me a strange look. "Who hit you? Maggie?" He sounded perplexed.

I just stared at him for a moment before I said, "Yes." Despite the aches and pains, the whole event was beginning to feel like a bad dream.

My father turned so white I thought he'd pass out. Adam grabbed his arm and said, "Maybe you should go to the hospital, too."

He nodded and the three of us went out to find a taxi.

We went to the casualty section, where I was looked over and pronounced "lucky."

"Why lucky?" I asked, the booming now reduced to a whopping headache.

The doctor looked up from the notes he was writing. "You were injured at Millhaven House, weren't you? The other lady didn't fare as well as you, I'm afraid."

"What do you mean?"

"She's dead," came from the doorway. Detective Inspector Guess stood there in his perpetually rumpled suit.

"Dead? No. She can't be." Tears rolled down my cheeks. I looked at Adam, who had entered behind the detective.

He came over and silently wrapped his arms around me.

"No. She can't be. This is my fault." I sobbed into Adam's shirt. I was so very grateful he was there.

"Ssh, Livvy. It's not your fault. She knew you believed in her," slid in between the pain and the noise in my head.

I was shattered, and the only reason I didn't fly apart was Adam's careful, all-encompassing embrace.

I peeked out to see Inspector Guess walk over to the doctor. "I have a report this woman was injured before the other woman fell down the stairs."

"I don't know what order anything happened. This woman was struck on the top of her head with something heavy. There was a moderate amount of bleeding that is now stopped."

"Were her injuries consistent with unconsciousness?"

"Most certainly. Is there anything else, Inspector?"

"No. Thank you, doctor."

The doctor left the examination room and I hopped down from the table. My legs were still rubbery, and Adam had to catch me. I leaned into him, discovering there were some good things about being attacked.

"I'm going to need a statement from you, Mrs. Denis."

"Can it wait until tomorrow? I'm very tired." And I hadn't decided how much I should say.

"She's had a terrible injury, Inspector." Adam put his arm around me and ushered me out of the room into the hall where my father waited.

"Maggie's dead," he said.

"They told me."

"We need to take you home," my father said and took my other arm, helping me put distance between me and Inspector Guess.

"I'll call on you tomorrow," the policeman said.

I nodded. Adam and my father hurried me out and into a taxi. My father gave the cabbie my address and then settled back. I knew I would get a grilling when we reached my flat.

Adam had me propped up on the sofa with a cup of tea in my hand and an ice bag over my wound before he'd let my father ask a single question. However, once he got the nod from Adam, my father didn't seem to be able to stop.

"Why did Maggie hit you? She's always looked out for your best interests."

"She admitted to killing Lady Amelia. I accused her of killing her father as well as poisoning herself and Lord Eustace. Once I did that, she wasn't going to let me out of her room alive." At least the hot tea was helping my head.

"Preposterous," my father thundered. I wished he wouldn't talk so loudly. "She would never have killed anyone. She was a lady."

"Aunt Margaret tried to blame her father's murder and the two attempts on Lady Amelia. And she said she killed Lady Amelia in self-defense."

"That sounds more likely," came through my father's clenched jaws, followed by a snort of derision.

"Then why did she try to kill me? And yes, she very definitely tried to kill me."

"What did you find in the garden? And did that have anything to do with this?" Adam asked.

"The night Lady Amelia was killed, Lady Margaret came in late saying she'd broken a strand of pearls."

My father nodded.

"I thought nothing of it at the time, but then I found a single pearl in the garden near where Lady Amelia's body was found. Amelia wasn't wearing pearls. I took the pearl upstairs and found the broken strand in Lady Margaret's room. The pearl matched in color and size."

"On the basis of a single pearl, you accused Maggie? Are you mad? You're certainly ungrateful. She's looked after your best interests ever since your mother died." My father started to pace the room.

"And she admitted killing Lady Amelia."

"In self-defense."

"And she must have stolen the countess's necklace because when it was returned, there was black soil on it. It was hidden in the greenhouse."

"Anyone can get in there."

"Then why try to kill me?" came out in a screech. A terrible headache, grief, and frustration made a bad combination for my temper.

"I can't believe it." My father kept pacing.

CHAPTER TWENTY-SEVEN

I gasped from the pain of my father's lack of trust in me. "I certainly didn't hit myself over the head. Do you really believe that I'd make something like this up? An event that ended in her death and my injuries." I was ready to send him away.

I loved Aunt Margaret. She'd always been good to me. Always treated me like I mattered to her. She was so important in my life. How had I failed to see how frightened and angry she must have been at the thought of losing her home?

He stopped and faced me. His shoulders slumped as he said, "No, I don't believe you'd make it up. And Edwin was upstairs and saw you with blood on your face. He also saw Maggie fall down the stairs. But I can't imagine Maggie killing anyone."

"She said it was up to me to tell the story. And she said to look in the library. Maybe the answer is there. We have to go back." I started to scoot off the sofa, trying not to move my head.

"I don't think they'll want to see us again today. I'll go with you tomorrow," my father said, his voice finally gentled.

"But the newspaper—"

"Can wait," Adam said. "I'll call Sir Henry and tell him you've had an accident and won't be in tomorrow. Then you and your father can go out there and see if there's anything in the library."

I didn't like the way he worded this idea. "You don't think we'll find anything?"

Adam took my hand. "She was dying when she said

it. I've found people don't always make sense when they're dying."

I wondered what Adam had been faced with in his counterintelligence work.

"I'll see you tomorrow, Olivia. Redmond, good luck back at your base."

"Thank you, sir." The two men shook hands and my father left.

Adam called Sir Henry and then came back to join me on the sofa. "You're cleared for tomorrow, with more time off if necessary."

I stared at him for a moment before I said, "Am I reading too much into it, or did my father just give you permission to stay here?"

"Guess he thinks you need a minder after the crack you received on your head." Adam's smile widened as he watched my astonishment. "I believe I've been given the green light to court you."

I reached out to him, in need of comforting. "Good. Come here and hold me, Adam."

* * *

The next day, my father came over to take me to lunch at his club before we ventured out to Millhaven House. He asked me if Adam had got off all right on his way back to his unit. I told him he had. After that, the silence between us was broken only by questions concerning lunch or the cab ride.

After a slow walk to the door, my father keeping a stranglehold on my arm, Watkins was waiting in the open doorway to admit us.

"Aunt Margaret told me there was something in the library she wanted me to find," I said, entering the house without asking to be invited. I was afraid I'd be told to leave.

"The family would like to see you in the parlor first. If you'll follow me?" Watkins walked to the door and opened it.

I followed my father in, feeling unwelcome. Lady Beatrice turned away with her nose in the air, but Uncle Humphrey and his boys faced us.

"I told everyone what I saw from upstairs," Edwin said. "It's not your fault, Livvy. And I'm glad to see you doing better today."

"Aunt Margaret told me she'd left something for me in the library. Do you want to help me hunt, Edwin?"

"I think we all do, Olivia," the earl said. "We want to make sense out of this tragedy." He looked around. "These tragedies."

We squeezed into the library. I took Aunt Margaret's desk chair, something I'd never dared do in her lifetime. My father, Earl Humphrey, Thomas, and Edwin took the bookcases. Charlie sat in another chair and watched.

Lady Beatrice didn't make an appearance.

After what felt like a long search, Edwin said, "There're two envelopes stuck in this volume of poetry called *Grasses in the Wind*. One's addressed to you, Livvy."

"And the other?" his father asked.

"Uncle Ronald."

My father and I took our envelopes and opened them. After reading the first paragraph, I stopped, blinking away tears, and looked up. My father, not taking his eyes off the page, felt his way into a chair and collapsed into it.

"Well, what do the letters say?" Thomas demanded.

My father just shook his head as if he couldn't believe what he was reading in his. I cleared my throat and read aloud from mine.

"Dear Livvy, if anyone has figured out what happened, it will be you. And if you are reading this, I am either dead

or I escaped. I planned to take the necklace and run, but the garden and then Walter kept calling me back. I hope I have vanished, but I suspect I left it until too late.

"You have a cool, analytical mind coupled with a warm heart. I would have been honored to be your mother instead of an honorary aunt."

"Oh, God," my father sobbed and then fell silent.

"My father never valued my mind, and as I didn't marry, didn't value me at all. That was why I fought so hard on your behalf with your father to see you received a university education instead of having to take random classes in London as I did.

"I knew Father was dying, and when he presented his new will naming the grandchildren as the keepers of the family coffers, something inside me broke. Why could he never see Beatrice and Walter and me as intelligent adults?"

I read the next part silently before I swallowed and read aloud, *"I surprised him by coming into his room unannounced, but the knife surprised him more. He told me I had no right to threaten him; his mind was made up. I told him that on the contrary, his day of reckoning had come for all the hateful, hurtful things he had done to his children.*

"And then I plunged the knife into his chest."

"Golly," Edwin and Charlie said in unison.

"I poisoned myself to throw suspicion away from me. You were getting too close to the truth, Livvy, and I suspected my work here wasn't done yet. I didn't realize you would become more involved in the case in an effort to protect me. I hadn't known how dear I was to you."

I loosed a sob before I pulled myself together to read on.

"I could tell you saw the import of my being in the

bathing room at the time Philip saw me. I tried to change the time, thinking the drunkard would go along with it. He did, but only up to a point. I'd forgotten how honest he used to be.

"I tried to poison Philip to stop him from doing any more damage, but Ronnie knocked the glass out of his hand before he'd had enough strychnine. Ronnie always was the hero."

"Not this time," my father muttered, sounding miserable.

"Amelia told me her plans to sell the house and get something stylish and modern in town. She said Bea, Walter, and I would get nothing from the proceeds. We could earn our own way and stop being useless. Useless. The same word Father used to describe us.

"I couldn't let her do that."

"I told you nothing good would come of her plans," Thomas snapped at his brothers. They both studied the floor. I saw Edwin's ears turn pink.

"I convinced her to meet me in the garden. I told her I'd found a better offer from a contact of mine and I wanted half the difference before I'd put her in touch with them. She was so greedy she believed that silly tale. Who would I know with enough money to buy Millhaven House?

"After she met me, she became angry and pushed me, breaking the strand of pearls I'd had since my debut into society at King Edward's court. Perhaps it's time to break everything from before the war, but they weren't hers to break. When she had the temerity to turn her back on me, I struck her down."

"I should have stopped her. This house has been ours for generations," Uncle Humphrey said before slumping against a bookcase. Charlie rose and he and Thomas set their unresisting father down in the empty chair.

"I was surprised you never realized the significance of the countess's necklace. If I was going to be thrown out of my home, I was going to have the ability to buy another. Somewhere small that would be mine, a place that greedy, uncaring people couldn't steal.

"You almost caught me hiding it, Livvy dear. I'd just put it in the pot under the dirt when you came into the greenhouse the day after the wedding. I knew the police wouldn't unearth all my plants.

"Once Amelia, Countess Millhaven, was dead, I no longer needed such a large amount of money. I retrieved the necklace and hid it in the back of Philip's wardrobe, thinking he wouldn't notice it. Once again, I underestimated him."

"I would have gladly made a home for her," my father said.

After hearing his words, this part of the letter hurt me to read. *"I know your father would have made a home for me. Dear, dear Ronnie. And while I appreciate the thought, I could never move in with him without becoming his wife. It was partly my Victorian upbringing, but partly my desire for him to love me as I love him. In this situation, charity would have been bitter."*

"Why didn't you marry Maggie? We all thought you would," Uncle Humphrey said.

"Because I fell in love with Anne. And I've never stopped loving her." My father looked at me with a sad smile.

I was amazed. "All this time I thought you didn't get along with my mother. You never spoke of her."

"I couldn't speak of her. First the war, then her death. They became one huge ache deep inside me." He buried his face in his hands.

Not knowing where else to look, I continued the

letter. "*Livvy, please don't think badly of me. I have always loved you as a daughter and always wanted the best for you. If I was silent on your marriage to Reggie, it was because I knew no one could have talked you out of it. I won't be silent now. Marry Adam. You and he are very much in love, and with the war coming, you will regret not marrying him.*

"*I regret not running away and marrying George. Even though he died, it would have been worth it for a little happiness.*"

A sob escaped my throat. Then tears slid down my cheeks and made reading the note impossible.

Edwin slid it out of my fingers and read, "*Tell the boys I know they will grow up to be fine men if they survive the coming war. They need to take care of their father, and Humphrey, you need to take care of Walter. It won't be much longer.*"

I saw the look that passed between Humphrey and his youngest son, but I wasn't sure I understood it. I suspected Edwin knew more about what went on in the house than both of his brothers combined.

I took over the reading again. "*Don't feel sorry for Bea and Philip. They have each other and they'll be fine. I was shocked to learn you'd been invited to assist Celia on her wedding day. I suspect she knew her father was staying in the house and saw him near her grandfather's room that morning. Then she checked on Father and found him stabbed. She couldn't let anything come between her and 'I do' that day. Robert had nearly escaped marrying her once; she couldn't let it happen again. If Robert learned of the murder and that her father would be chief suspect, he would have called off the wedding 'until a better time.'*

"*I think Robert would have made sure that time never came.*

"*After Ames called the police as soon as everyone left for the church, Celia suggested to Amelia that she could cut down on staff by firing Ames. Celia is a sharp cookie. I never understood her hold on you. I hope you never let her control you again.*

"*I wish you all the best, Livvy. Don't judge me too harshly, because I have always loved you.*

"*Aunt Margaret*"

I looked around the room. "What do I do with this?"

"Throw it in the fire," Charlie said.

His father shook his head.

My father said, "We'll have to show it to that Inspector Guess. Then he can close the book on this whole awful—well, the police won't bother you anymore."

"They won't have to make public the personal parts, will they? I'd like to have the letter returned when the police are through with it." Not for the details of her crimes, but for the asides meant only for me.

"I wouldn't think they'd report the parts that have nothing to do with the crime, Olivia. There obviously won't be a prosecution. And once they're satisfied, I should think we can get the letter back for you," my father said.

His letter sat open in his hand. I could tell it was only one sheet of paper, but I wasn't certain if he'd read it. "What about your letter?"

"It is purely private. There's nothing more to explain any of these crimes." He hastily refolded it and replaced it in the envelope.

After Inspector Guess left with my letter and a promise to return it sometime soon, we went into the parlor. It was nearly the dinner hour, but Uncle Humphrey as earl declared that first we would toast the old earl, Lady Amelia, and Lady Margaret.

It was somber. Even Charlie, the most indifferent of the lot, had damp eyes. Uncle Walter, Lady Beatrice, and Lord Eustace joined us in time for the toast, and afterward, Humphrey as head of the family told them what the letter said.

"How extraordinary that she should leave it for you," Lady Beatrice said in her customary lady-of-the-manor tone.

"She cared about Livvy more than any of us," Edwin told her.

And when her will was read a few days later, Isaak Rothenberger was gifted with her collection of books. I received her cash and investments, which were minimal, was called on to be her literary executor, and was given a strand of pearls she'd had since her debutante days in the Edwardian era. The solicitor added, "The string appears to be broken."

Adam offered to have the pearls restrung, knowing how much they meant to me. That was sweet of him, but I've never had the heart to have them repaired.

Author's Notes

My first introduction to the efforts to help Jews escape Nazi Germany came from an article in Parade Magazine back in the 1970s. A reporter interviewed two elderly British women who had traveled several times to Germany before the outbreak of World War II to smuggle furs and jewels into Britain for their owners who then were able to follow their goods.

The women would fly over in their normal clothes for the weekend to attend the opera, pick up the goods, and take the ferry back to Britain dripping in furs and jewels. They reasoned that the passengers on airplanes didn't travel by boat and vice versa, so this change in wardrobe was never commented on. They saved thirty-eight lives.

Their response? It was only thirty-eight. They wished they had done more.

I was impressed and the story stayed with me.

About this same time there was a comic strip in the newspapers called Brenda Starr, star reporter. She handled national news and frequently got the scoop away from male colleagues. She was leggy and red haired and I thought she was marvelous.

Combine the two, travel forty years into the future, and you find me writing Olivia Denis's stories. She's slender, auburn haired, and a mild-mannered sort of society reporter with equal parts loyalty and sass. But give her a special assignment from her editor in chief, or a murder to solve, and she becomes daring and resourceful.

My thanks to Jen Parker, Elizabeth Flynn, and Jennifer Brown for their help in making this a better story. Now Les Floyd has edited this for Americanisms so

Olivia sounds more British. As always, my mistakes are my own.

I hope you've enjoyed Olivia's newest adventure. If you have, please leave a review at your book retailer of choice or tell a friend. Word of mouth is still the best way to learn about terrific new stories.

About the Author

Kate Parker grew up reading her mother's collection of mystery books and her father's library of history and biography books. Now she can't write a story that isn't set in the past with a few decent corpses littered about. It took her years to convince her husband she hadn't poisoned dinner; that funny taste is because she can't cook. Now she can read books on poisons and other lethal means at the dinner table and he doesn't blink.

Their children have grown up to be surprisingly normal, but two of them are developing their own love of creating literary mayhem, so the term "normal" may have to be revised.

Living in a nineteenth century town has further inspired Kate's love of history. But as much as she loves stately architecture and vintage clothing, she has also developed an appreciation of central heating and air conditioning. She's discovered life in coastal Carolina requires her to wear shorts and T-shirts while drinking hot tea and it takes a great deal of imagination to picture cool, misty weather when it's 90 degrees out and sunny.

Follow Kate and her deadly examination of history at www.KateParkerbooks.com
and www.Facebook.com/Author.Kate.Parker/
and www.Bookbub.com/authors/kate-parker

Made in the USA
Las Vegas, NV
04 January 2024

83916227R00174